balance of fragile things

balance of fragile things

a novel by

Olivia Chadha

www.ashlandcreekpress.com

Balance of Fragile Things

A novel by Olivia Chadha

Published by Ashland Creek Press

www.ashlandcreekpress.com

ISBN 978-1-61822-009-7

Library of Congress Control Number: 2012931270

Printed in the United States of America on acid-free paper. All paper products used to create this book are Sustainable Forestry Initiative (SFI) Certified Sourcing.

Cover and book design by John Yunker.

Cover painting, “On the Wings of Butterflies,” by Pegi Smith.

For my mother, father, and brother.

"The past is never dead; it's not even past."

— William Faulkner

ON THE WING

Watching the Butterfly

Posted on October 4

Today, people are blind. Our age is less introspective than the previous. We worry neither for the small things nor the large things but rather for the *now* things.

In order to observe her closely, one must make amends with solitude. Not by walking alone but by approaching her with a singularity of mind and the purest of intentions. She delights in our awe, when we come to her without vanity or an architect's eye. She mourns us, too. You can see it in the wings of the swallowtail as she soars with a melancholic flight from one flower to the next. There is a desire for an audience that somehow is lost on those who can no longer see the smallest things. Does she wish for sun? It is wrong to assume she has disconnected from us. Each time we walk past an oak, mourning cloak, field of springtime grass, or newly snowcapped mountain, she sees.

To be human is to be a part of nature. To feel separate is to be the anomaly. In her presence we feel the sorrows of modernity fall away like the chrysalis giving way to time. In her presence we feel once more hers, a thing belonging—simultaneously a child and an elder.

Why would we watch a butterfly? When we don't have time to look up and cannot let go of modernity, why would we try? These delicate things are indicators of the forest's health. They tell stories of flood and drought. Their wings are maps to worlds unseen. They are cartographers and pollinators. When the forest and soil are healthy, they are, too. Adults lay their eggs on one kind of plant. The caterpillars eat that one kind of plant. They mummify themselves on one type of plant. The adult then flies in that area eating the nectar from flowers, rotting fruit, or mineral-rich rainwater collecting on the ground. If the host plant is suffering, water is toxic, ground quality is poor—then the butterflies are directly affected. Watch them, and watch the health of the forest and land. When we watch a butterfly flutter from flower to leaf to sky, teasingly, as though its wings are attached to invisible thread that some unseen puppeteer is pulling, we can also see the strength of those living things around it.

When we see an ancient butterfly nearing the end of its life with wings tattered like sails, still searching for nourishment, we may come to a greater understanding of what connects us all. Even battle-scarred, we all still seek the sun, try to avoid pain, and attempt to find food. Thus, all life is connected: Insecta, Lepidoptera, Mammalia.

The insects beneath your feet are managing the earth on which you walk. The trees you pass are providing food and shelter for hundreds of living things in addition to the shade they provide you and your home. The bees busy in your flower bed are carrying with them saddlebags of pollen and pollinating every other flower, including vegetables growing in your area. What most people don't know is that butterflies and moths aren't just flying flowers: They are the second most important pollinator next to bees. They, too, have a job in the world, and looking pretty is one of their lesser engagements. What we choose to notice about these connections differentiates us as a species. Perhaps many of us no longer see her as she is; rather, she has become a reflection of how we see ourselves.

0 COMMENTS

Vic

When Joe Balestrieri landed a solid right on Vic Singh's nose, the entire student body of Cobalt High probably heard the crack. The sound echoed in Vic's ears as his face went hot, stomach dropped, tears gushed, and copious amounts of blood splattered the front of his T-shirt as well as his assailant's.

Vic's first reaction was worry as he gingerly put his hand in the pocket of his corduroy jacket and felt for something. Then, relieved, he balanced himself against the lockers so he wouldn't faint. The blow had loosened the *patka* that enclosed his unshorn hair; it fell like an autumn leaf to the linoleum floor among blackened splotches of gum. His braid tumbled halfway down his back, a precursor to an imminent turban-wearing future. The length of his hair shocked even Vic as he stood with it naked to the world. He could have dodged the punch and prevented a broken nose; he actually thought of this option as he watched Joe's fist—in slow motion, like a heat-seeking missile—follow the trajectory to his face. But Vic was more concerned with what was in his pocket than with Joe's simian fist.

Vic spit blood, and the crowd of rubbernecking students *ooh*'d and *ahh*'d, then moved closer. The pain from his septum sped through his nerves and reached his toes. This had been the worst day of his life, and at that precise moment, he wondered why he'd gotten out of bed at all. It had begun with a freak rainstorm that had drenched him on his walk through the abandoned industrial park on his way to school. He'd taken refuge under a gathering of trees.

"Jerk," Vic said under his breath. He looked at Joe and imagined what it would be like to grow four inches and be able to stare down into his soulless eyes. It wasn't fair. Vic was just trying to get by, like everyone else, but Joe had singled him out long ago with tired teasing and insults like "Ali Baba" and "Babu"—though this was the first time he'd physically assaulted him. Joe was Goliath, and he had to have a weakness. Today Vic's EYE FOR AN EYE AND THE WHOLE WORLD'S BLIND T-shirt had ironically attracted Joe to him like a huffer to an open jar of glue.

"You need glasses or something?" Vic said.

Joe laughed, though he took a few steps back.

Vic would get his revenge. He wouldn't react carelessly. He'd craft a plan that would show up Joe in the end. If he couldn't best him with strength, he'd take him down with his brains. Like Batman, who went full-throttle against any and all evil in Gotham, Vic would have his day, he vowed to himself.

He adjusted his nose and realized that this already large feature on his face was now even larger from the swelling. Vic had his father's nose. It was a sometimes trunk-like proboscis, depending on the time of day and allotment of shadow. His mother had told him his profile illustrated his relation to great rulers across oceans and time. These rulers, she said, were conquerors who led their people to victory. Vic had never learned more about these rulers, their names, or their empires, so his mind had constructed disembodied kingly faces with enormous noses, lips with wide moustaches, and heads with heavy crowns. Vic's eyebrows, soft as tufts of rabbit fur and bushy like the wool behind the ear of a yak, were also the exact eyebrows that framed the moon-shaped face of his grandfather, Sardar

Harbans Singh. Vic knew this only from photographs; his grandfather lived in India, and they had never met. But here, now, on this North American continent in the tenth month of the year, the vessels that kept Vic's beak alive were bringing forth a torrent of blood.

"Oh my God." Katie, the freckle-faced object of Vic's affection, put her hands over her mouth.

"I'm okay," Vic said through the blood and tried to smile, which made Katie cringe again. The posse scattered, though Joe stood frozen.

For once Vic was thankful for the robust size of his nose, as he assumed the size allowed a particularly shocking amount of blood to flow. To him, it seemed, his dissimilarity was the cause of his bully magnetism. He'd never cut his hair, because *kesh* was one of The Five Ks of Sikhism, and he wore a *patka* to keep his hair neat and clean. Or perhaps it was the language Vic spoke when he'd first entered school, something he called *Engjabi* that was halfway between English and Punjabi. He uttered words that no teacher could translate when he was in first grade and just beginning to learn that the first letter of the alphabet looked like an apple and the second letter could be turned into a bumblebee if doubled on its side. Or perhaps it was the fact that his father made him follow the traditions of Sikhism when most kids were taking their fashion tips from MTV, not Guru Gobind Singh of the seventeenth century. Every time his parents were called into the school to discuss matters pertaining to Vic, they defended their son passionately with more foreign words like *starpība* and *jhuthá*, but the principal would have no idea they were pointing out the finer points of their family's culture, or that they thought what was being said was mostly untrue. Vic thought they'd set him up for the worst thing any teen could endure—*difference*.

All of these thoughts flooded his mind as the blood poured out. One of Joe's friends pulled him away from the sight of Vic's gore.

"Stupid camel jockey can't even bleed right." The brilliant Joe

Balestrieri had to say something. He didn't know that Vic wasn't even 100 percent Indian.

Joe's racial slur made Vic's face burn with an unearthly desire to defend his culture, his father's religion, his mother's heritage, and his grandparents' existence. But he would not throw a punch. He imagined what his father would want him to do: Vic would let out a war cry—*"Jo bole so nihal!"*—and with juggernaut speed he would charge Joe and hit him, dead on. Then he'd unsheathe his knife and stab Joe in the gut. But in this reality, Vic simply smiled at Joe with fire in his eyes and stuffed his anger down deep in his belly.

"See ya round," Joe said.

Joe walked away with a sneer, and Vic stared at his back; he hoped his eyes would ignite a flame that would lead everyone to believe that Joe spontaneously combusted. Paranormal scientists would use Joe's remains for proof of the phenomenon and add Joe Balestrieri as a footnote to a contemporary version of the *De Incendiis Corporis Humani Spontaneis*. Vic imagined them standing over a glass table that was lit from beneath, each holding a different scalpel or knife while they pieced together what little was left of Joe's adolescent combustion. Vic laughed because he imagined that would be all Joe would amount to one day—a pile of volatile organic garbage.

"Come on, let's get some ice." Mrs. Stein, the English teacher, took Vic by the arm. The gym teacher, Mr. Smith, grabbed Joe as he made his way down the hall and dragged him forcefully to his office without saying a word.

When Vic and Mrs. Stein arrived in the nurse's office, she let him go into the bathroom to clean up. After he closed the door behind him, he opened his jacket once more and retrieved a very small blue butterfly from his pocket. No larger than a nickel, its light blue luminescent scales sparkled. Vic puzzled over the markings and the difference between the left and right forewings and hind wings.

This inconsistency made Vic uneasy. He analyzed the antennae. Looking more closely, he realized that it was not moving as much as it had been when he'd first found it, at lunch, in the gutter outside of Cobalt High on a pile of dead leaves. It had appeared injured then, but he assumed if he got it home he could give it some rotten fruit or salt water to revive it. But now, noticing its broken antennae, he felt the need to rush home to get it under his microscope. The previous year Vic had identified a Red-Spotted Purple, and it had been, up until this moment, the most amazing butterfly he'd seen. Its wings were akin to majestic glass windows, with shades of burnt orange, sky blue, and eggplant all framed in black. The butterfly had been so enthralled in drinking juices from a sap flow on a deciduous tree that it had barely moved while Vic observed it.

This one, though, was different from anything he'd ever seen. The left and right wings were slightly dissimilar in shape. It was so very fragile. Science usually offered Vic comfort because it explained the world. But this—this was unexpected, and the sight of it made him anxious.

He sighed, folded a large piece of paper towel into an envelope, and slipped the butterfly inside. He changed into his PE shirt and threw his favorite one, now bloodied beyond repair, in the wastebasket. Then he twisted his long braid on top of his head and wrapped the dusty *patka* around it before exiting.

Ms. McClasky, the nurse, handed him an ice pack and said, "Sit down and let me take a look." She lifted his face into the light and looked into his nostrils. After she packed them with gauze, she said, "Put pressure on your nose with the ice."

Vic's wandering eyes landed on a poster on the corkboard to the right of the door. The flyer read: YEARBOOK CONTEST. ART, PHOTOS, ALL SUBMISSIONS CONSIDERED. WIN $20 AND SEE YOUR ART ON THIS YEAR'S INSIDE COVER! Katie was in charge of the yearbook, and Vic thought of the possibilities. Maybe he could finally speak with Katie properly and, well, bask in her honey-colored aura.

"Stay still, head back, Mr. Singh," the nurse said. Just then the principal, Mrs. Cohen, whose disapproving look spoke volumes, entered the room.

"At least school is nearly over for the day. Here." Mrs. Cohen handed him a letter. "Give this to your parents when you get home. I will call this evening to make certain they received it."

Vic's thoughts turned to his father, who, in his mind, was going to kill him, not because he was in a fight but because he was injured—which very specifically meant that he *didn't* break his opponent's nose.

Paul

Ikpaul Singh looked out the window of his Kwicki Fill gas station. His eyes traveled down Sycamore Road, across the graying asphalt and beyond the line of cars that had been rerouted around the massive hole in the road. He noticed the frost had arrived early this year, and he tried to rub the serpentine ice patterns from the double-paned windows with his shirt's cuff. The ice wouldn't budge; he realized he was rubbing from the wrong side of the glass. He looked above the trees that grew perilously close to the power lines and frowned at the bruise of clouds gathering. As his longing for a glimpse of the sun grew, he wondered how long it would take to walk to the Punjab if, of course, he could walk on water. He imagined walking with extraordinarily large feet the length of battleships. He would cross seas, continents, and mountains. In an old oak he saw a *pippal* tree, with a trunk the size of an elephant's waist and bark the texture of a riverbed in drought. Paul saw beyond concrete; he saw the suffocated earth under the palimpsest asphalt and gravel.

The construction on Sycamore was as constant as the cloud coverage. And now the prehistoric machines were at it again, with their shovel-toothed mouths and their smoke-puffing blowholes, right outside his gas station. This time the traffic wasn't caused by the new construction in the Heights. The title of the article on page A9 in the *Daily Mirror* in Paul's hands said the hole was the beginning of a sinkhole. He couldn't believe it. A sinkhole in Cobalt, New York? What next, he thought, an earthquake? The mess was already preventing drivers from entering his station from Sycamore. It caused business to decline, as it always did every time they ripped up the road, even though he'd climbed up the ladder at five that morning to lower his gas prices below the Stop and Go station's by nine-tenths of a cent. Those stupid-bastard city councilmen were just wasting money lifting and repaving roads every year, he thought. The title of the article was "Sinkholes, Man vs. Nature: Who's to Blame?"

"It'd better be nature," Paul grumbled, "or else I'll chase down the idiot who started this mess. Pothole, sinkhole, asshole, same difference." He decided to write a letter to the *Daily Mirror*; his wife, Maija, had a friend who worked there. She'd be obligated to rescue his letter from the slush pile.

He glared at the expanding pile of debris and soil alongside the gaping hole. What they were digging up, he had no idea. What he did know was that he would send another e-mail to the city complaining of his loss of business since the construction began. His station's peripheral location, like a useless appendix to Main Street, already had poor traffic. It now suffered aesthetically from the dust and debris, and he feared the Kwicki Fill was beginning to look like a halfway house for construction workers and their temporary defecation rooms. He would have to do something clever to draw the customers inside the convenience store, and quick. Winter would cut the construction project short, as it usually did, and when the snow melted in the spring he'd see the gash in the road once more. Where were the moderate seasons, like autumn? Seems we have only two seasons in this town, Paul thought: sticky-hot summer and freeze-your-*tatte*-off winter.

He shrugged, used a pencil to scratch his scalp under his turban, and flattened his blue dress shirt down a stomach that was just beginning to show the roundness of middle age. Then he stuffed the newspaper into the drawer under the counter and turned his attention to the boxes of windshield fluid that needed unpacking. Today he would make a pyramid of the blue bottles that would entice everyone to make an impulse purchase in his c-store. Perhaps he could sell the whole lot of them in one day. He smiled. Goals made his day speed by.

His knife was in his back pocket, as always. He took it out gingerly, holding it weightlessly, like a child, and unfolded the blade from the handle. He'd bought this knife with his own money when he was a young man. He ran his thumb along the blade. It was getting dull; he would sharpen it soon. On the silver handle was a poorly sketched chain of elephants carrying a man and woman atop their backs. The vendor had said it had special powers, but Paul just liked the handle. He dug the blade into the flesh of the cardboard, then moved it down and away from himself until the box surrendered its contents. He would usually display the first case of windshield fluid at the earliest sign of winter, but today he knew that the debris from the construction would stick to motorists' windshields when they passed by, which would in turn remind them to check their fluid levels. He would be ready. They would buy his windshield fluid. Maybe, if he was really lucky, they'd get flat tires and have to purchase new ones from Paul's inventory.

When he bent toward the first group of blue bottles, something crunched in his back pocket. He pulled out the nuisance, an envelope. One quarter of its face was covered in stamps, and the rest displayed the gaudy handwriting of someone who had recently learned English.

It was another letter from his father.

PLEASE RESPOND was written in bold on the back of the envelope near the adhesive lip. Paul's heart sank. Even from across the world, his father could make him feel inadequate. Paul's father had been nicknamed "Papaji" decades earlier by a British-educated head of their Punjab village as a term of endearment. Even when relatives attempted to use the common "Dadda" or "Daddaji," the man scoffed and protested, demanding to be called Papaji by all. Paul had yet to open any of the letters, and they were beginning to pile up. He wondered what Mr. Sardar Harbans Singh wanted so desperately that he'd felt the need to mail one letter per week for the past two months. Paul wanted to leave India and his father behind him—that's why he'd come to America years earlier. The letter rustled when he shoved it back into his pocket. The sound was familiar, like wind rushing through wheat.

At least there aren't any snakes here in this village, he thought. This barely comforted him. He looked at the sinkhole and imagined a monstrous basilisk jutting through the surface and swallowing the construction workers. The bell on the convenience store door jingled him back to the present, and he returned to his position behind the counter.

"Marlboro Mediums." A gruff teenager stared at Paul's crimson turban as if it were a second head and handed him a wad of crumpled dollars.

Paul sized up his customer with a pointedly critical squint and ran his fingers through his beard in contemplation. He saw his torn jeans and stringy blond hair; he saw a blue jacket with a license-plate-shaped patch on the lapel that read Joe. He saw his buddies waiting for him in an old Mazda outside. Joe smelled as if his backpack were filled with garbage. Who would let their child leave the house looking like this? No shower? No clean clothes? Paul couldn't understand, even after twenty years of living in this little town, what went on, if anything, in parents' heads to just give up on their offspring. He told Maija the other day, *These kids smoke like it is some sort of privilege. And their parents think they can blame our little stores for selling to minors? Their precious children dress like no-good beggars on the street. And here they have been given so much.* Paul lifted a pack of cigarettes from the display and slid them across the counter without taking an eye off the grungy kid.

"I'm eighteen, man."

"And I'm not your father, *samajhna?*" Paul turned his back to his customer and mumbled, "And don't read the warning label."

"What did you say?"

"Have a nice day."

As he got the kid his change, Paul reread the form that the corporate Kwicki Fill office sent last month, which stated the four Ks of customer service: kindness, konsideration, kalm, and kare. Paul didn't find the misuse of the letter K particularly funny, but since his station was just a drop in the Kwicki Fill bucket he had to post the list where he could see it at all times. His religion's use of the letter K was meaningful, not vulgar (*kaccha*, *kesh*, *kangha*, *kirpan*, and *kara*). By the time he finished reading the list, Joe had already disappeared into the Mazda. The car coughed black smoke out of its tailpipe as it cut off an old lady turning into the station.

The green Salem Lights clock read two-thirty. Paul looked outside and saw his fifteen-year-old son walking past on his way home from school. He decided Vic looked more like a twelve-year-old, but his growth spurt would surely be on its way. This was going to be his big year. He looked at Vic, who had his backpack on and his tidy jacket zipped up all the way. Now, that's how children should look. They should be proud to be seen, not filthy and smelly, he thought. But today there was something different: His *patka* was dirty, and his nose was no longer symmetrical.

Vic waved and kept walking.

"Oi, *puttar*, where are you going? Come here!"

Vic stopped before crossing the road construction and turned toward his father.

"What happened? Come inside!"

"I tripped and fell at lunch." He moved slowly toward his father.

Unlikely, Paul thought. "Who did this?"

Vic's lips tightened until they turned white.

Paul put the BACK IN A MINUTE sign on the door, then inspected his son's face, bruised and broken as it was, just like his own had been after a fight. "Assholes are a dime a handful."

Paul took him quickly into the unisex bathroom inside the station and locked the door. After washing his hands, Paul straightened his son's back and brought him closer to eye level. He placed his large hand flush against Vic's nose.

"Brace yourself. This will hurt, but only for a second, *puttar*."

Vic leaned against the tiled wall.

"Don't worry; I've done this to myself twice." Paul rested his large hand across Vic's nose and, in one quick movement, he thrust it back to center of his face.

Vic screamed. Tears poured. Paul handed his son a towel for the tears and blood. Paul removed the stained *patka* and took out a white handkerchief from the back pocket of his brown slacks.

"*Puttar,* you need to cover your hair and keep it clean. Otherwise you're going to have to wash it like the Americans, okay? There are ten gurus, Vic; the first one brought us peace and education, but Gobind, the tenth, brought the *Khalsa*."

He spoke of the sacrifices the gurus had made to better their lives, and how this unshorn hair, this *kesh*, was a symbol of his connection to their martyrdom and willingness to protect those who were unable to protect themselves. He tucked the handkerchief around the braid that was wound into a bun at the very top of Vic's head, took a pin from his own turban, and bisected the small yet adequate pile of hair and fabric.

"*Puttar*, you will stand up to the *págals* that have been tormenting you. Yes, you will fight back." Paul's hands dug into Vic's shoulders a little too deeply.

"Papa, just—"

Paul took out his knife and held it to his son. "Sometimes the only way to protect yourself is to make others fear you first."

Vic put his hands in his pockets. The ancient-looking blade glimmered dangerously.

"Take it."

"No." Vic's voice cracked.

"Look"—Paul put the knife on the counter and sucked in his stomach—"I want you to remember that running only makes them chase you faster. They are like hyenas. Stand your ground. Aim for their weaknesses: their knees, their necks, and their feet. It's not the biggest one that you should attack first but the smallest. Once they see you defeat one of their own, they will back off."

"Papa?" Vic motioned to the door.

"Yes, *puttar*?"

"Um, nothing." Vic cleaned his glasses with the edge of his shirt.

"Okay then. Now go home; your mother is waiting. Where's your sister? You're supposed to walk with her."

"She has play practice." They reentered the store.

"Oh, *achchhá.* She's your responsibility, you know."

"I have to study, Papa. I have an exam tomorrow."

Paul held Vic's face in his hands. He looked forward to the day when his son would become a man. It was difficult for Paul. How could his son—the son of an ex-boxer, an ex-farmer, and an ex-warrior—allow someone to break his nose? This was not possible. He thought of his Papaji, with the shotgun slung over his shoulder and his knife at the ready to cut whatever needed cutting. Vic's snake was this bully, and Paul was going to help him stand up to him regardless of the consequence. They would both have their day, and the other kids would fear his name: Varunesh Dzintar Singh. Paul's eyes glowed, his large nose tingled, and his calloused hands pressed the cheeks of his son just a little too firmly.

"I will make you stronger, *puttar.* Tonight I will show you how to fight." Paul beamed; Vic looked terrified. "Okay then, *chaliá.* Go home and see your mother. I will be home later."

He watched Vic maneuver across the construction and turn onto their street, a cul-de-sac. He noticed that Vic bounced on his toes just a little bit. That would not do. Not for his son. Paul would teach him how to walk, talk, punch, and box. He would show him how to have honor. Paul opened the cabinet under the cash register and caressed his cricket bat; he'd never used it, not once since they'd moved here. He had wanted to whack many of his customers on the noggin several times over the past week, but it wouldn't have been right. But defending oneself, yes, that would be acceptable. The bell on the door jingled, and an old lady entered.

"Hi, Paul. How's life treating ya?"

"Living the dream, Mrs. Carmichael, as always." He gave her his million-dollar smile.

Mrs. Carmichael, an octogenarian, walked around the convenience store, checking the expiration dates on each bottle of milk before pouring a small cup of coffee and topping it off with the freshest milk, which she then returned to the refrigerated section.

"That racket outside is going to raise the dead!"

"You're telling me." Paul stretched his arm out and looked at the foreman through the inch of space between his pointer finger and thumb. Then he squished the man in the distance.

"One day they're going to dig too deep and find what they're looking for."

"Eh, what do you mean?"

"Oh, you know." She slurped her hot coffee. "Every town keeps their secrets in the ground. You've heard the rumors about PMI, right?"

Paul's blank look said it all.

"Never mind. Hey, am I going to win that trip to Mexico this week?"

"Guaranteed—I see it in your future."

"Did your wife tell you that? Then it'd mean something. Otherwise, I'd think you just want a cut of my winnings!"

Mrs. Carmichael placed the correct change on the counter, took a sip of her coffee, and tucked the scratchers in her purse. "Keep the change."

"Have a nice day."

"All righty. See you next week, Mr. Singh."

Paul Singh knew two things: One, he would train his son to defend himself; and, two, he would find out if his psychic wife could see what was written on lottery tickets.

Maija

Empress of Multitasking, Goddess of Kitchen and Garden, Countess of Costco—in her mind, Maija Mazur Singh listed all the appropriate titles that she could stitch on her zip-up cardigan's lapel. On this, her day off, she'd cooked, cleaned, and learned a few things—and it was only the afternoon, which meant she still had time to appraise her children's secret lives before they returned from school.

Maija had managed to concoct a beautiful sauerbraten and had even remembered to add a few extra peppercorns to quench Paul's incessant need for spice. To Maija, it seemed he had long burned all the taste buds from his tongue, that the little buds had all waved their white flags after decades of interpreting the scorch of raw chili peppers. Paul claimed capsicum was good for his gums, and Maija wondered what good gums were when the tongue was collateral damage.

She'd also baked an Alexander cake and glazed it to perfection. She'd vacuumed the house and even spent an hour watching Montel Williams's self-help parenting program. Maija felt as if she could do it all, at least when she was the only one at home. The other inhabitants, her family, made getting things done difficult. No matter what she did or how hard she tried, she could not control everything; she was far from all-knowing, and she had not been blessed with strong parental communication skills. She had the sight, that was certain, but she rarely saw futures for her family, which was even more frustrating and led to her snooping. Instead of inquiring about Isabella's female changes and Vic's experiences at school, Maija held it in. Birds and bees remained bottled up, and they stung and ate each other. Since she couldn't discuss these difficult topics, she was forced to infiltrate their personal things and read them like runes.

Maija inspected the shoebox that she'd found tucked deep beneath Isabella's bed. It was, of course, more than a box—it was a portal into Isabella's brain, and Maija, mother of no words, parented as she mushroomed: once in a while and when no one was looking. She told herself it was out of love, but deep down she knew that entering dresser drawers and lifting dust ruffles with the intention of unearthing clusters of fleshy chanterelle fragrant with teen angst was necessary. Maija's mother, whom she called Ma while almost everyone else referred to her as Oma, wouldn't have even paused before looking, Maija reassured herself. If she'd bothered at all.

Oma's interest had always been, in Maija's eyes, in the lives of others. After Papa had passed away, it was as though Oma's identity as a mother had vanished along with her identity as a wife, leaving Maija alone. When they had first immigrated to Cleveland through the sponsorship of a Latvian Baptist church, Maija would go through Oma's things in hopes of feeling closer to her. Sneaking Oma's cameo around her neck had comforted her as she'd fought through the Ohio school system's remedial classes with disabled students, students branded as "slow" and other immigrants who struggled with the English language.

Oma would open this box and say that everything in her house was hers anyway, Maija thought as she sat at the foot of Isabella's bed. But still she hesitated.

She could still hear Montel Williams telling mothers that snooping was not right. His eyes had glimmered, his teeth had glistened, and his hairless head had glowed. Though she knew Montel meant to defend teen privacy to an audience of mothers, his piece only motivated her to scour Vic's and Isabella's bedrooms for secrets.

She imagined all the possible terrors stashed within Isabella's box: marijuana (the devil's weed), weapons (perhaps a gun), or, worse, the Pill. Like Pandora, whose all-gifted hands released the evils of the world and left poor Elpis, hope, in the jar, Maija opened the lid. She puzzled at the contents. If they were emblematic of her daughter's inner self, they weren't going to expose their secrets easily. She perused the items that belonged in the garbage: bottle caps, bits of string, paper clips linked together in a circle, a leaf, a ball of used rubber bands, Band-Aids, and gauze pads. Maija caressed the ordinary office supplies, searching for signs of rebellion. What did these items say about Isabella? It could mean she had a strange desire to collect dirty things; there was a term for that affliction—yes, hoarding. Or perhaps these were simply here to throw someone like Maija off a trail; she was a clever girl.

Maija dug further, and under the odd collection of stickers she found the treasure of all parenting treasures: a diary. She opened the first page and shut it immediately. Then she slowly opened it again and flipped quickly through the whole book. She saw some sort of code: BFF, 2GTBT, 459, 4EAE, BTWIAILWU. None of these codes made sense to Maija. Was Isabella in trouble? The only codes that Maija knew were pharmacological: OTC (over the counter), QOD (every other day), PO (for the mouth), and BID (twice a day). She closed the book and tried to forget everything that had taken place over the previous few minutes. She wished she'd never opened it in the first place.

The phone rang, and Maija jumped. In a rush, she rearranged the box the way she had found it and put it back under Isabella's bed in the same place. Guilt and regret began to build in her heart. She wished she could forget what just happened and pretend that there wasn't a code to decipher. It was her deepest flaw, that she could see the futures of others but not of her loved ones. What good was being a psychic at all? She shuffled her slipper-clad feet to the piss-yellow kitchen to the phone. The walls looked dreadful during the afternoon, when the fluorescent lights had to be turned on above the sink. "Summer Apricot, my *dūre*." Maija rolled her Rs. "Curse you, Lowe's employee who sold me this paint."

The phone rang a third time, and Maija picked it up.

"Hallo? Yes, Paul, my dear, what did you say?" Her heart pounded in her chest. "No, I've never played the lottery. Well—" Maija squinted, hoping the adjustment would increase the acuteness of her large ears, which hid beneath piles of thick brown curls.

"You want me to look at some lottery tickets? Why, darling? You know *it* doesn't work that way." She scrunched her nose into a button-sized embellishment between her two high cheekbones. Maija's blue eyes were murky like the sea, and her hair, particularly on humid fall days like this one, would mat together like seaweed tossed in a ruthless current. But an ocean goddess she was not. She was no mermaid or undine. She was stout, like her favorite beer, which she drank warm.

"Fine, yes, sweetie, I will look at them. Oh, bring home a gallon of milk, will you, dear?"

She cradled the phone between her ear and shoulder as she stacked the mail in a neat pile next to the computer in the kitchen nook. There was a notice from Cobalt High inviting parents to join the PTA, a few coupons from Dante's Hops and Pies, and another letter from India. "What? My *putns!* Poor Vicki. Okay, I will wait for him." News that her son was coming home with an injury was upsetting. At that moment her heart raced, and the letter from India began emanating light. It flickered opal like a small galaxy. It was irresistible to Maija.

"*Uz redzēšanos*," she said, then hung up.

This letter was different than the others from Paul's father. She lifted it to the fluorescent light and looked at the thin piece of parchment folded into a square inside. Maija had never met Paul's family because, he'd told her, they were poor and couldn't afford the plane tickets from India. Paul and Maija had met in a pharmacy in Cobalt years and years ago. He'd crushed his hand while fixing his car, and he'd been getting antibiotics to ward off infection. She'd fallen in love with him after their first picnic date in the park, when he told her she was the prettiest girl he'd ever seen and then kissed her. He told her she tasted like strawberries. They were married in the Cobalt courthouse by a justice, and only a couple friends were in attendance along with Oma. Her day was far from the wedding she'd imagined, but they were in love. Yet every time Maija asked him about his family, Paul turned to ice. Once, he'd mentioned something vague about his father's anger, and she took it to mean that his abusive nature had caused Paul to immigrate to America. Not knowing the details allowed Maija's imagination to run without reins.

Don't you think it would be good to make amends now? she'd asked years earlier. *Whatever happened, happened so long ago.*

Piyar, *you should be thankful I am not speaking to them,* he replied. *Otherwise they might decide to move in with us like other Indian in-laws.*

She'd kept her mouth shut after that.

The letters had begun to arrive a couple months ago, and their frequency was increasing. Why didn't Paul's father just call like a normal person? Maija shrugged and took a deep sniff from the letter's edge. The glue on the envelope's lip smelled like a journey across a sea by steamship.

At that moment, everything within Maija's vision froze, and her lips became icy, as though a cool breeze had blown across her face. The saliva in her mouth vanished. Her perspective was slipping, and she was being pulled gently backward into herself. It was an uncanny feeling. She thought it must be similar to the sensation Alice felt as she grew taller in the bottom of the rabbit hole.

Inside her mind, Maija came upon a scene. She felt rain pelt her face as she approached a dense forest. The trees bent and swayed under the wind, then parted to expose a dirt path. Maija moved forward, frightened. Her feet were bare. It felt as if the trees were watching her as she intruded into their home. A lion appeared up ahead, and she knew to follow. The dirt beneath her feet turned to water that began to rise. The lion vanished under the water, and in its place was something shiny in the soil. Maija was pushed into the water, which turned into an ocean. She swam under the water toward the shiny object, and when she reached for it, the edge cut her finger. Suddenly the water rushed away, and she was left, cheek down, in the mud. A small aluminum butterfly lay in her hand. She heard a tearing sound. A tall man wearing a *kurta pajama* was dragging a long *kirpan* along the forest ground in the distance. The blade was slicing open the land as he walked. Reddish brown soil bubbled up from the gash.

The vibrations of his steps shook Maija back into her kitchen. She sat up on the floor in front of the open refrigerator. A pitcher on the top shelf lay on its side; iced tea pooled around her bare feet. The slippers were across the room.

"*Vīratēvs.*"

From her vision, she knew that her father-in-law was coming to her home, and there was nothing she could do about it. She shook her head. Maija hoped he wouldn't pollute her home with his violence. Now she knew what was written in the letter: The man whom Paul called Papaji was coming. There was more, much more to decipher, but one thing was clear: His presence would change her home.

Maija wiped up the iced tea and threw the dishtowel in the sink. Dammit, she could work and plan and cook, and still she felt she had no control over life. She could see silly things in the future—the way she saw Mrs. Carmichael win fifty dollars on her scratcher, and now the strange vision about her father-in-law—but rarely anything to do with her immediate family.

Maija took off her reading glasses and looked at the letter. She focused her eyes, those penetrating steel orbs set perfectly apart with almond-shaped lids that suggested her relation to Mongolia. She was a woman of few words; she spoke through grin or sneer. Slow to warm, her stare, chilly as though it trickled from some mountain up on high, would grip others' smiles and greetings. And no, her eyebrows wouldn't curl, her eyelashes wouldn't flutter, and the uncanny, unabashed line one could draw from her eyes to those of her acquaintances could have been traveled by icicle. Maija's corneas, irises, lenses, retinas, and optic nerves rested precariously atop centuries of Latvian political oppression—they were the peaks of glaciers of her forced suspicion for all who were free to flash their teeth, for they might be the ones reporting to the KGB.

Okay, she said to herself, deep breath in, and deep breath out. Focus on the positive. Be present. She chanted a slogan: Where is my happy place? She dodged images in her head of Vic being beaten at school and of Papaji hitting Paul as a child.

Maija curled her toes and relaxed them, donned her slippers, and shuffled along to the pots with the makings of *sivēna galerts*, her favorite aspic loaf, on the stove. She relished the few days a week she could spend at home from her part-time job as a pharmacy technician—and nothing would ruin her day. Her feet would swell to a half size larger when she worked; during one shift, she would stand for at least ten hours. So, over the four days a week she spent at home, she kept her prettily painted toes nestled deep within her fuzzy, size-eight sheepskin slippers. Her feet were a size six. As she shuffled in the too-big slippers, she made a rhythm with her feet: one-two-three, one-two-three. She loved dancing. And though Paul did, too, they literally moved to beats from very different drummers: his was a *tabla* and sitar, hers a *kokle* and woodwind. As she shuffled across the kitchen floor, she wondered whether she should tell Paul what she'd seen. Better not, she thought; he needed to read the letters himself. Maybe she'd ask him about them. And in her kitchen, with the aroma of her sauerbraten wafting in the nostrils of her button-sized nose, she waltzed across the linoleum floor and directly, accidentally, into Vic.

"Oh, *mans zvirbulis*, you are home."

When Vic was born, he'd weighed only a few pounds, and as Maija held him in her arms she decided he resembled a little bird. Now, she gasped at her son's battered face and had to steady herself against the counter. "Vicki, who did this?"

She lifted his face under the light. His nose had been broken. Black eyes were forming. His cheek was bruised and swollen. Maija began to cry without a sound. This was the work of a villain. "Oh, my baby!"

"Mama, can we talk about this later? Ouch!" Vic's voice was nasally, and Maija pushed him to sit at a kitchen stool and turned his face this way and that. She looked into his nostrils, cut pieces off a new sponge, and carefully shoved the sponge inside. Then she piled a bag of frozen lima beans on his face and told him to sit still.

"Oh dear, does it hurt much?"

He did not respond.

"Where is your sissy Queen Isabella?" Maija asked while nervously dumping a pile of ibuprofen into her hand; a few fell to the floor, and she didn't pick them up.

"Rehearsal. The play."

"Ah, yes, will Michelle give her a ride home, then?" She tried her hardest not to say anything about the fight because that was Paul's department, though it was difficult. "You know, you are lucky to have such a nice little sissy, Vicki; you should take care of her. Ninth grade can be very difficult for kids these days."

Maija's fountain of parenting knowledge reached the end. She considered the archetypes she'd learned from television, including the troubled teens, pregnant teens, druggy teens, and even prostituting teens. Just earlier that day, she'd watched a special on the Internet and teens, and she was thankful neither of her children spent much time on their one family computer in the kitchen, except when papers were due. Oh yes, Vic had an obsession with a video game that had something to do with building a city, an entire simulated world. That and his blog he told her about. This sounded nice to Maija—so creative, not destructive—but Vic would never show his mother his creations.

"Please don't call me Vicki, Mama. Call me Vic."

"Oh yes. Sorry, *mazs dēls*." Maija put her hands on Vic's cheeks and concentrated in an attempt to see something, anything—but the other world gave her nothing, as usual.

"Mama, quit it!"

"Who did this to you?"

"I don't want to talk about it."

"Your father will fix it."

"It's like I'm asking for it, wearing this stupid thing on my head and all."

"Vicki!"

"There isn't even a *gurdwárá* in this town—why should I have to wear this?"

"You want I should start one? You're lucky I don't send you to

Latvian camp. There's one in Pennsylvania, you know. Or maybe you'd rather." Maija's cold eyes found Vic's pupils.

He looked unfazed. "You don't get it. Do kids in Latvia wear this?"

"I know how difficult the teen years are."

Vic went to his room without looking back at his mother. She knew he wouldn't emerge until his father requested his presence in the backyard later. She knew he thought it was unfair that his sister didn't have to display an element of their father's orthodox religion. But wasn't that part of being a teenager, thinking the world's against you and wondering why it's so unfair?

Maija wondered how having a grandparent in the house would change her children. She went to his bedroom; the door wasn't closed all the way, so she peeked inside. His hair was flowing down his back in curls, rebelling against the turban. He looked small under all that hair. He was sitting on the edge of his bed reading a comic. She wanted to go in, wanted to talk, but she wouldn't. What was he reading? A story about a rabbit samurai? She couldn't read the rest of the cover. *Ach*, she wanted to enter, but she remembered hearing somewhere that it was best to give space to teens. She just hoped he wasn't imagining what it would feel like to hold a sword in his own hands. But then she remembered his aversion to sharp objects and felt better.

Isabella

The stage was a collection of loosely assembled wood, nails, and glue, its floor covered in thick black paint, dulled and scratched by a thousand feet that crossed it in productions of *A Midsummer Night's Dream* and *The Crucible*. Behind the curtained walls: four metal chairs, six bowler hats, broken track lights, a working stepladder, and a podium. Stage left: a wooden cutout of a leafless willow tree painted black and gray. Stage right: petite Isabella Singh, with long black hair and caramel eyes hidden behind glasses, and sixteen-year-old Erik Fritjof, who looked like a scrawny descendant of Vikings.

Isabella's surroundings were standard as far as high school theaters went, but she had never been inside a real theater. The Royal Cineplex 5 didn't count; that was where she'd sneak in the back door with a bag of sour gummy worms tucked in her pocket and stay all day long, bouncing from one movie to the next as if it was her job. This theater was different. Its smell, for one thing, was a combination of dense mothballs and Elmer's glue. Isabella imagined that the stage was pasted together and wondered if it might collapse under the six drama club members and one rotund teacher. She estimated the distance to the exit was thirty seconds away at a sprint, and she wondered, if she ran fast enough, whether she could defy the space-time continuum and go back in time to three weeks earlier and not join the drama club.

"Are we square? One more time." Mr. Tewkesbury rubbed his belly over his red flannel shirt. Mr. Tewkesbury's Worcester accent caused him to avoid Rs as though they were arsenic, so his *square* sounded like *sk-way.*

Isabella adjusted the bowler hat tipped on her head. The black circle drawn over her left eye with face paint was running down her cheek. Rumor had it that the face paint was left over from when Tewks had done a stint in the circus as a clown. That was after his off-Broadway days, which he reminded his students of often. They'd been practicing the scene from *Waiting for Godot* because it would, as Tewks put it, help them intellectually understand his own play, *1,001 Cries*, which they would be performing in three weeks. Each week, he'd cast a different actor as Vladimir or Estragon. Now it was Isabella's turn as Estragon.

Isabella read her line. "Where are the leaves?"

Erik said, "It must be dead."

Isabella said, "No more weeping."

Tewks screamed, "No, no, no! You both sound like robots. Put some feeling into it. Remember what I told you earlier."

Isabella pushed her glasses higher on her nose. The rest of the club held its breath, too afraid to express their lack of comprehension. "Um, no, Mr. Tewkesbury. What do you mean by 'defiling plot,' and what does, er, something about 'rupturing representations of reality' mean?"

He growled and clumsily cleaned his round spectacles on the edge of his shirt. "I knew my gift to you all would go unappreciated." He twisted his copy of *Waiting for Godot* into an object appropriate for hitting students, then spread his hands and pushed outward at the students, as if through this action he could blast them all off the stage and out the rear door. "The author is a postmodernist. He is destroying the grand narrative."

"I get it, Mr. Tewkesbury. They don't, but I do." Tracy Finch's voice was cotton candy.

"No, I understand that part," Isabella said. "It's minimalist. But what's the point? Is it a play about nothing?" Isabella moved closer to Erik for support. Michelle, her best friend, moved toward her as well.

"Well—in a way." Tewks squinted.

"Like *Seinfeld*?" Erik ventured.

"Nothing like *Seinfeld.* Take five." Tewks clapped his hands, then pointed to Tracy, and they both went toward his office.

"Fun, fun," Michelle said to Isabella.

"What's he thinking, anyway? High school theater is about the big five." Erik shrugged.

"Big five?"

"*The Crucible, A Midsummer Night's Dream, A Christmas Carol, Beauty and the Beast*, and of course, if you're daring, *Arsenic and Old Lace.* I didn't sign up for postmodern drama. I hate the way that Tewks is forcing it down our throats. And, like, we should be spending time rehearsing *1,001 Cries.*"

"Yeah, and what's up with Tracy? She's so obviously his lap dog." Michelle tousled her blonde pixie haircut and stuck her finger down her throat in a faux gag.

Isabella nodded in agreement. She thought about Tracy. Isabella found herself hesitant around Tracy, always afraid she would see signs of the girl who had lived next door when they were children. What if Isabella got the urge to remind Tracy of the day they'd played hide-and-seek and Isabella had lost her pink My Little Pony in Tracy's backyard? What might happen if she mentioned the time they'd dressed in Mrs. Finch's clothes and pretended to be mommies to their baby dolls?

Reminiscing was only meaningful between two friends. Isabella would be a fool to ask Tracy how she liked living in the Heights, across the river. She would be even more foolish to ask how her life had changed since PMI closed and her father, who was a PMI director, was laid off and given enough severance to begin building the Heights development. The Finch flock had sold their house next to the Singhs on Peregrine Court, moved to their gated community across the river, and ascended the social ladder into the upper echelon of Cobalt. Isabella's father used to obsess about what Mr. Finch did to receive such a massive severance. It gave him little comfort to know the Finches had inherited the land on which they'd built the development from Mr. Finch's great-grandfather.

As Tewks and Tracy returned, Isabella looked at Tracy—in spite of the downpour of doubt, not because of it. Tracy's golden hair cascaded over her shoulders and down her slender back. Aside from the hair and eyes, Isabella couldn't find a trace of the girl she had known five years earlier. It was strange to realize that so much time had passed, yet this was the first moment Isabella had studied her ex-friend unabashedly. The sightings in the school halls were fleeting. Getting a good look at Tracy was like trying to spot a gazelle in a field of reeds. The divide between the microcosms of student society didn't allow them to interact.

Tewks had returned with a stack of paper, sweaty with determination. The students gathered around him eagerly.

"This should be good." Erik nudged Isabella's arm. She felt sparks all over her body.

Michelle gripped Isabella's arm. "Isabella, I have to tell you something."

"What, Michelle?"

Her friend looked nervous.

"Now," Tewks said, "I have to reassign the lead role, since the lead will no longer be with us. No complaining, no trading, and no crying."

Tracy scowled at Isabella.

"Isabella," Tewks continued, "since you've shown some promise, and I assume you've spent time with Michelle as she worked on this role, you will play Samantha from now on."

Gasps rose from the group.

"What? Me? Why?" Isabella turned to her friend. "Michelle?" Samantha was the President's daughter, who during the play was trapped in the bomb shelter with the Vice President, trying to talk him out of pressing the doomsday button.

"You will be perfect." Tewks grinned and clapped his hands together, making it so.

"I'm sorry," Michelle whispered. "I just found out and wanted to tell you before this, but all my teachers got a letter from my dad. I'm moving."

Isabella felt as if she'd been hit twice by a truck: Her best friend was moving, and she had to take her role. She'd signed up for drama club for three reasons: Michelle, Mrs. Stein, and Erik. First Michelle had wanted her to join. Then Mrs. Stein had ultimately convinced her to join after Isabella had neglected to turn in a paper about Charlotte Brontë. Isabella had tried to use "religious holiday" and "my grandmother's sick" as excuses, but Mrs. Stein had seen through it and suggested that she join the drama club for extra credit, adding that this extra credit would, in fact, be required in order to receive a decent grade in the class. And then Isabella had met Erik and decided she wanted to stay.

"You've made a mistake," Isabella said to Tewks. She was fine with a bit part like Girl #3 or the Explosion, which stood to the rear of the stage and didn't have to do much but scream *Bam* and shake a tambourine at a particular moment.

"Why, are you not comfortable playing the lead?"

"No, it's just—"

"Look, figure out if you want it by tomorrow morning. I'd really like to see you as Samantha. She's the Lolita of the play, okay, and you're perfect for the part."

Isabella blushed. Erik whispered, "That's hot."

"I'll have to think about it." She fought the urge to vomit; her heart raced.

"Okay." Tewks rolled his eyes. "You have one day. The show is scheduled to begin in three weeks. And now that we've changed things, we are in a crunch." He continued reassigning a few of the smaller roles.

Dammit! Isabella's thoughts were so loud she wondered if others could hear her. She couldn't possibly manage the lead role. She couldn't even remember her homework, much less an entire script. It was Tewks's fault they were behind schedule; now they all were going to be punished for his lack of connection to reality.

"No, not okay, Tewks." Tracy was the only student who had the permission to call him by his nickname. "She's all wrong for the part. I should be Samantha. Look at her! She totally can't even handle us looking at her right now. How is she supposed to manage an entire audience?"

Isabella laughed nervously. Her nose, which was a smaller, feminine version of her brother's, turned scarlet. When she was born, Isabella had looked just like her father's second cousin's mother—a woman named Rani who everyone said was *sohná*. When Isabella was eight, she began to look more like her mother's side of the family; her eyes appeared more unintentionally intense day by day. Now, as a teen, she finally looked like herself, independent of the Singh or Mazur tribes, aside from the nose.

"Shush up, Tracy. Samantha's Best Friend is a great role for you." He turned back to Isabella. "We'll have to do something about that overly responsive nose of yours. Do you have contacts?"

"You'll be great," Erik said before tossing his backpack over his shoulder and leaving with the other students.

In the hallway, Michelle held her hand and said, "Remember that time we told our moms we were sleeping at each other's houses and went to the haunted house in Oswego instead?"

"Yeah, brilliant idea. We didn't even make it until dark." Isabella rolled her eyes.

"And we thought we were going to sleep there through the night and take pictures of the old woman ghost."

"Mrs. Fletcher. Yeah, that was super creepy."

Then Michelle changed the subject. "I'm sorry I didn't get a chance to tell you first," she said. "My dad had to tell Tewks because he's a teacher."

"What's going on?"

"It's my immune system. They don't know what's wrong with me. They think I'm—"

"Don't even say it."

Michelle had been sick for months, but Isabella had just assumed it was mono or the flu or something that teenagers get. She never thought it was serious.

"I don't know. Maybe I've got something bad in my blood."

"Where are you going?"

"New York City. My dad got transferred there so we can be close to NYU and Columbia hospitals. I'm scared, Iz."

Isabella hugged her friend. "It'll be okay. I know it will." She said a prayer in her mind. She held Michelle's hand as they walked. "The city isn't far. I can take a bus there in three hours."

"Promise?"

"Promise. I'll ride the bus even if I have to sit next to a weirdo."

"You're gonna do great as Samantha."

"I can't."

"You can. Do it for me."

Isabella's stomach turned, and her head shook no.

"You want to come over?"

"I should head home. Mom's all into QT together. I'll walk."

"I have to pack anyway. I'll call you before I leave."

"I can't believe—" Isabella stopped, her words flat in her mouth.

She walked the long way home from school. The cold air was heavy with moisture. Isabella let the tears come without fight. They rolled warmly down her cheeks and around her mouth, then collected at the delicate point of her chin. She wished her run-down suburban surroundings were a desert, ocean, or forest. The houses she passed in the neighborhood around Cobalt High seemed to be watching her, judging her with their chipped-paint faces. Instead of inducing visions of comfort and apple pie, the word *neighborhood* twisted Isabella's stomach into knots.

She ducked into the clearing that ran between an old factory and the river near the Flats. Nature ignores us, she thought; it doesn't watch us. The wild had reclaimed the factory-turned-brownfield. Concrete slabs, rebar, and other remnants of the booming assembly of computer parts were almost fully appropriated. Tall grasses, young sycamores, and ivy sprouted from gaps in the walls and tilted cement blocks. A steel rod stabbed an oak tree that had grown too close to a wall. How slow the pain must have been, Isabella thought. The bark looked as if it had parted and made way for the metal that embedded itself into it—but it grew beyond that point; its branch made a detour around the steel. The tree continued.

She slowed her steps and peered into a glassless window of the factory. It smelled sweet inside, as if the last person who'd left had dumped a barrel of clover honey on the floor. They must have left quickly, she noted, because telephones, folders, desks, and other typical office equipment were still inside, as if an atom bomb had vaporized all the humans. She heard the *whoo-whoo* of a barn owl that was perched high in the rafters. It stared down at her with its ghostly, heart-shaped face. Humans leave permanent stains on the spaces they use, she thought, then turned her back to the brownfield and walked toward the thicket.

She'd learned in fourth grade that the cougar, *felis concolor,* and the wolf, *canis lupus*, were common in New York State—even here in the Southern Tier. Isabella looked for an imprint of these animals, but they'd left nothing. She imagined the cougar slinking through the tall grass and the wolf leaping through the forest. The image was so foreign, like trying to imagine an elephant or a grazing triceratops. She'd also completed a report on the Iroquois in that same class. Her mind was filling with absent lives. She took in her surroundings, extinct and otherwise.

As she continued along, the ground grew wet because of the Chautauqua River. A large black willow moaned with the wind. It looked nothing like the black cutout on the stage; this one still had most of its leaves. The wind blew, but the tree stood still. The roots ruptured the earth as though the spine of a creature were rising to the surface. Then Isabella noticed the long thin branches lift gently with the breeze. Just a moment before, she hadn't noticed this slight movement. She refocused her eyes, as though she were watching it for the first time, and was amazed: A beetle dove under a root. Ants marched in a line to the water's edge. Her shadow caused night to fall upon a forest of reeds. If she focused too hard, she could no longer see the details, but if she allowed her peripheral vision to lead, everything moved—like when she tried to count the number of stars in the Pleiades and they would disappear, then playfully reappear a moment later when she focused on something else.

Isabella bent over and picked up a rock at her feet. The rock wasn't special, but the moment was. She memorized the rough, reddish-gray surface. The rock would find a place among her collection in the shoebox or her locker at school. She wanted to remember this moment because she felt present. Some moments she wanted to remember because of their pain—like the ball of rubber bands she'd "borrowed" from Ms. Simm's desk after she'd passed away at ninety—or because of their joy, as in the paper clips she'd "borrowed" from Erik. These items embodied the essence of people, and when she perused her collection, it felt like communing with friends. She'd collected so many little things, and she never forgot the feeling of the moment to which it was attached.

Her path took her along the river; in this light the water looked black as tar. She met up with Main Street in the Flats and followed it all the way to her house on Peregrine Court, the split-level at the end of the cul-de-sac. As she turned her key in the lock, she heard strange metallic noises *twang* and *ting* from the backyard. She didn't check to see what it was; she just stood and listened instead.

Paul

From his chair at the head of the table, Paul surveyed the dining room as an emperor might his empire. He cast his eyes across the various dishes his wife had prepared for their dinner: sauerbraten, cabbage salad, *spec piragi,* and Alexander cake for dessert. His family sat in the designated chairs Maija had assigned at the beginning of time, after she'd bought the table-and-chair set, sanded them down, and stained them this deep walnut color.

Paul perused his offspring's cleanliness, noting Izzy's frizzy hair and Vic's face, which appeared more masculine because of his broken nose. He looked at his wife, his love, and noticed she looked tired. He remembered when he first saw Maija—how every part of her glowed as if there were something she knew about the world, some secret no one else knew about how it all was going to turn out. His love for Maija had grown exponentially every year since the first moment he'd kissed her in the park. He put his hand on hers and squeezed. She squeezed back.

Paul wiped his lips with his handkerchief. His mouth was watering.

Maija said, "Isabella, perhaps you should say it tonight for us."

Grace wasn't common in the Singh household—and Paul did not like it when Maija asked the children to say it—but Maija seemed happier after doing this ceremony, so he never interrupted. Maija arched her eyebrows over her granite eyes, but Isabella was quiet; only the sauerbraten bubbled.

Paul cleared his throat theatrically. Isabella sighed and closed her eyes; Vic did, too. But Paul sat twisting the moustache above his lip, as he often did, watching all of them.

"Thank you for the food, God," Isabella said, "and may you watch over all of us and"—she fought for words—"may you forgive us all. Amen."

Maija pursed her full lips. "What do we need forgiveness for?"

Isabella shrugged her shoulders. "I dunno. It just sounded right."

Paul thought that was silly. Forgiveness. For what? For being alive? Silly, but Isabella was a young woman, and, well, she was still learning.

"Did you find the letters from your father, Paul?" Maija ladled some *jus* onto the beef on Paul's plate.

"Not now, *piyar*," Paul said.

Paul kept his eyes locked on his plate. He thought about the pile of letters, one of which, he'd noticed, had already been opened and resealed poorly. He looked at Vic. No, his son had too many other important things going on. Then he looked at Maija—but she wouldn't be so anxious to see the contents if she'd already opened it. His eyes fell on his daughter, and right away he knew she was the culprit because her nose was red, which was a dead giveaway. But why she might do such a thing? Could it be because she wondered why his letters were being handled like a gift jewel sent from a maharaja? Paul imagined she'd opened the letter with the steam from her hot peppermint tea the week before, marveling at the careful up-and-down strokes of a ballpoint pen that made symbols—the Punjabi writing was a cross between ancient Greek and Chinese—and at how much like saltwater the parchment smelled. Or perhaps she'd thought nothing at all.

"What happened to your nose, Vic?" Isabella said. "It's bigger than it was yesterday."

"What happened to your face, Izzy?"

"Paul, darling? The letters—have you read them?"

Paul ignored his wife. He ignored his children. Instead, he relished the rich beef juice that filled his mouth. Paul thought Vic was looking even more handsome now. The bruises added a certain depth to his face. He knew, too, that having such scars while at school would be beneficial to his son's persona. Though he had been the recipient of the damage, he would be now considered a little dangerous, devil-may-care. Girls would find him more attractive and reckless. Paul watched his son eat as if he'd never seen food before, and added eating properly to the list of things he wished to teach him before too long.

Paul looked at Vic's hands as he shoved more and more food in his mouth. The bandages around his son's fingers told a deeper story. When Paul had returned home from the station earlier that evening, he'd decided that he would instruct Vic in the ways of Punjabi martial arts. Paul began with sword training. He kept his *kirpans* in the garage, above the chainsaw near a box with the Christmas ornaments. After he'd dusted them off, he'd taken Vic into the backyard and taught him to swing them and slice the air, though Vic had only managed to flail wildly and shear the tops off of Maija's roses.

Then they moved to sprinting; Paul joyfully showed Vic how to extend his neck and back synchronically with his calves and knees. They bounded like antelope along the fence until Paul was winded. Then there was hand-to-hand combat, which was most difficult for Vic. Paul insisted he should learn how to box, not to instigate a brawl but rather to be prepared in the event of one breaking out. He'd told him bullies were like locusts—they don't stop until you smash them underfoot—and he felt smart saying that. Paul had held up his hands and made Vic punch them repeatedly then alternately hit him in the stomach: right jab, left jab, right hook, left hook, body blow. One punch in particular turned Paul's complexion green. To hide the bout of nausea, Paul had blocked a punch and accidentally bent one of his son's fingers halfway backward.

Jesus, Papa, you wanna break my hand, too?

It's not broken, just sprained, it's okay, Paul said. *Let's do push-ups now, all right? One-handed.*

Paul had been so cheerful during the calisthenics that he'd barely noticed his burning muscles and strained back. As he watched his son, a harsh truth showered down upon him: How was he supposed to best his bully now, with an injured finger? Vic wasn't great at arm wrestling even with a healthy hand, and his punches were weak. Paul knew that the bully wouldn't stop until Vic fought back. Vic would have to use his brain. Intelligence was an asset in times like these. Paul had heard about the business of outsourcing for protection at Cobalt High: One kid traded his newest video game to be able to sit near another kid at lunch and walk home near him after school. Enlisting the support of others in his defense was an option, but that was far from heroic. No son of his would buy protection like that wimpy kid.

"Paul?" Maija pleaded.

"Um hum," Paul mumbled.

"The letters, darling. Did you find them?"

"I did. I found them."

"Oh, good, good. I wonder what they say."

Paul watched Maija survey the placement of the dishes on their doilies, which were supposed to prevent humid stains from appearing on the surface of the wood dining table. She adjusted them with care. Up to this point in their marriage, Paul had appreciated the fact that

Maija had allowed him to manage Vic, just as she would manage Queen Isabella. Paul and Maija had discussed, when she was pregnant with Vic, that their parental duties would be divided equally. *You are good with the emotional, but perhaps I should handle the boy myself,* na? he'd said. One boy and one girl later, they had become this thing he'd read about in the *Daily Mirror* called a nuclear family—almost.

"Paul, dear"—Maija swallowed her food—"do you think that these exercises you do with Vic are, what is it, extreme? Doesn't he get exercise in his gym class?"

"Mai-*ja*." Paul's voice separated her name into two distinct scolding syllables, but she didn't waver. Vic, on the other hand, dropped his head.

"Well, then, maybe you could explain exactly what you were doing out there with my son."

"Mama, it's fine."

"See, Maija, *it's fine*. The boy likes spending time with his father." Paul shook his head. He was not going to give her any clues about his logic. In his mind, it wasn't her place to wonder about such things.

"Okay, yes, fine." Maija offered a soft smile. "Have you read them?"

Paul looked out the window at the rain, which tattooed a rhythm on the concrete patio in their backyard. He took to shredding beef on his plate with his fork and knife. Why was Maija pushing him, here, now, in front of the children, for heaven's sake? He did not know. Any conversation about his father was sure to give him indigestion. He already ate several rolls of Tums every week. Even the suggestion of the letters triggered an unpleasant taste of blood in the back of his mouth. The beef turned to metal.

He found himself suddenly in different surroundings, reminiscing about a faraway place he was beginning to forget. He remembered his childhood in the village, which felt to him a distant memory of someone else's life—1955, Punjab: He was chasing his big brother, Kamal, under a dry, dusty sun through a wheat field that stretched all the way into tomorrow. The wheat, six feet in the air, was ready for harvest. Papaji was cutting it with a *dátrí,* his handheld sickle. Paul and Kamal went to get a closer look at the bundles of wheat.

Come on, yár, *you're too slow!* Kamal teased Paul.

Paul was smaller than his older brother. He stretched his body until sinews strained and muscles cramped. Kamal ran faster. His legs were longer, and his body was sleek like a panther's. Kamal had Papaji's countenance and would have his size, too. Paul hoped for the growth spurt that his Bebbeji said would come in time, though he knew even then that height alone wouldn't fill the crevasse between them; his differences would become more apparent as he grew. That secret was buried in the blood, and no one ever talked about it.

That day, as Paul and Kamal ran through the field that rose above their heads, they accidentally separated. Paul turned round and round to locate his brother, but all he could see was a golden wall of wheat. Then he heard Kamal scream. The wheat parted as Paul ran in the direction of the desperate voice. The tall grass whipped his cheeks and cut his chin. When Paul found Kamal, he was prostrate on the ground, shaking, a brown-and-black snake writhing nearby.

It bit me! Kill it, bhái! Kamal tossed him a knife. His nine-year-old hands clenched his foot as if pressure would make the serpent withdraw its poison. Snakes hid everywhere on their property, under beds, beneath bales of wheat—loathed demons of the earth.

Paul lifted the knife and dug his heel into the soil for balance, but he froze when the snake hissed. It buckled back into itself, threatening to uncoil in his direction. Fear consumed Paul, and he dropped the knife and ran to get his father.

Papaji wiped his forehead with the back of his rough and

calloused hand, tucked the edge of his turban back into its form, and slung his shotgun over his shoulder. Kamal was sweating when they found him amidst the forest of wheat. His foot, bloodied by the fangs that had entered his skin, was now twice its normal size and purple.

Where is it? Papaji aimed his shotgun at the ground around them, but Kamal said it had gone back into the thicket. Papaji smacked Paul across his cheek and told him he should have killed the snake so it would not bite again. *Or do you want it come out of the earth and bite you too,* na*? What good are you,* puttar*?* He addressed Paul in the same tone he used to speak with the washer boy.

Papaji pushed up the sleeves of his *kurta*, leaned over Kamal, and took his injured foot in his hand. *Hold your brother steady*, he said. Like a skilled surgeon, he flicked open his knife and cut a sizeable hole around the two deep bite marks. Kamal screamed. Papaji put his mouth to the wound, now rushing with blood, sucked the venom, and then spat.

Hurry, puttar. *Follow me.*

Papaji carried Kamal back to the *haveli* and asked his wife to fetch the nearest doctor. Paul's little sister, Prithi, cried amidst the commotion. It was five hours before anyone came to look at Kamal, five hours of writhing pain and prayer. *Wahe guru, wahe guru*—his mother's prayers steadied everyone. But when he came, the doctor was pleased by Papaji's method of venom extraction and thought Kamal had a good chance of healing on his own after his body dealt with the fever and poison. The doctor cleaned the wound with iodine and hot water, then tied it up while instructing Kamal to remain upright to keep the venom away from his heart. The doctor gave Papaji a small flask of whiskey to administer to Kamal for the pain and told him to clean the dressing on the wound each day. He said he would return in a week.

Kamal beat the poison; the snake wouldn't be his murderer.

Yet Papaji still blamed Paul for Kamal's tragic life; Paul felt guilty just by touching the letter. Though he was now a man with children of his own, the whisper of memory drew Paul back into a world of childhood regret and guilt. Paul grew frightened of the day when he would trip over that snake and have his turn with the fangs because he'd failed to kill it in the wheat fields of his youth. Paul had always hoped to find likeness with his family in his own appearance, but instead it set him apart. His face was round; Kamal's was thin. His nose was large; Kamal's was a perfect symmetrical slope. His hair was soft; Kamal's was thick, like a horse's tail. They were foils. Not to mention the terrible scar that ran up Paul's body from mid-thigh to his upper arm. He'd been told that when he was two, in a fit of curiosity he'd pulled a pot of boiling oil down onto himself. His torso today still looked as though it had gone through a meat grinder, as the scar stretched across his broadening adult form.

"Darling?" Maija's voice jarred Paul into the present.

"This—what is this, broiled beef?—lacks flavor and spice." Paul spoke angrily through his full mouth.

"Did you hear me? Have you read—?" Maija asked.

Vic shoved food into his mouth at an alarming speed.

"*Mundá*, slow down or you'll choke." Paul placed his large hand on Vic's hand.

"My head hurts," Vic said. "May I please be excused?"

"Yes, darling, of course." Maija turned to Vic when she spoke.

"No, *puttar*, stay." Paul dropped his fork on his plate.

Paul noticed Isabella's face change from white to green. She put her hands over her mouth and seemed to win the battle with a beast in her stomach, but then lost the war. She ran to the bathroom, and Paul heard the purge

Maija looked at Vic. "Tell me, Vic, darling, does she have boyfriend?"

Vic shrugged his shoulders, made a gross-out face, and mouthed, "I don't know."

"She'll be fine," Paul said. "It's probably nerves, the play."

"Darling, the letters." Maija sighed.

Paul growled, stood, pushed the chair behind him to the floor, and walked out of the room. He returned with the tall stack of letters, which he threw on the table, tipping the salt and pepper shakers. He tore open the envelopes one by one, occasionally tearing the letter inside. He read, took large draughts of his beer, grunted, and stabbed his wife with *kirpan*-sharp glares.

Then Paul lifted his chair from the ground, sat back down, and asked for the good scotch. Vic brought the bottle to the table with a glass. He asked for two more glasses, poured an inch into each glass, and passed one to his wife and one to his son.

"Sardar Harbans Singh is coming. We will need to prepare."

No one pressed him for details, and for that Paul was thankful.

ON THE WING

Metamorphosis

Posted on October 7

Some people hate the winters here because they expand across six of the twelve months of the year. Others find only the early summer exciting, with the end of school and ignition of fireflies, like fairies, floating through a transformed and magical night. I don't have a favorite season, but the in-between days when nature prepares for change have a special place in my heart. When seasons change, nature shows us who she really is. She's vulnerable at the end of summer when the grasses have grown too high and face decay and drought. Things go in reverse—leaves experience vertigo as they fall from their royal seats at the tops of willows, oaks, and other deciduous relatives. Flowers retract their blooms; petals turn mushroom-brown. Nature begins to shut her doors as bears prepare for hibernation, and many late-season butterflies reach their Spartan-esque pupa, which will remain frozen in stasis until the springtime thaw. Autumn is a time of en masse preparation.

Now, here in Cobalt, New York, the clouds have begun to darken and wrap fog around us like a wool scarf. There's little left for us to do other than self-soothe with long walks trampling through the fallen leaves. After the sun escapes the day, on a fairly clear night, I climb out my window and lie on the roof under the stars. The return of my friend Orion with his canine companions makes me happy. Every fall I wait for him to appear; throughout the year my eyes search an empty night sky for his figure, even though I know he is not there. Signs of consistency bring my mind peace.

The metamorphosis must bring the caterpillar comfort. After she consumes more than 2,700 times her weight, her tired jaws must celebrate when she hears her internal scale telling her she's fattened enough. Then, she casts a silken thread from her mouth, lassos a branch, flips around like a tiny acrobat, and holds the thread with her toes. Then she unzips her exoskeleton coat of caterpillar skin and exposes her hard chrysalis self underneath. Inside, during her longest rest, cells rearrange and move into different order. I wonder what it feels like to change, to truly morph like that. I wish I could rearrange into something like a grizzly bear or wolf—not a werewolf with its full moon limits but to shape-shift into something wild and strong forever, something that belongs only to nature.

I wonder if the unnamed butterfly I found earlier is endemic to Cobalt; it looks quite similar to the one I found a week ago except for the difference in color and shape on each side. It must be a part of the blue family because of the color, though it's possible it is a copper because I've been wrong about identifying them before.

It reminds me of the Spring Azure I saw months ago. I was sitting atop a clump of mud near a puddle of rain-water on the path I was taking beside the Chautauqua River; I thought my eyes were tricking me. I thought a piece of bright blue sky had fallen to the ground. The sun lit its wings in a way that reflected its slightly powder-blue iridescence. It must have been a male because they tend to be flashier to the human eye than the females. I kneeled down and lay flat on the damp ground about one foot away. It couldn't have been larger than my thumbnail, wings open. As it was so consumed with its meal of salt and nutrients from the wet earth, it didn't even seem to notice my presence. We spent nearly two minutes next to each other. I could also make out its drinking straw, the proboscis. Its wings were still warming to the world as they weren't fully uncurled and were still moist from its chrysalis. I read that Spring Azures only live for a few days before they lay eggs and die. Most of us think of the life of a butterfly as only the time when they are in the adult stage, in flight. The time it lives as an egg, caterpillar, in chrysalis to pupa, should be considered its infancy. If its life was three days long, and I spent two minutes with it, then we were more than passersby, perhaps acquaintances.

It would be a shame if the nameless blue remains so. I will take it on as my special duty to find out what it was like when it was alive, so that in death, it can find peace. I've spent a great deal of time searching through the Internet and the limited books I have here at my fingertips, and I still haven't found what I'm looking for. If anyone is reading this, if you have any idea what this butterfly is called, please post a comment below. Here is a brief description: one inch across the full body, maybe less, outer margins of the forewings and hind wings have a whitish fringe, the left side of the body is mostly an iridescent blue and the right side is an earthy brown, and there are white circles filled with black scattered along the post-median area of the wings. The left side has slightly sharper edges than the right. I have found butterflies that match parts of this description. Perhaps it's a new breed I've found, or perhaps nature has created a freak, like me.

Please post a comment below if you know what I've found.

0 COMMENTS

Maija

Maija saw tiles. From behind her counter in Jones Drugs, she looked at Mrs. Eleanora Finch and saw marble, glass, porcelain, and travertine. There were so many shapes and sizes, from the smallest and most variegated used to craft classical Italian mosaics to the sapphire squares that allowed Eleanora's kitchen and bathroom floors to match. How far had the little blue gems traveled to arrive in such a place? Were they made in China or Taiwan, or had some skillful Mexican or Italian man flattened a lump of clay into perfect thickness, sliced it into squares, and then fired it in a kiln? Maija wondered if he would hand paint each one or simply cover the squares with blue glaze and place them into the kiln's inferno once more. She could see him bending slightly and sliding the tray into the fire, a movement not unlike a child from a fairy tale his grandmother had told him about, a curious boy who was pushed into the oven and baked in the dough. Would he even have guessed that his tiles, from far across the Pacific or Atlantic and then a series of smaller seas, would arrive in a small town and play such a central role in a life so unaware of the importance of tile density and resistance? Maija couldn't just come out and ask her. She couldn't control the images and thoughts that poured into her mind as she stared across the counter at Eleanora Finch.

Maija took one look at Eleanora and knew she would die soon. She would have a heart attack.

Eleanora was the head of Cobalt High's PTA. And here, this Sunday, Eleanora's clogged arteries wouldn't be death's agent provocateur—no, it would be the blue-gray tiles that covered her shower that would crack her skull as her chest tightened and her feet slipped on the water.

As Eleanora handed her the small piece of paper from Dr. Green's office, her hand grazed Maija's wrist, and through this teensy touch, Maija saw something worrisome. What she saw without her eyes was not a complete and total picture but a series of images and flashes of sounds: Eleanora's floral Sunday dress hanging on a towel rack to loosen the wrinkles with steam; a shower running; a thud; blood mixing with water. It felt like a presage whispered to her from an inaudible voice. Maija took Eleanora's prescription and told her it would be ready in ten to fifteen minutes if she wanted to wait. Hoping Eleanora would wait, Maija attempted to sound as pleasant as she could and even added a sappy smile at the end of her sentence. Eleanora smiled at Maija, asked her how she was, then turned her back to her before Maija could reply.

Maija could never bring herself to truly rely on her visions. Sometimes the presage was dead on, and she felt it in every scruple of her being. She'd see something, and it would happen. Like the time she got up in the middle of the night with the feeling she should lock the door and in the morning heard that the neighbor's house had been robbed. Other times, particularly when dealing with death, these phantasms of her mind were more imprecise and symbolic, as the recent one with Papaji seemed to be. They could also be a manifestation of her anxieties and fears. She'd never understood why she couldn't see her family's futures. That was a cruel joke. Or perhaps the sight had to have limitations. Without vulnerability, her ability would be too powerful. This gift was a curse. But perhaps the disturbing image of Eleanora lying like a dead fish on the floor of her shower, breathing in the water that had puddled around her body, meant only that she would have an awful fall. Maija's mind may have altered the vision to include her latent feelings about Eleanora, who, since she had moved from the house next door five years ago, hadn't called her once.

No, she realized, this forecast was true. She had felt Eleanora's heart stop and her throat close.

Maija both believed and didn't believe her visions. If she doubted them too much, she would doubt herself, and it would be maddening to think that she was lying to herself. Still, Maija's confidence regarding her sight was waning because of her recent divination malfunction, the case of Mr. Bozeman. He came in last month as a new patient to fill a Viagra prescription. She had a terrible vision of a dark room in his house on Monroe Avenue, where he kept a girl no more than five years old tied to a chair and dressed in provocative clothes. She'd assumed from her vision that he was molesting a little girl and called the police with an anonymous tip that led nowhere. She even stole his address from his medical records and sat in her car one night across the street from his house, just in case she saw a child in need. It nearly drove her mad for a whole week, until she convinced the police anonymously that she was a neighbor and heard a fight and glass breaking. It turned out, the police said, that Mr. Bozeman was just babysitting his granddaughter. Why Maija saw what she had seen was beyond her. Regardless, a moment of misleading clairvoyance had been a blow to her self-esteem, not to mention her conscience, because she rarely acted upon the visions. If the images in her mind were becoming questionable, Maija feared the worst: that her sanity was finally giving way to the imagined future.

Perhaps Eleanora's demise would not come to pass, but still

Maija felt the urgency to try to save her former friend from a potentially painful end. Maybe the Plavix would thin her blood enough to give her another season, but medicine was about as accurate as soothsaying. Everything is theory, she thought, and most medicine had a success rate similar to the placebo in trials. The pills considered actual medicine were guesses that made large corporations piles of cash. If you popped a pill, your world of troubles nearly vanished, along with your liver. Nothing was ever truly certain; this was the only fact that Maija truly believed.

Maija watched Eleanora spin the display of plastic reading glasses. She was, as her surname suggested, avian in shape, with a face that drew to a slight point in the center and long fingers that mocked feathers. She seemed so young and didn't appear sick.

Maija typed Eleanora's information into the computer and put the slip of paper in a plastic basket behind her. She glanced at a postcard that a chain pharmacy recently mailed to her offering relocation to their newest store and top salary for experienced technicians. She propped up the card next to her screen so she could read more about it while she worked. The store was in Orlando, Florida, and she'd always wanted to see a white-sand beach. Beside the postcard was her favorite photo of Paul, taken during Christmas a few years ago at the Jones Drugs company party. He'd had a few eggnogs and looked like he was having a great time, smiling, laughing. Someone had dared him to put the plush antlers atop of his turban, and he never was one to pass up a dare. It was the small things Maija kept in her station that distracted her from the reality of her day-to-day. Palm trees and plush antlers were powerful numbing agents, as powerful as cocaine eye drops.

"Hey, lady. I'm next."

A lumpy-looking man stood at the counter. He came in from time to time to fill his antipsychotic drug, and today he looked worse than usual. His prescription was lost among his banana-length fingers as he held it out to where Maija had been standing earlier. The line had grown during the mere moments her back had been turned. Of course, the phone began to ring as well—line one, line two, and then line five were all on hold while she accepted a glare from the man with the big hands. This pharmacy had only one pharmacist, Tom Tingle, a man who on some days resembled Santa Claus and on others a truck driver. A girl named Shandy, whom Tom called their intern though it had been more than ten years since she'd walked through the doors of any school, managed the register. The pharmacy also had a drive-through window, but, thankfully, few of their customers had discovered this additional convenience.

Maija left the phone lines blinking and gave her physically present customer her attention. Tom Tingle was sitting on his stool as usual, not filling prescriptions but ready to check Maija's work after she was through. He smiled impatiently at her and moved the toothpick from corner to corner in his mouth. Today he looked like he drove a big rig.

"Can I help you, sir?"

The man responded by shoving his scrip forward once more and grunting with his mouth closed. His breath reeked even through his pursed lips. Maija looked at the scrip; it was the anti-seizure medicine Dilantin. She didn't need her power of insight to know that the dosage was extremely high, even for a man of his size.

"Sir, I have to call your doctor. It'll just be one moment."

"Why do you need to call her? I brought the paper like I'm supposed to, right? You think I'm stupid?"

Maija was tempted to say yes but forced her face into a smile instead. "Not at all; this is only protocol." She ignored the blinking lights as she dialed the doctor's number.

"What kind of call?" The man yelled this in a voice that bordered on hysterical.

The other customers were unimpressed by his antics, and they continued to stare impatiently at Maija over his shoulder. Maija heard the phone ring once through the receiver, but then she heard a familiar and unfortunate sound: three multi-tonal beeps followed by *I'm sorry, the number has been disconnected or*—and she hung up.

She looked up at the man, then toward the exit door that led to the rear parking lot. For one millisecond she considered the shoes on her swollen feet and wondered if she could make it to the safety of the Cutlass before the man noticed her absence. For one moment she imagined an alternate reality where her ankles had wings and she could tell Tom Tingle that he was an ass as she flitted away. It was the worry she felt for Eleanora that jarred her back into reality once more.

She went to the man at the counter and said, quietly but clearly, "I'm sorry, I cannot fill it. Your doctor is no longer in service. High dose."

The man seemed stupefied by her quick and fearless response, but he held his ground through confused eyes. "Can't fill it? This is legit, and you are required by law to fill it for me."

"No, I'm not." And she really wasn't. She had that one and only eject button in her back pocket that allowed her to toss out the crass, the slovenly, and the frighteningly rude. She'd never refused before—but Mr. Halitosis was different. He scared her. She could tell he was a drug user.

He asked to talk to her boss as he scowled at her. The man's open mouth allowed Maija to glance at the source of his gutter breath. He suffered from oral dental hyperplasia, a strange and off-putting condition that could have been brought on by his medicine. His gums grew halfway over his teeth, leaving the enamel looking like lumps of pebbles. And his saliva had all but dried up, which created a warm, dry nest where bacteria could grow. Maija sympathized, or tried; he needed better medical treatment because he obviously couldn't take care of himself.

"Boss, yes, well, I am sure he would be happy to—" Maija turned and saw only an empty stool spinning around. Tom was gone. Shandy was biting her chipped purple fingernails and reading a magazine behind the register. Maija stood alone.

"Where's Tom?"

"Huh?" Shandy replied with a digit wedged between her lips.

"Tom—where is he?"

Shandy shrugged and went back to her article. Maija glimpsed the article: "Swine-Child," about a forty-pound baby born with the head of a pig. She never had seen such articles in Latvia. Here anyone could say anything and make money from it. But, she thought, that is one of the reasons she'd immigrated.

She told the man that her boss was gone at the moment, but that he was welcome to come back later or try a different pharmacy. He grabbed the slip of paper, crumpled it up, and threw it at Maija's face without saying a word. Relieved by his exit, she went to work on Eleanora's medicine. Like a confident cuckoo that clucks an hour late, Tom reappeared with a sub sandwich in his hand—it was only ten in the morning.

Maija took a deep breath. This was the first hour of her day; she would have to stand here in the medicinal trenches behind the counter wearing her white god coat for at least nine more hours. She dug her heels into the rubber mat that helped her stand for hours on end and counted pills with a metal spatula. Eleanora was conducting a one-person fashion show in the slim, two-by-four-inch mirror on the side of the reading glasses display. She fluffed her wispy hair with her thin fingers, flashed a diamond the size of a walnut that couldn't have been real, and puckered her thin, almost nonexistent lips.

Mr. Herbert Finch, her husband, was a small and quiet man. Maija had only seen him a few times, years ago when she'd visit

Eleanora for tea. The Finch flock had never accepted any of her dinner invitations, so she hadn't had the chance to speak with him a great deal, or graze his hand for a tidbit of his future. He was shorter than Eleanora and much older. The gossipers in town whispered about how Eleanora had only married him for his potential fortune. Maija marveled at how ironic it would be if Eleanora died before her older husband. She felt a little sorry for Herbert.

She finished her prescription and handed it to Tom for inspection. Tom, lifting his nose from his sandwich, gave the bottle a hurried nod.

"Eleanora? It's ready." Maija stood at the receiving end at the window under a sign that read Pick up. Maija saw Tom pull a stack of official-looking papers on top of his sub. Even Shandy took a moment to look up from her magazine to acknowledge Eleanora.

"Can I pay for these here?" Eleanora handed Maija five pairs of reading glasses. "I just can't keep track of my glasses; if I stash a pair in every drawer, maybe I'd be able to read my day planner."

"Sure, no problem."

Maija attempted to touch Eleanora's hand again as she took the glasses from her, but her fingers fumbled and missed their chance. She just wanted to be sure of what she'd seen; if she spent any sleepless nights drowning in guilt, she wanted to know whether she deserved it or not. But her insight was stubborn and defiant and refused to give her any further image or message.

So Maija rang up the glasses and asked Eleanora if she was familiar with the medicine. She said she was, though she never looked up from the depths of her purse. Maija paused and told her it was very important for her to follow the instructions on the bottle. Eleanora waved her on, pulled out her overstuffed wallet, and dealt her a credit card out of a stack. Maija knelt down to swipe the Visa through the card machine under the counter. As she did so, she heard tires swerving on the rain-soaked road outside. The machine beeped at Maija, and she saw, much to her dismay, that the card was declined. She desperately swiped the card through the machine again, and again. It was social suicide, but she had to find the courage to efficiently ask Eleanora for another card. Maija stood with a board-straight back and gave a reassuring smile.

As she was about to open her mouth and let the words march professionally from her tongue, an explosion sent her falling to the floor. The drive-through window had shattered and sprayed shards of thin glass across the pharmacy and everyone within a twenty-foot radius. The brick that had broken the window landed right on the counter and smashed the bag that held Eleanora's medicine, denting the countertop.

Shandy held her hand to her right eye and screamed, while Tom ran into the back room again. Maija looked up, through the broken window, and saw the man with the Dilantin prescription standing in the fog with his mouth contorted into a pout.

Maija stood up, shaking, and yelled, "Asshole!"

The man jumped in his car and disappeared.

Maija cursed at the man in Latvian as she picked pieces of glass from her thick locks. Her net of hair had caught the majority of the glass and, thankfully, protected her face.

Eleanora took her card and bag with the smashed prescription and glasses from Maija and ran out the door. *Crap*, Maija thought. She would put the pills and glasses on Eleanora's growing tab.

In only a few minutes, the police arrived and Maija gave them a description of the assailant. "He was like a beast—ugly, sick, and a drug user."

"Any idea what triggered this?" The office took notes.

"He's on an antipsychotic. I can't imagine how he sees the world."

Shandy and Tom did not back her up. They said they hadn't seen a thing. By the end of all the brouhaha, Maija's watch only read two o'clock.

After the police left, Maija took refuge in the break room and locked the door by shoving a chair under the doorknob. Her hands quivered as she drank tinny-tasting water out of a Styrofoam cup. The fake wood paneling that seemed to cover every surface in the room, from table to cabinets to the sides of the ancient microwave, felt as if they were pushing in against her. The fluorescent tube light flickered. As she sat in a cold plastic chair, she lifted her knees to her chest and held them tight for a moment. Her breath left her lips dry and cold. Why, she thought, hadn't she seen the man's attack coming? Her sight was really off, and it had taken her intuition as well. She should have known that he would explode. She should have smelled it, if not dreamt it. She looked at the clock that smirked at her. Two o'clock! She'd promised to take Isabella to her first gynecological appointment today. This was one of those moments for which bottling up emotions came in handy.

She would also have to find an inconspicuous way to contact Eleanora to find out if she was healthy. She couldn't just call her up as a pharmacy technician because that could lead to unnecessary questions. It was curiosity that really got to Maija. She could deal with emotions like anger, frustration, sadness, and happiness quite well, but she could not manage to quell curiosity once it made itself known. Curiosity would sit in the center of her thoughts like a shiny red box with a big gold bow, begging to be opened. She hated the suggestion of being haunted by a person who wasn't even dead yet; perhaps she would attend the new member meeting for the PTA. She would have to find a way to speak with her.

At least no one had been injured. Her thoughts were erratic, and her chest felt tight. Maija left the break room and told Tom that she was taking a sick day. Tom mumbled something about telling corporate, but Maija held her hand up to his face, which stopped the flow of words. She walked out of the pharmacy with her purse slung over her shoulder and looked under her car before she climbed in. *Ach*, she needed a cup of tea.

Isabella

Birds and bees, fowl and insect: Isabella tried to understand the connection between these two flying creatures and human reproduction. Euphemisms only complicated the transmission of knowledge. She prayed her mother wouldn't feel the need to tell her about the birds and the bees, as she'd learned about sex long ago through a friend's older sister. As her mom drove the Cutlass through the fog, Isabella bit a hangnail and drew blood. She sat stiffly in the passenger seat, holding her backpack in her lap like a life preserver. Her mother turned on the windshield wipers to clear the mist.

"Oh, my God, Mama! Turn it off!" Isabella yelled. A large brown moth had gotten caught against the glass, only an inch from the wiper's path. Her mother switched them off.

"Poor creature." Her mother slowed the car, and the moth escaped.

Potholes punctuated the remainder of the ride to Dr. Gott's office. Her mother seemed tenser than usual. Isabella's stomachaches were worsening, and in a female form there were so many other organs down there, from ovaries to fallopian tubes, that Dr. Foster, their family physician, suggested Isabella make her first gynecological appointment to rule out ectopic pregnancy, cysts, and endometriosis. She could only imagine what her mother must've felt and thought when Dr. Foster even said the word *pregnant.* She must have freaked out. Isabella had no desire to have sex. Kissing, however, she thought of often when she saw Erik.

Her mother had told her that Oma had never mentioned to her how babies were made but that she'd managed to make two. When Isabella woke at thirteen to blood in her panties, her mother said, *Don't fret,* meita. *This is a part of your life now. You are a woman now.* And she left a box of tampons under the bathroom sink.

"So, Izzy," her mother said. "The exam might feel strange, but it only takes a second, and before you know it we'll be on our way home."

"Okay, Mama." Isabella clenched her jaw.

Her mother inhaled, gripped the wheel, and said, "Do you have any questions you'd like to ask me? I mean, about, you know, the—sex." She whispered the word *sex.*

"No." Isabella wished she had never heard the word *sex* from her mother's mouth.

"Because you know it is only meant for people who are married."

"Yeah, I get that."

"For making of the babies."

"Uh huh."

"You're too young to have a baby."

"Mama!"

Isabella wiped the small beads of sweat from her upper lip and daydreamed about being anywhere but locked in a moving vehicle with her mother skating around a sex talk. When they arrived at the doctor's office and were assigned an exam room, Isabella said, "Mama, maybe you can wait in the car or the waiting room?"

"No, no, I should come in with you."

"I don't know, Mama." Isabella imagined her mother's awkwardness making the exam even worse.

"I'll come in."

"Mama, I just—"

"Izzy, fine, go on and change and I will come in afterward."

Isabella sighed, frustrated by her mother's cluelessness. She wanted to tell her she needed to do this alone. Instead she said, "Whatever."

Isabella entered the room, closed the door behind her, and put on the gown. She left her green-striped tube socks on as a remnant of a less naked world. The mint-green gown did not feel fresh, and it was rough against her skin. They'd said "take off everything," so she had, almost.

Now she examined the room: Q-tips and cotton balls, tongue depressors and a box of gloves, size extra-large. Dr. Gott must have big hands, Isabella thought, big paws. She opened the first drawer and found open boxes of syringes, small bottles with soft plastic lids, and a cream she couldn't pronounce. She took a syringe and put it in the pocket of her jeans, which were folded up on a chair with the rest of her clothes.

The next drawer was full of tubes of lotion, most with the word *glide* integrated into the brand name: AstroGlide, SureGlide, GlideRight. She looked at the biohazard waste can and noticed a scrap of tissue hanging out of the top. Doctor's offices should be sterile so you forget about all the other butts that have sat on the table before yours, Isabella thought—like a thin piece of white paper can actually protect us from one another anyway. Might as well be sitting butt to butt with Mrs. Mulch (who she'd seen in the lobby making a follow-up appointment for something contagious) or Ms. Charlotte (who smelled as though she needed immediate attention). Isabella tore a few sheets of paper towels from the dispenser and put them bum-level on the table, then rested her bare back against the paper. Her gown left much to be desired, as it was nothing like a dress. They should call them aprons instead, or chaps perhaps, she thought.

There was a knock on the door.

"Mama?"

Her mother entered the room and sat down with a stack of *People* magazines. Isabella gripped the crunchy paper. They wouldn't find anything inside her unless she could get pregnant just by looking at someone. She remembered seventh grade, when the principal separated the girls and boys for reproductive abstinence education. Coach Seibel, chapped-lipped and red-faced, led the boys, and Ms. Johovic, an ex-army nurse, led the girls. Ms. Johovic was brutal in her description of the female anatomy as an "overly fertile fruit tree that would take the pollen from any bee to make a crabapple." So romantic, Isabella thought. Ms. Johovic's chalk drawing of the uterus looked like a cross-section of a fly.

Thank God for the mobile that hung from the popcorn ceiling and the little origami horses that dangled from a carousel-type structure. Isabella wondered if the horses would keep her from freaking out during the examination. She had no idea how cold the forceps would be and how strange it would feel to shoot the breeze with someone while they opened you up inside and scraped your cervix with a tiny metal brush. Yet the horses danced, and Isabella watched. She heard metallic carousel music playing in her mind. She heard the organ puffing thick notes against the *oompa-oompa* of the tuba and the twang of a flute. She remembered the Mad Hatter's un-birthday tea party. The air smelled of candy. Her skin grew dewy with midsummer humidity. The origami horses' pulpy forms were shocking pink, blue, and yellow. She almost succeeded in leaving the fluorescent confines of the paper-toweled table. Then, with one shiver, she psychically returned to Dr. Gott's examination room, awaiting Her Divinity's presence.

She didn't know how much longer she could stand to wait. Her jeans looked so inviting and warm on the chair next to her mother. She wanted to get dressed. Her mother would understand; she obviously didn't want to be here either. But then the door opened, and in walked the long-awaited white coat.

"So." The doctor looked Isabella up and down. "I am Dr. Gott, but you can call me Polly." She shook her mother's hand.

Polly was an adult-shaped person, not tall but taller than Isabella, and she smelled of vanilla perfume. Isabella couldn't get a good look at her hands. "It says here that you're having pains in your abdomen?"

"I guess. I mean, yes. Dr. Foster said it could just be food allergies or something, but that since I am fourteen, I should get checked out." Isabella blushed.

"And when did your last menstrual cycle begin?"

"Oh, um, two weeks ago."

"Okay, and how long have you had pain in your abdomen?"

"How long?"

"When did this start?"

"I don't remember."

"About two months, I'd say," her mother interjected. "That's when I had to start making peppermint tea for her every night. Yes, two months."

"How long does the pain last when it happens?"

"I don't know."

"An evening. It lasts the whole evening." Her mother put down her magazine.

"Okay, Isabella, is that true?"

She shrugged a yes.

"Well, let's take a look then, okay? Just lie back for me and tell me when it hurts." Dr. Gott pulled out the table extension, which allowed Isabella to rest her legs as Dr. Gott pressed her abdomen in various areas, beginning with the middle. Isabella could feel her lunch still sitting there in her stomach, and she hoped Dr. Gott didn't think it was a tumor growing inside. The doctor's large hands moved to the right, then the left, the lower center, the lower left. Her hands were huge. The nails were short. The mobile watched her as this woman pressed her belly. When she reached the lower right, Isabella lurched forward and upright.

"Sorry," Dr. Gott said. "Now, does it hurt worse once my hands lifted or when they first pushed down?"

"I don't know; it just hurts." Now she really wanted to leave.

"Have you been feeling sick to your stomach?"

"Yes. For weeks."

"Since the play," her mother said. "It's stage fright, I think."

"Okay, now relax. I am going to take a look inside, okay?"

Isabella had *never* felt such a deep pain before, nor had she felt more uncomfortable with another human being. She'd had her period, sure; she'd heard about these kinds of gynecological tests, but she wasn't prepared.

"What are you looking for?" she asked and peeked over her blue paper apron down at the doctor, holding on to the table with both hands. Maybe it wasn't such a good idea to have let her mother into the room with her. Her mother was looking away, sitting in the furthest corner of her chair as though she, too, wanted out of the small room.

"I'm just taking a sample to be sure that everything is as it should be. It'll only take a second. We women have more than just stomachs in there, you know."

When she was done, Dr. Gott slid off her extremely large gloves from her extremely large hands and told Isabella she could sit up. It was wet between her legs. Now she was truly cold.

Dr. Gott smiled. "Everything looks fine. We'll call if the test shows anything abnormal. I doubt you have a cyst. I'd say you might want to eat more fiber and drink more water. Perhaps your system is out of balance. Try this." She handed Isabella some samples of fiber supplements. "Let me know how you feel in a month. If the pain becomes acute or you get a fever, call me."

After her mother stepped out into the hall, Isabella got dressed in under a minute and dumped her gown in the trash. They were quiet on the ride home. Isabella was relieved. Dr. Gott must have assured her mother that she was not having sex. She was pleased with this small victory.

"I don't think anything is wrong with me. Just a stomachache."

"Yes, that's great. Take the fiber supplements and drink more water."

When they arrived home, Isabella looked at her mother and wished, for once, that she'd open up or close completely. She felt her mother teetered somewhere between the two stages, which made her nervous. She envied the fictional relationships characters on sitcoms had with their mothers as friends or buddies.

Isabella changed into her pajamas when they got home, even though it was only late afternoon. Her mother took a nap that lasted for hours. When her father came home from the station, she felt his curiosity as to why she was wearing flannel pajamas during the day. Isabella was thankful for once that her father pretended not to notice her at this particular moment because, she knew, he ignored things that could potentially be uniquely female, as that was outside his department.

Paul

As Paul stood on the concrete step leading into his dingy garage, he imagined how it would feel to stand on a porch gazing into the expansive Western wilderness. Where those boxes lined the walls three deep, tumbleweed would be rolling. The unfinished ceiling of exposed wood and wires would be a tangle of manzanita branches through which he would watch a hawk against a blue sky dive skillfully toward the sandy earth after a rabbit or rodent. He squinted, though the space was already dimly lit.

Paul went back inside to his bedroom closet and traded his slippers for his cowboy boots. He returned to his garage with a cowboy's swagger. His strut was smooth because he'd practiced before; it was just like Eastwood's in *The Good, the Bad and the Ugly*. Paul had studied the movie as a child when he visited the city with his family. He'd seen every western he could get his hands on. *Hang 'Em High*, *A Fistful of Dollars*, and *For a Few Dollars More* were his favorites. He'd always wanted to be a real American cowboy. He imagined he was a loner wandering into a skeleton of a town. Wind had blown dust into the air and turned the midday light to the shades of sunset, and the silence was ear piercing. Paul smiled and sat down on the concrete step leading to his garage, took his knife from his back pocket, and used the edge of the blade to trim his fingernails. Maybe he'd pick up whittling.

He looked around the room, and his imagined surroundings vanished; the mess confronted his eyes as a vulgar contrast to the Wild West. There hadn't been room to park their car in the garage for years. He had no idea what they kept in these boxes. The one thing in the garage that he always kept a watchful eye on was the small gray lockbox with his pistol inside. It was set high on the shelf above the door leading back to the house and was always locked for safety. But besides this, the whole family could go almost an entire year without retrieving anything from the garage.

Paul stood, sizing up a box at the bottom of the pile, then kicking it with the metal tipped toe of his boot. A large crack opened on the cardboard seam. He bent to see what was inside: a few hunter-green files filled with old receipts, a stack of photos he'd never seen, and a beer stein with Ikpaul Singh #1 engraved on a sliver of nickel in an old-English font. He'd won it through the regional Service Station of the Year contest. He shoved his hand into the hole to free the stein from the jungle of papers, but its size denied him the return journey. He used his knife to widen the split cardboard seam by slicing a circle around the gash, but still it wouldn't come out. Something must be wrapped around the handle.

Though there were several more practical methods for retrieving the stein, such as disassembling the piles of boxes or moving the ones that impeded his box's freedom, when he saw his ax he remembered how Indians used the tomahawk in battle in *The Last of the Mohicans* and couldn't resist the smooth handle. He hadn't used it since that old sycamore fell in their backyard and he'd decided to chop it up, bit by bit. He lifted the ax from the hook on the wall, planted his feet firmly into the concrete floor, and took a conservative swipe at the box. He missed the crease by an inch or two and instead decapitated pale pink buds from a silk flower arrangement. He tried once more and this time delivered a messy wound. Sweat poured from his brow as he focused. Again he struck the box, and again. Injuries were inflicted on the surrounding tchotchkes, and two smaller boxes collapsed completely and expelled their scraps and books and knick-knacks: a water testing kit, two identical pairs of gardening gloves, and a few feet of non-specific plastic tubing. He hit the two-by-four in the wall three times. He even slammed the blade into the concrete, but the only evidence of that mistake was a twang of pain inside his rotator cuff.

"Hey, Papa. I found them." Isabella stood in the doorway between the garage and the house. In her hand was a small, shiny object: nail clippers. "What happened in here?"

Paul placed the ax back on the wall hook, wiped his forehead, and said, "Just cleaning."

"Now I know why Mama doesn't let you clean the kitchen."

"Did she say something about that?"

"No, I was just kidding, Papa."

"How was your doctor's appointment?"

"Fine."

Paul waited for more information, but nothing came.

"Well, I'll be inside then, Papa."

Paul looked at the mess, made out the location of the stein, and dug in with both hands. He pulled it free as the precarious tower of boxes crumbled. He spit-shined his prize and sat down again on his concrete step. He doubted that Papaji had ever seen a stein before—or won an award.

The activity had been a good stress reliever—his father's pending arrival had put Paul on edge. After he'd read the letters, in which the same information was written in variations, Paul had kept the last one in his pocket at all times. Papaji's letters, formally signed *Mr. Harbans Singh*, were written in Punjabi and usually began with a fragment of gossip. "Massey Sukminder thinks the servant stole her shoes; the woman is losing her mind." Or "Uncle Chand is going in for stomach surgery. Thanks be to God. The man smells of old age. We can only hope for the best."

Papaji had moved from the village into his cousin's home in New Delhi because of a bad foot. The four-story flat had become a convalescent space for all the related aging elders. Admitting he needed help walking had not been easy for Papaji—Paul understood this from the letters. He was a man who liked the outdoors, his shotgun, and his *haveli*. Living in New Delhi was akin to living in an unpaved New York City. The pain in his foot must have truly become unbearable, Paul thought, for him to trade his wheat fields for the oppressive congestion of the city streets.

And when he arrived, what would they talk about? Would Papaji judge his family as he'd judged Paul his whole life? Papaji had barely acknowledged Paul since the accident, and now his presence would force Paul to remember things that he wished had passed with the dead. Paul could do nothing but prepare himself for the stoic presence of his father by reminding himself that this was his home, not Papaji's, and he belonged here.

He'd studied the intricate characters that he missed and was thankful he could still read Punjabi. The most recent one read:

To Mr. Ikpaul Singh:

You would be interested to learn that Gurumukh Uncle did well after his visit to the apothecary. They managed to heal his blinding headaches with a homeopathic tincture. I know it has been long since we've spoken. I believe you have now received at least one of the letters I've sent in duplicate because I was not confident of the address. My son, I now see, nearing the end of my life, that I wasted the time I was given with you. I hope that you receive me now, at this late hour, as my flight to America is fast approaching. I've enclosed my flight information below. My injury has almost crippled me, son, and I am coming in hopes that a good American doctor will be able to help my ailing limb. I've saved money to pay for the medical care.

Signed,

Sardar Harbans Singh

American Airlines, New Delhi to NYC La Guardia, 3:00 p.m.

US Airways, NYC La Guardia to Cobalt, 5:00 p.m.

Papaji had not mentioned his mother, Bebbeji, in the letters. No one had mentioned her since Paul had left for America. She'd passed away right after he'd left—and he hadn't had the money saved then to return home for the funeral. Papaji and Bebbeji had been estranged and hadn't lived together since before Paul was a teenager; divorce hadn't been an option. They had been too young when they married. She had been barely fifteen; he'd turned seventeen the day before their wedding ceremony. The pressures of adulthood and the damaging events that transpired during the Partition had taken a toll on their relationship. Paul had been relieved when they separated—the silence he felt between his mother and father had been so unbearable that he had to move all the way to America to escape the void.

Paul made his way into the house with a prize in his hands. "Maija, look what I found! Who packed my German stein away?"

Isabella came out of her room and whispered that Maija was napping. And finally, Paul realized that Maija was indeed tired. He'd wondered why she had taken a nap—this was out of character. Before they'd decided to have children, Paul and Maija had a talk about children and how it would change their lives forever. She was worried that he wouldn't find her attractive after she put on baby weight, but he assured her he would, and his affections had never waned. He was worried that he wouldn't be a good father because, well, his father was such a phantasm of a figure in his life. Maija made it clear to him that they would do as others had done for centuries and figure it out as they went along. They made love that night with such passion that they saw the sun rise. A few weeks later, Maija had come to him and whispered that they were going to have a baby.

Now, Paul walked into the bedroom to watch Maija sleep. Her arm was draped over her eyes as though she wanted to keep the light out. He went to the bed beside her, carefully, so as not to wake her, and kissed her cheek. Maija smiled without lifting her arm from her eyes.

"*Piyar*, you okay?" he asked.

"Headache."

"Okay. Rest well." He left the room quietly.

In the kitchen, Paul sat down and turned on the old PC. He placed the stein gently next to the screen, where he suspected it would remain until Maija managed to pack it away secretly once more. Paul appraised his nail cutting job and tapped his two pointer fingers against the keys. In the search engine, he typed: *road construction Cobalt*. The first link led him to the local paper, the *Daily Mirror*. He began to sort through the various articles in hopes of finding a report about the mess in front of his station, but because it was a side road, nothing came up. What had apparently begun as a village improvement had ended up an enormous hole in the ground with a gigantic pile of debris beside it. He wanted to know how repaving the road or repairing the sinkhole could lead to such destruction, and whether there was any way he could be compensated for his lost business.

The journalists at the *Daily Mirror*, however, were not so

concerned with side roads in the city. Paul skipped over the next story, about a ten-year-old girl not far from their neighborhood who recently won a national spelling bee.

"Papa, um, what are you looking for?" Isabella stood behind him, her eyes squinting at the screen through her glasses.

"*Dhí*, what are these *um*s? All the time *um*. Be sure of yourself, or don't say anything." Then, after making note of her red-and-green plaid pajamas, he said in a different tone, "Just reading the paper."

Isabella shrugged her shoulders, got a glass of water, and went back to her room. As soon as he heard her door close, Paul typed *construction* into the newspaper's search box. There were several links to the Chautauqua Bridge reconstruction and the recent upgrades at the water treatment plant, but nothing much about the road construction on Sycamore Road. As he clicked through the archives, his mind wandered.

He imagined sitting behind a podium, shuffling several sheets of loose-leaf paper. There were important men, like the mayor and Dante Espirito of Dante's Hops and Pies, wearing black and navy wool suits, sitting behind microphoned tables waiting for his speech to begin. The wood-paneled walls in the hall rivaled the courtroom in a *Law & Order* episode. He cleared his throat and began to speak knowledgeably about the thickness of asphalt and the benefits of creating a working construction plan before beginning a demolition process. Behind him on a screen, a projector illuminated charts and graphs and maps that Paul pointed to at the perfect time to highlight his plan. The suited men nodded and applauded Paul as he bowed and shook hands. He would be the hero of the town. Paul would find a way to fix the road. He would become a politician.

Finally, his search brought him to an archived article that contained a city map, so he clicked on the magnification icon. The crossroads were clear enough—but what was that large rectangle surrounding the entire block? It was shaded in a light green and unlabeled. The rectangle extended across the railroad tracks, behind the gas station, across the street into the residential area, and down Main Street right where the construction was taking place. His station was in the center of the rectangle. At the very bottom of the map he found a copyright that read COBALT HISTORICAL SOCIETY, 2000. He found the Historical Society's website, located the hours of operation, and decided he had time to go there before Maija woke from her nap.

He remembered how his father was the one honest man in the village and, because of his knack for truth, became a sort of counselor for all. He sat in on first meetings when a wedding would be arranged: He sat in the background and listened to the way the groom's family spoke (or the bride's) and could decipher whether the family was hiding behind a dowry or behind greasy smiles, and sometimes he'd inquire about filial illness or ask to see the teeth of the girl or boy to be engaged to ensure they were healthy. People trusted him, Harbans Singh, as his beard was the longest, and he was the tallest and the most vocally reserved—these qualities together made him honorable to all. Paul straightened his back, smoothed his moustache like wings on his upper lip, and left the house.

~

The Cobalt Historical Society was located on a street that once was residential but had been consumed by industry, then spat out. Skeleton structures and buildings that no longer functioned as either home or business lined Monroe Avenue. Paul parked and looked out across an empty parking lot the size of a city block, perpendicular to where he stood. It looked like a hurried graveyard, as the asphalt was lumpy and uneven. The stretch of black was empty, and the Kmart for which it had been constructed was going out of business. The Historical Society, housed within a whitewashed Victorian house, was the only structure around that looked as though it contained life. Paul thought if he could pretend it was the nineteenth century and look away from the industrial ugliness, perhaps he could find beauty in his surroundings. He wondered if this town had been a Pleasantville when it was first settled. Or if it had always been just a scab on the earth's surface, a blacktop Band-Aid suffocating the grass.

He entered the building, and an older woman behind the desk introduced herself as Nancy and guided him on a photo tour of the town. As they went from room to room, she pointed to the life-sized images on the walls of the first bank in town, the first carousel, and ghostly figures in turn-of-the-century attire, and she told him how Cobalt was the first stop for any Italian or Irish immigrant who landed in New York City.

"There was a train that brought them all right here," she said. "There was a factory that employed more than twenty thousand men, women and children. They made shoes."

Paul thought about how any association with feet as a profession was characteristic of the lowest caste in India. Though Gandhi had metaphorically ousted the caste system, remnants of it still remained. Paul questioned what the harm was in making shoes—everyone needed them—but he couldn't get past the caste crisis. That was an entirely different problem.

He noticed one fellow that showed up in almost all of the photos.

"Oh, that's our founder, Heathrow Johnson," Nancy said. "He built this town on a strong work ethic." She pointed to a photograph from at least one hundred years earlier of the gray stone arch that curved over Main Street. There was a freemason's symbol at the highest point and an inscription that read: HOME OF THE SQUARE DEAL. The arch was still there; Paul passed it each time he went down Main

Street. It was now directly next to the golden arches of a McDonald's, which cast a shadow over the stone structure.

Nancy told him that Cobalt was first a mining community but that all of the digging in the earth had been long since abandoned because a catastrophic flood had brought the natural water table higher more than a century ago.

"Do you keep maps of the town?" he asked. "Can I look at them?"

She was delighted to have someone interested in the layout of the town—so delighted, in fact, that she smiled as she unlocked the back room, which she said hadn't been opened in years. She turned on the flickering fluorescent lights and pulled out several maps protected by a thin plastic film. As Paul sat down, she spread the maps across the table and said, "These are originals. Say, where are you from?"

"India."

"That's interesting. So far away." She leaned in too close over Paul's shoulder as he perused the map. He could smell the hairspray that she'd sprayed on her white hair. This closeness made him uncomfortable, so he twisted his wedding band to make certain Nancy could see it clearly. He was thankful when the phone rang and she excused herself.

The map that interested Paul most was the one that illustrated the different underground goings-on: the drainage, sewer systems, and water. A complicated web of snakes twisted around everything. He placed the underground map beside a very simple map of the natural area, which depicted the hills, the low points, and the bodies of water. He didn't notice anything unusual except for the web of pipes that tangled under the town in several different areas.

Nancy came back into the room.

"Ms. Nancy, do you know of any other maps that would show what is under the ground here?"

"Maybe I could help you better if you told me what you were

looking for."

"I'm a history buff. This is my neighborhood, here. Just want to know what came before us."

She wrinkled her forehead and went to the back room. When she returned, she brought three maps of different sizes. "These are from around the time Progressive Machines International came to town, in 1908, but it wasn't called that yet. A lot of things changed since then. Be careful with these; they are the only ones that PMI left."

The PMI campus sprawled across the base of the hillside, contained only by the borders of South Street and the forest line. It ran about four full city blocks. Paul saw now how close his home on Peregrine was to the site. Every building on the PMI campus was white: white concrete, marble, frosted glass. It dominated the surrounding area like an industrial ice city. It had shut down about five years ago, and many of the streets had closed as well. Everyone assumed that PMI, like many corporations in a changing world, found it cheaper to outsource.

Paul shook his head. The Cobalt community had depended on PMI. Families moved into town because of Progressive Machines International's promise: *Our machines make your life easier.* Then, suddenly, as though it was only a phantom, the company dissolved after sixty or so years of operation. No more bustling about. Thousands of people—mothers, fathers, brothers, sisters, and friends—without jobs and without decent severance packages flooded the unemployment lines in downtown Cobalt. Some had worked their entire lives at the plant and had no other skills other than the specific placement of a particular chip in a particular slot, that key into that typewriter. Even Paul had worked there for a short time, until he decided he wanted to run his own business. He'd gotten a good deal on the gas station from a family who'd inherited it and didn't want it, and that was that.

The phone rang once more, and Nancy went into the lobby to answer. Paul looked at the map. He put his finger on Main Street and walked it toward his station. There were things he couldn't make out along the pipeline. Oh, how he wanted to make a copy of this map. Perhaps Nancy would allow it. No—she wanted to be the gatekeeper of Cobalt's history. Paul squinted, cleared his throat, and made up his mind. He looked toward the lobby and saw Nancy twirling the phone cord in her hand, her back to him. He gently rolled the map into a tube and covered it with his Members Only jacket. He waved to Nancy as though he were saying *It's all right* and left with the jacket under his arm. He walked with a swagger, slow and methodical. He was a renegade.

Vic

It wasn't long before Vic gave in to the ache in his knees and knelt on the ground. The grass was cool and a bit moist. He tried to prevent grass stains on his knees by keeping his movement down to a minimum. It was quiet in Vic's favorite pasture—he had to walk nearly a mile from the closest street before he came to the first hill, then across a short span of bog and then over another hill to finally arrive at the stretch of earth that stood just in front of the thick red pine and hemlock forest.

Vic enjoyed visiting this place he called *his land* for many reasons. Though homesteading was a thing of America's distant past, and he knew claiming open land and building a home was now a romantic chapter in a history book, he still dreamed of such a life, in which he'd have the freedom to live near an untouched forest that would provide deer to observe and berries to pick. His land was beautiful in a sigh-inducing way. Little insects and butterflies coasted above the tall grasses, and if he squinted, they would become fairies or gnomes. Although it was fall, and there had been a particularly odd first frost, there were still a few airborne mayflies. Vic adjusted the brown baseball cap atop his *patka* and narrowed his eyes. He was watching the few coasting insects, hoping to spot a butterfly, a grass skipper or small satyr. He would love to see a satyr to inspect the small dots on its wings, which mock a many-eyed creature of a much larger size. Maybe he would finally spot that strange blue butterfly in his shadow box that books failed to identify. He knew that there were various blues in the area, but he had only seen them in the spring months.

Just earlier that day, Vic had made one of his more fascinating discoveries while researching the area's butterflies in the public library: Some caterpillars allowed themselves to be raised by ants. Myrmecophily was the term that explained how ants nurtured and protected certain caterpillars as they grew in exchange for the sweet juice they excreted just for them. Some caterpillars returned the hospitality by eating their nurse ants. Vic would think twice before stepping on one, or wiping out an entire hill, for that matter. The strange word he wasn't certain how to pronounce rang out in syllables in his mind: *mer-me-co-fily.* Vic was relieved to realize that his interior was a secret place that no one could hear if they were simply walking past. No one disturbed him in the library; not even the librarian looked up from her large stack of books to notice him. Vic's collection comprised *Essential Lepidoptera; History of the Sikhs Vol. I; How to Tie Knots, Vol. II; Walden Pond*; and *Lives of a Cell.* The Cobalt Public Library was his favorite after-school stop; he had to take two buses out of his way to get there. Cobalt High only had a couple of bookshelves, but in the public library, he could stack books around himself and manufacture invisibility. After he read as much as he could about butterfly habitats and habits, he jumped onto the next bus from downtown Cobalt to *his land* to inspect the invertebrate life firsthand because books could only teach him so much.

The afternoon light hung shadows behind every leaf of grass. Vic saw only one Little Yellow butterfly flitting wildly around a clump of weeds. He took out his notebook, and on a new page he wrote: *Little Yellow, perhaps a sulphur.* The book was half-full of his notations and sketches, and he transcribed his notes onto his blog.

Vic's fascination with winged insects began when he was seven years old; his parents had given him a ladybug farm for his birthday. He set up the small plastic dome, arranged the leaves and fake plastic trees, and mailed away for his fifteen to twenty ladybug larvae. Ladybug Land looked like a fun place. It was a bug amusement park, where the ladybugs could slide down the gray plastic volcano into the green plastic forest as though it were a water slide. The front of the stickered base read: *Watch the magic of metamorphosis!* The bugs grew up quickly, as larvae are accustomed to do, and soon Vic watched the red-and-black bugs fly around inside the clear dome. One day, however, he noticed one particularly small bug fly repeatedly against Ladybug Land's plastic walls. Again and again, the flying bug rammed against the plastic until Vic realized that he just wanted out. He took the whole lot out to his mother's rose garden and released all of his little friends. He watched as some flew, some crawled, and most escaped alive. From then on, Vic always found himself watching the ground closely for insects. Butterflies became a natural fascination when he realized how variegated they were.

He put his sketchbook down on a tree stump. A breeze rustled the tree limbs, and one yellowed and wrinkled sycamore leaf fell to the ground. The changing light played with the bark of the trunks in the forest, and Vic could have sworn there was something moving within. One low-hanging branch of hemlock jostled in the wind and exposed a stake in the ground. The branch fell upon the stake once more, covering it up. There wasn't a house for miles. He never saw a person around here, but all this must belong to someone. As he pondered this idea of land ownership, the sound of a firecracker fractured the air.

His neck burned from moving so quickly in reaction. He crouched low to the ground and turned around, searching the horizon atop the hill for movement. He couldn't see over the hill, which made him nervous. The air tingled and pinched sounds to a different tone. Vic knew that anyone he'd run into out here would mean trouble, but the villains from his imagination were the worst: a witch who'd trap him in a cage and eat him for dinner, a toothless serial killer who'd escaped Sing Sing, or the revenge-seeking ghost of a Civil War soldier. He picked up his backpack and made a beeline for the forest, creepy branches be damned.

He was well camouflaged by the densely needled red pine. He thanked the gods he wore the brown baseball hat today over his *patka*—the white fabric would have been a beacon. He crouched behind a massive tree trunk and waited. And there! He saw tops of heads coming over the hill. Three—no, four—guys. They were throwing things at each other teasingly.

He heard, "Hey, dipshit!" and "I'm going to kick your ass!"

Unfortunately for Vic, it was Joe Balestrieri and his friends. They were the kind who'd dismember small animals for kicks and break their neighbor's window just to hear the glass shatter. Joe lit a match and touched the flame to something in his hand, then threw it at one of his mindless soldiers of mayhem. The firecracker exploded in midair. Vic hoped they would kill each other.

It's not their land, he thought. How'd they manage to find this place? Joe, their leader, bent down to where Vic had just been thinking about butterflies and picked something up from the ground.

"Hey, what's this?"

His notebook. In his rush he must have left it there, exposed, alone. The mob looked at his entries, which dated back to early spring, and laughed. Vic was relieved he hadn't put his name anywhere inside the book. Maybe they would just think some old man had dropped it. Maybe they wouldn't think about looking in the forest for a recent passerby to torment. The posse circled around the notebook, tore pages out, and crumpled them into a pile. Then, each lit a firecracker and stepped back. The whole thing exploded. Sheets became yellow flames, then quickly metamorphosed into black wisps of ash in the air. The thugs let the flames continue unattended and continued their path of destruction directly in front of Vic. He held his breath, clenched his teeth, and grasped the branches of the tree tightly. Time stood still until they were out of sight.

The fire left nothing more than a scorch of black on the grass. Vic could see the small wisp of smoke trundle into the air above his sketchbook's corpse. He smelled its burned pages. He wished he hadn't forgotten his notebook. Now he was truly thankful for his blog; no one could destroy that, at least, unless they had his password.

When he was certain the thugs were long gone, he backed up from the tree trunk and shook out his hands, as his palms were white from holding onto the bark so tightly. Vic picked up his pack and took a large step backward, deeper into the forest. As he did so, he felt the strangest sensation he'd ever felt: The earth moved under his feet.

The sound that escaped the ground wasn't loud at all. It was more like a *whoosh* than a crack. And suddenly everything turned black.

Vic fell for so long that his stomach hit the back of his throat. His arms and legs flailed in the darkness, but only air and dirt slipped between his fingers. When he landed, his bottom skidded to a stop along a rocky strip of land, and he wondered if he was still alive. Whether something was physically covering his eyes or there was simply not enough light to see, he didn't know. The air was musky and thick with sweet-smelling moisture; he had fallen into a hole of some sort, of this he was certain. Like Dante in the forest, he, too, had fallen into hell. His heart raced, and he tried to quiet his thoughts. What kinds of monsters lurked here? As his eyes adjusted to the darkness, he felt vulnerable, like a small mammal fumbling stupidly near a snake's hole at night. He reached blindly into his backpack. He now knew why he kept the emergency kit with him at all times: Swiss army knife, six feet of rope, tweezers, a plastic rain tarp, and the waterproof matches that he'd hoped to be able to use someday. Today was the day.

He lit one of the matches and looked around. He'd landed on a ledge over a deep crevasse. If he'd moved one more foot in the other direction, he'd have kept going down who knows how far. A metal ladder was screwed into rock and led back up, and another ladder led down. This place was manmade.

The match burned out and singed his fingers, and now Vic found himself in a darker place than before. He needed to light something *with* the match, but he hadn't thought that one through when planning his emergency kit, and the Dark Knight he was not. His hands moved through the darkness, and he grabbed in the direction of the ladder. It was cold down here. He tried not to think about the things that would like to live in this complete darkness. He tried so hard that he almost forgot to breathe. Got it. With both hands on the ladder, he pulled his feet up, moving higher and higher until he could see a sliver of light from above. It was as though the earth had swallowed him. He thrust his hand through the pile of leaves that had blanketed the opening, and lifted himself up and out into the light once more. He paused at the surface and realized that he had just found one terrific hiding place. Joe's posse had passed it by, so they couldn't know about it. He smiled; this place would be his fort from now on. After, of course, he equipped himself with defensive weapons and lanterns, lots of lanterns.

Maija

Maija applied another coat of lipstick as though this shade of red would make her feel brighter and more cheerful. She was getting ready to retrieve her father-in-law from the airport, and she still couldn't figure out what to wear. If she wore a dress, it would appear she was trying too hard to look feminine. If she wore what she wore every day—jeans and a sweater—it would appear that she was treating this day like any other, which would illustrate her disdain. She needed to be an example for her children, but at the same time, she wanted to be herself. She was sitting at the dressing table in her bra and underwear, painting her face with soft brushstrokes of lipstick, when she heard Paul calling from the foyer again. She couldn't move. This was an identity crisis, after all.

Maija knew this arrival would unsettle their happy little home. Papaji was a mythical creature—someone who'd affected her life from afar since she'd first married Paul, even though they'd never met. She knew this man would bring answers to questions that she'd carried all these years. Here she was, a grown woman, nervous about the arrival of her in-law, or, as her friend Adelaide called him, The Outlaw. Adelaide was witty; she was good for venting. Maija had convinced Adelaide to come with her to the PTA meeting the previous day by telling her she could write a story about it for the *Daily Mirror*.

Though she hadn't known what she would do when she arrived at the PTA's new members meeting, Maija had to attend. She couldn't ignore the vision that entirely consumed her life. Everywhere she looked, Maija could see only the way Eleanora's expression was tortured as she took her last breath, a mixture of warm shower water, blood, and air. Her wide eyes looked as though she were questioning her very own death as the walls closed around her. It was as though even Maija, in her vision, knew there was something she could do to break the line toward this future. She had to try; Eleanora's eyes pleaded with her every time Maija closed her own lids.

There had been twenty women in Cobalt High's music room that night. Maija didn't see the small man in attendance, Herbert, until he moved from behind the upright piano. The others Maija recognized were Eleanora; Jennifer Thomas, a mother of triplets in the first grade; Harmony Tingle, wife to Tom Tingle and mother to their two middle school–aged children; and Deborah Espirito, wife to Dante Espirito and mother to their four children. Sheets of music for "Mary Had a Little Lamb," "Away in the Manger," and the four verses of "The Star-Spangled Banner" with the notes colored in crayon hung on the walls. Maija was not comfortable making small talk because to her it was pointless. She knew what people were really asking in their seemingly harmless questions. *Where do you live?* meant *How much money do you make?* And *What grade are your kids in?* meant *How old are you, really?* She was on psychic business here and had no time to make friends.

Thank you all for coming to the new members meeting. Eleanora had paused to take a Styrofoam cup of coffee from Jennifer Thomas. *The PTA depends on your participation. Without you, there wouldn't be an association at all. Please take a moment to fill out this form with your information.* Eleanora passed around copies of the PTA Individual Member Form, which asked for basic contact information. *Then we'll all introduce ourselves.*

Maija hadn't been sure what to do. If she filled it out, Eleanora would have her information, and she'd be forced to commit to these silly meetings. If she didn't fill it out, she'd look suspicious. There were far too many attentive eyes evaluating the new members, as though they were joining an elite book club run by Oprah herself.

Maija had dressed casually: slacks and a sweater. She saw how new money had changed her old neighbor. Instead of the ratty tracksuits she used to wear, Eleanora wore a fitted Ann Taylor suit. It looked uncomfortable. The Heights trend was an anomaly in Cobalt. Maija had heard of the McMansion phenomenon in America as it had infected the suburbs of larger cities, but Cobalt was a modest village with little pretense. Until now, there hadn't been a gated community within the city borders. Maija couldn't help but wonder what they were trying to keep in or out of those gates.

Maija had taken a leisurely drive into the Heights one day out of curiosity. The street leading up to the Heights' entrance seemed to wind needlessly. Between the young pines and willows she'd caught glimpses of the enormous wrought iron gate. She recalled how the Vatican was designed; as leaders would enter the structure on either side, they would get only a hint of the enormity of St. Peter's Basilica between the Roman colonnades. Each peek would deliver a sensation akin to that of arriving closer to God himself. Every step the kings and emperors took would remind them of their place below the church. This winding drive on Heights Way was designed to induce a similar sensation, though it did nothing more than increase Maija's frustration. Small, manmade hills complicated the three-mile drive that would only have been one mile as the crow flies. It was a sad attempt at a labyrinth; Daedalus would have stomped directly through the development. When she arrived at the locked gate and realized that she did not have the code to enter, she pulled her car to the side and got out to take a look around, peering through the bars. The entire community was closer to the old Cobalt village and PMI's campus than she had thought. The neatly arranged houses appeared to have swallowed steroids. They were massive clones, all born from the same gray and white palette, and had small, unnaturally green, manicured lawns. She thought it strange that there weren't any sidewalks at all, as though the outdoors were not to be explored. It seemed empty, a ghost town. There weren't any children riding their bikes or parents mowing their lawns. But the eeriest attribute of the community was the blaring silence. Not a fly flew, nor bee buzzed. The street signs, with grandiose names like Prominence Point and Grand Terrace Drive, were rusting. Maija had left quickly, wondering what the Finch family saw in such a soulless place.

At the PTA meeting, she'd taken a pen from her purse and pretended to jot down her name, address, and phone number. Instead, while Jennifer, Eleanora, and Harmony were discussing the new fall clothes at Talbot's, she wrote a note:

Dear Mrs. Finch,

You are in danger. Please be careful to take your medicine and watch your footing on slippery surfaces. I only want to help.

—A Friend

She'd stashed the form on top of the pile and gone to the restroom, signaling to Adelaide with a wink that it was time to go.

The mirror into which Maija peered was cracked. She pressed her palms to either side of the glass and said aloud, *What were you thinking, Maija dear? You actually believe Eleanora's going to read that note and not call the police? She'll know it was you, Maija. It was you who told her she was going to die this weekend.*

She fidgeted with her wild curls, and, just as she was planning her escape to the parking lot, saw that Adelaide had entered the bathroom.

Addie was shaped like a bubble. Her blonde, curly hair was piled in a bun at the top of her head. Everything about her was round, without an edge in sight. Like Maija, she, too, was dressed in jeans and a sweater. *You're not an idiot. She deserves it, you know. Being so high and mighty all the time.*

They'd walked to the parking lot together. *So, she's going to die, huh?* Adelaide continued. *Tomorrow, you say?*

I don't know anything anymore.

Serves her right. Adelaide chuckled.

Oh, dear. Maija didn't think Eleanora deserved to die just because she was nasty. Most nasty people lived longer than nice ones. That was the law of the universe.

Over coffee and pie at the Thunderbird Diner, they discussed Maija's seeing life.

I've always wondered about that psychic stuff, Adelaide said. *I read Sylvia Browne. Do you know who she is? Of course you do.*

Maija told Adelaide about how sometimes the dearly departed would come to her to make peace with their unsolved problems they left on earth. One memory that still haunted her was that of Vic and Isabella's babysitter, Alex, who died suddenly in a car crash near their house many years ago. That night, Alex had appeared in Maija's bedroom wearing that big red bandana in her hair, waving and smiling. Maija thought she was really in the house and waved back at her. She didn't find out until the next night that Alex was dead, that she'd come to say good-bye.

Maija's grandparents, neighbors, friends, random people she'd never met—all came to say their good-byes. Her favorite Sunday section of the newspaper was, of course, the obituaries. It surprised her how many times they chose to print the deceased's high school yearbook photos, even if they were in their nineties. The shades of people that Maija would see were a blend of their younger and older selves. They were a moving form within time and space, uncontained. She'd never tried to explain this to anyone outside of her family.

That night at the diner, Maija had even told Adelaide about the recent dreams that didn't feel like her own. In her nightly imaginings, the ones in which Eleanora Finch was not the main character, she felt as if she had been walking through Latvia. She had dreams of Riga and the countryside, marsh and forest, rivers and sand. The birch trees were somewhat familiar. She could hear soldiers marching. In these dreams, she looked down at her feet and they weren't hers; perhaps they were Oma's. Maija, now more than ever, needed a friend, and was grateful to have Adelaide in her waking life.

Now, still sitting at her dressing table, Maija looked at her watch and realized that if they didn't get to the airport soon, they might be late. She'd heard Paul call everyone down into the foyer ten minutes ago, but her legs were molasses.

Paul

Paul stood alone in the foyer with his back to the front door and fiddled with the scrap of paper in his hands. The well-folded creases on Papaji's itinerary had been softened to a fabric-like flexibility. The last time he held an itinerary in his hand that read *New Delhi to New York* was long, long ago. Paul thought of his twenty-year-old self as a pioneer, a frontiersman of sorts, with a turban rather than a coonskin hat, charting his path across oceans and through forests. And he knew that Papaji's visit would bring all memories, desired or not, into the present.

Paul's arrival in America hadn't been one of singing swallows and trumpeting youths. He'd landed in Cobalt exhausted, with a small bag over his shoulder and a twenty-dollar bill in his pocket. His distant cousin, Baba, was the point man for immigration from their village. Baba had come to America on his own and found work, a Herculean feat that had lifted him to mythic status in the village. Now all who wanted to immigrate to the new world had to go through him. Paul had sent him a letter and asked if he could sponsor his visit for a work visa.

He'd gotten a reply almost immediately via phone. *Oi,* bháí! *Come out here. We will have a first-class job waiting for you. Take the next flight.*

Though the word *Cobalt* was on his ticket, he thought he was going to New York City—the only New York he'd ever heard of. He'd never seen it, but he'd heard it was a wild place where people made piles of money from a shouting gallery and where a person could get anything delivered at any hour. He'd heard you could order toilet paper when you ran out, and someone would bring it to your bathroom. When Paul arrived, after piles of paperwork and months of waiting for his visa, he found himself alone. No one met him in the airport as he stepped into the terminal. And the New York that he landed in was not the metropolis he'd hoped for. There was a state called New York, he'd learned, with a small village named Cobalt that had a population smaller than his village in India. He was at least a three-hour drive from the mega-city of his dreams. He was terrified and vulnerable, and his surroundings did nothing to comfort his foreignness. All of his senses told Paul that this place into which he had just entered was not home. It was not a town where he'd be able to find *pakoras* for a snack or *khichuri* when he was sick. Here he would not find a good glass of chai or pick up a game of cricket with other young men his age. No, Cobalt would be nothing like his village. Of all the emotions Paul had felt at that moment, the one he did not expect was relief.

He remembered where he'd slept that night: near Gate Two. What he ate for dinner: a bag of Cheesie Crunchies from the vending machine. He remembered the smell of cleaning supplies in the men's room where he'd washed his face and rinsed his mouth. Baba came the following night. He nonchalantly told Paul he'd gotten the days mixed up. Paul had sat in the airport for forty-eight hours by then and was still jet-lagged from his flight. He was getting strange looks from the security guard. Paul forgot to be angry with Baba when he arrived to claim him. The delight of seeing someone who knew him trumped all.

The joy of this new experience began to fade after a few months of sleeping on the floor of Baba's studio apartment. He ate pasta and soup with small balls of meat from a can, while his taste buds longed for cumin and cardamom. This was a new life for Paul, and he had to remind himself of the various exchanges he would have to make in the new culture. Chef Boyardee was just another thing he'd grow to love.

A few days after he'd arrived, Baba dressed Paul in one of his polyester suits and took him to meet Mr. Charleston, the head of manufacturing at PMI. Though Paul's English was rough, he could understand the verbal exchange between Baba and Mr. Charleston through their hand gestures: A flip of the wrist upward from Baba meant something positive; downward meant pleading; a pointer finger waggling left and right was something potentially disastrous; a finger standing tall and proud was something promising. From the sidelines, Paul watched his future unfold, curious as to what he'd be doing here.

Of course he has machining experience. Worked on a farm his whole life. He can run anything. Fix anything. He's smarter than he looks! Green card all the way! One hundred percent. A tall and taut finger rose into the air.

Mr. Charleston acquiesced. A few overly vigorous handshakes later, Paul was given a short tour of the facilities and told to come the next morning to begin. His eight to ten hours were spent pressing the tiny tip of a hot metal wire to a very specific spot on a computer motherboard. Some days he'd actually slip a small chip into place on the big jigsaw puzzle of a motherboard. He saved up as much money as he could and stashed it under his mattress, in old coffee cans and pickle jars. It was almost a year before he and Baba could afford to rent a larger, one-bedroom apartment. More cousins came shortly after they'd moved. The larger apartment wasn't big enough for Baba's ten new relatives, even with the breakfast nook. Paul took his pickle jars to the bank and got a cashier's check for a deposit on his own apartment. Lucky for him, too, because not long after Paul had moved, Baba was picked up for harboring illegals from India. From his apartment down the street, Paul had heard that the authorities took his other "cousins" and dropped them off at the airport with one-way tickets. He watched until he was the only one left. Paul had never considered returning home. He didn't answer any letters from the village. He wanted to be forward moving, like the machines he was making, so he continued.

Folds of time concealed sections of Paul's past, covering events and years of his life. He moved on quickly from difficult situations, and his willingness to sever ties left him alone much of the time, with impossible questions dangling around him. His departure from India had been a final snip to the village umbilical cord. This was the most difficult separation he'd ever made—not because he regretted it but because images and people continued to haunt him long after he left.

Now, in the foyer, Paul straightened his collar in the oversized mirror on the wall above the key bowl. He recalled the day of his secondary school portrait. The student body, thirty in all, had stood still, dressed in starched slacks and shirts and lined up in rows. Expressions were frozen awkwardly, almost frightened, almost proud. His brother, Kamal, sat in the front row on a chair, his eyes sparkling. Paul was just a dot in the back. Paul hadn't taken the sepia-toned photo with him when he'd come to America.

He wondered what his brother would have looked like as an adult. He couldn't see Kamal as a man because death had cut his life short. The loss of his brother had changed his family forever. Paul's heart had filled with thick concrete before it had a chance to expand on its own. Kamal's ghost visited Paul in his dreams. Perhaps it was because he could not recall in complete detail the one thing that truly mattered: how his brother died. And so he fought long and hard to erase all memories of his brother from his mind. If he'd never existed, he couldn't have died and left Paul the only son to receive his parents' bitterness.

Paul dabbed the sweat from his forehead with a white handkerchief, then refolded it and slid it into his back pocket. Maybe the old man wasn't coming as the letter had said. Maybe he'd wrote the wrong date and time on the loose-leaf paper.

"*Chalo!*" Paul called for his family, but no one came. "We are going to be late." He listened but no one responded. "*Piyar*? Vic? Izzy? I'll be in the car."

Vic

Vic looked out the window of the car as they drove to the airport. His mother had forced him to wear a periwinkle embroidered tunic that she believed his grandfather had given him years earlier—the shirt had traveled the world in order to arrive on Vic's doorstep—and it was too tight. His grandfather had passed it to his neighbor in New Delhi who had a son who was visiting America to interview for a position as an engineer. This neighbor's son, whom the Singhs had addressed as *cousin*, arrived in New York City and drove over three hours to their home in Cobalt. Cousin didn't realize how far the Singhs lived from Manhattan, or even that there was a state connected to the city, but when he arrived he was rewarded with a lengthy conversation with Maija and Paul about their relations, whether it was marriage or blood, and a mention of American girls who they knew would love to meet an *Indian* Indian. He filled his belly with plenty of tea and fried, sugary things and finally delivered the long-awaited package of gifts. Inside the brown paper was a set of glass bangles for Isabella, a tea cozy for Maija, a small chess set and tie that was made in China for Paul, and this most desirable shirt for Vic. The shirt didn't fit his shoulders, and the Nehru-style neck was a little tight. But still he wore it, and along with his *patka*, Vic looked more Indian than American.

Though it had been difficult at first, he'd finally come to grips with idea that he would be sharing his room with his sister to give Papaji his own space. In addition to the duct tape he'd adhered poorly to the carpet, he tacked a sheet to the ceiling with Isabella's help so they couldn't see each other undress. He also didn't want his sister to see the artifacts he'd found underground. He'd moved most of his findings back into the hole in the ground and put the rest under his bed. He could only look at the bits of metal and rock when she was at rehearsal.

He'd managed to go back to the hole several times and even figured out how best to descend into the shaft without hurting himself. Armed with a fluorescent lantern hanging from his teeth, a slingshot, and rocks in his pockets, Vic climbed carefully down the ladder for what felt like a solid five minutes. He continued downward, with his eyes squeezed shut until he finally felt his feet arrive at a level surface. It took a few moments for his eyes to adjust, but when they did, he was glad he'd followed his adventurous side. His feet were on sandy mud, and above him was a low ceiling of curved rock. A tunnel stretched in two directions. He bent down and entered.

The ground was damp. Vic rubbed his fingers along the cold walls. Veins of different minerals made jagged patterns in the sandstone. He walked in both directions for a few steps until he felt more of the same. To make the cave more inhabitable, he'd brought a rain tarp, a blanket, a box of crackers, a milk crate, a bottle of water, and a few comic books he didn't mind getting wet. He'd also brought cans of food he didn't think anyone would miss, like navy beans and baby corn, though he didn't have a can opener yet. Vic built a shelf out of a pile of rocks and hardened soil. On it he kept his most prized possession: the shadow box with his blue butterflies.

He would never have killed to peruse a butterfly like other collectors; he felt fortunate to have found them so close to their natural deaths. Some collectors paid tens of thousands of dollars to smugglers for rare and endangered species of butterflies and moths. He thought those villains should all die by the same torture they inflict on the butterflies—impalement. He looked at his shadow box. There they sat, almost glowing blue in the dim light as though their wings were phosphorescent and still living.

Though he'd agreed to have *time with Papa* once a week, when his father continued to train him in the finer points of combat, he still didn't feel comfortable enough to tell his father of his new fort. Vic wondered how their small three-bedroom home would change with Papaji in the house. He hoped he wouldn't have to have *time with Papaji*, too. At least he had somewhere else he could be if things got to be too much at home.

At the airport, Vic fiddled with the matches he'd grabbed from the market. These, too, would end up in his underground palace. He noticed that he still had a pile of rocks in a pocket in his trousers, which made him feel closer to his adventure even while fulfilling his filial duty in his light-blue collared shirt.

Isabella

They all stood shoulder to shoulder at the gate, as her father specified, but it was too close for Isabella's taste, so she shifted back and forth and finally went to the bathroom for the third time. She dropped her water bottle into the recycling bin en route. It was in the restroom that she discovered she actually enjoyed ocean-scented air freshener, though that all porcelain in public bathrooms reminded her of doctors and their exams. She saw a quarter on the ground and picked it up for her collection.

Isabella had moved her found treasures to her locker at school. She didn't want her brother to find her pilfered things. She wasn't a thief. She was a collector. She organized her collection in her locker with plastic bags, jars, and boxes and arranged the items in a tidy manner according to area of memory: medical (things she grabbed from doctor's offices), organic (things found in nature), Homo sapiens (objects belonging to people), strange (antiques), and things of unknown origin. There was bag of nails and a box with pieces of glass, a rainbow pencil topper with the name *Courtney* etched along side, and a new collection Isabella designated to all things pertaining to the play. So far these weren't particularly exciting: a receipt from Friendly's that she'd found onstage, dated January 12, 1987, for a fishwich; a piece of a chain probably having belonged at one point to a gold-plated necklace, which she'd found dangling from a Christmas tree prop; and the first page of a play with no title. The only words on the page had something to do with stealing a car and the good heart of a man named Thomas. It was, in general, melodramatic writing, she thought.

This reminded her that she still had to memorize her lines. Every time she opened her script she felt burned by Tewks's title page: *1,001 Cries* by Harry Tewkesbury. She wondered if he'd plagiarized the text from some unknown author, changed the title, and pasted his name on the title page. He made Isabella nervous. The way he spoke to the cast was a precise kind of condescension, as if he didn't realize they were older than sixth graders. When people were overly particular, they were built to pop, Isabella thought. Something was going to send him over the edge one day.

As she left the restroom, she took the script from her purse. Joining her family again, she read the cast of characters. Her name was first. The lead. The star. She blushed. Her name was written in pen on top of a mound of Wite-Out; it was obvious she hadn't been the first Samantha. She read the scene while they waited for her grandfather. It wasn't half bad. It began, like the work of Aeschylus, with a cryptic message from the chorus. The monologue belonged to Samantha; she had the distinguished role of the daughter of the President. After her short piece, in which she said something about the fragility of humankind and the ferocity of the horses of war, the play began with an intense scene of action.

"Multiple explosions and people screaming wildly" was the specific direction. Isabella imagined how she might design the stage. If she could freeze the opening scene, she'd light the stage delicately with floor lights shining upward to the scaffolding and ask the cast to freeze in their most uncomfortable positions. The shadows would become as large a presence as the four people in the scene. The audience would want to hear gunfire, helicopters, bombs, cries, though there would be none to hear. It would be like staring at *Guernica* through a microscope; one had to be patient and swallow the tragic images and moments, careful not to choke on it. To the right would be a large leather chair tipped on its side. All the books would be scattered at the base of the bookshelf. White papers that once held top-secret memos about the encroaching Third World War would be strewn across everything, crunching underfoot like yesterday's trash. Two half-destroyed walls would partition the room that had once been the Oval Office. High against the corner of the partial wall would be a shadow of the doomsday clock with its hands set at one minute to the hour. The cast would bustle about, papers would fly, bombs would explode, and Samantha would then throw herself at the Vice President's feet. His hand would reach for a button, red as a hot poker, ready to stab the earth's core. She would beg him not to press the doomsday trigger—and with this, the action again would slow and Samantha would drag the Vice President into the bomb shelter. The scene would freeze once more; stagehands dressed in black would rearrange the props like phantoms.

The previous day, she'd gone to rehearsal filled with curiosity.

All right, people—places. Tewks had come in wearing a strange, thrift-store knit scarf around his neck, so tight that Isabella wondered if he might cut off the oxygen to his brain and faint.

Butterflies had soared in her stomach. Erik, playing the Vice President, had smiled at her, and she'd tried to smile back but only managed to curl one side of her mouth into a smirk of sorts. Erik was skinny and tall and had longish hair that slipped into his field of vision every few minutes. In other words, he was cute. *You look nice*, he said.

Isabella hadn't been able to handle the compliment, as awkward and benign as it was, and her stomach flipped. She excused herself from the stage, with one hand over her mouth and the other waving a *hold on*, and ran to the nearest bathroom to throw up. Her stomach hurt in the same place it had in Dr. Gott's office. But she was not about to go back to see her again. She rinsed her mouth out in the green sink, read what had been written in marker on the mirror—IT'S NOT NICE TO WRITE ON SCHOOL PROPERTY—wiped the tears from her eyes, refilled her water bottle, shoved an Altoids mint into her mouth, and returned to the theater.

Sorry. Stomach bug.

Tewks had not been pleased, and he'd raised his hand in protest. *We have to learn to overcome these things in theater. You might have to get through a scene without running to the bathroom, Isabella.*

And hope that no one minds the throw-up all over my shirt?

The show must go on. Plays are about synergy, and if you can't manage to get through a scene in rehearsal without throwing up, then what are we to do?

Tracy Finch had stared at Isabella with her vicious eyes. *If you can't do it, I can.* She stretched the word *can* to wicked lengths. *I've already memorized your lines.* Tracy had just been killing time until her scene, hassling everyone and threatening to take their parts away from them like a director's hound.

Begin again, Tewks said.

The first attack took us by surprise—Isabella coughed.

Isabella! What do you think you're doing? Tewks leapt to his feet.

Huh? she asked.

Do you call that crying? You need to work on your believability. You can break the audience's spell if you remind them that they are watching a play.

At this Isabella had sighed, her hate for Tewks growing inside her heart like a blossoming, billowing balloon—ready to explode. She'd swallowed her pride and thought of the worst thing she possibly could. She saw flames rising from a house, her family trapped inside. The lump in her chest moved into her throat—and *voilà!* A tear. It rolled lazily from the corner of her eye. She felt its cool trail crossing her cheek to her lips and delivered her next line: *Is there anyone besides us left?*

Okay, cut! Well done. That's good. Maybe next time you can wear less mascara?

Isabella's hand went to her eyes; rivers of black ran down her face. She probably looked like Tammy Faye Bakker. Well, at least no one could deny whether she was crying or not. It was real. She actually felt a pit in her stomach and wondered for the first time how real actors did this for a living. How could they channel a different life for a period of time and then return to their own? Did the other world knock on their doors, like a doppelganger trapped behind the mind's transparent wall, and demand attention? She'd decided then and there that if she were going to act in the future, she'd only do comedies.

On their way out of the theater, after an hour-long lecture from Tewks on the importance of stage presence, which he described as something innate, Isabella and Erik had reentered the world of Cobalt High. The school in all of its concrete glory seemed dimmer and grimier than usual; the hallways were covered in old gum, and the tags of last names no one could read tattooed the lockers, walls, and, yes, even the ceiling, as if a marker or can of spray paint had been all it took to claim ownership of something inanimate. Isabella found that she preferred the world onstage: Though she and Erik had walked together, a wall resembling reality had grown once more between them; they couldn't touch or look at each other with longing eyes because no script directed them to do so. They did not speak. They were on their own. It had been awkward, but they'd continued on through the halls as though they were betrothed—until they reached the end of the front hall. Isabella thought she would act professionally, as she did this acting thing all the time, and she'd waved goodbye to Erik with an open hand, even though she wanted to touch him.

Hey, Erik called, and she'd turned.

Yeah?

Um—he moved closer—*Tewks is a total freak.*

Yeah, total freakazoid.

You wanna go to a movie or something, sometime soon?

Yeah, sure, okay.

Okay, well, see ya.

Remembering the moment, Isabella shivered and looked around at her surroundings in the airport. Her stomach turned.

"Isabella, put that play away. Your grandfather will be here soon." Her mother's eyebrows slanted down.

"Mama, he's late. What am I supposed to do?"

Her mother did not respond.

Paul

US Airways Flight 785 from La Guardia to Cobalt, New York, 5 p.m.: Delayed.

Paul wrapped his large hand around Maija's shoulder and squeezed. "I think that's his plane landing now."

They had prepared as best they could. That's all Paul could think to himself as they stood—a starched, creased, gelled, and straightened brood—waiting in their Sunday best for the last male elder of Paul's family to arrive at Cobalt's airport. If this moment were a photograph, as it should have been, the edges would curl in a rococo frame that would rest atop a great aunt's bureau covered in dust. If captured, this image would serve as evidence to future generations who might poke their fingers toward Great Aunt So-and-So's photo and exclaim, "Aren't those the American Singhs picking up their last patriarch from the Cobalt airport?" It was a scene like many others in any small airport. Sardar Harbans Singh was to arrive any minute now, and the entire Singh family was there with their clean-smelling clothes, smiles, and uncomfortable sighs.

Paul watched the commuter plane soar over the white-pine forest and coast along the slick black runway. The turboprop emerged from the mist like Gandaberunda, the mythological two-headed bird, ready to battle Shiva. History and the here and now crashed deep beneath

Paul's sternum; the collision caused acid reflux to coat the back of his esophagus. He focused his eyes on the busy carpet instead; he watched it crawl like burrowing worms and wished he could dive under it and disappear altogether. It wasn't Papaji he feared seeing, though he did not want to see him now or ever. It was the shade of himself he'd abandoned in the village and all the ghosts that chased him, which he knew were hitchhikers in his father's luggage.

"It'll be okay," Maija whispered, only for his ears.

Passengers filed like ants down the stairs along the tarmac to Gate Two and toward the security area. They were a weary yet organized swarm. Five, ten, twelve people passed with their wheeled bags and disheveled hair. Next came an elderly lady with a walker, shuffling slowly along the carpet. Paul searched with a poised smile and lungs inflated, anticipating a joyful release. Minutes expanded like an already over-full helium balloon, compounded by the pressure of high altitude. Two security guards and one policeman rushed past them toward the gate. Paul followed, his eyes squinting with inquiry.

A husky TSA lady stopped Paul from entering the gate. "You can't go in without a ticket."

"But I'm looking for a passenger."

The TSA lady pointed to a woman at the ticket counter. The woman's nametag read SHIRLEY. Shirley wore more makeup than you can find at a Walmart, Paul thought.

"Can I help you?" The added syllables in her accent were most certainly Texan. Paul liked Texans; they reminded him of Punjabis.

"Yes, I'm looking for my father. He was on that flight."

"Name?"

"Singh."

Shirley looked at Paul's turban, then the gate, then tapped the tips of her acrylic nails on her keyboard.

"Mr. Harbans Singh?"

"Yes, that's my father. Where is he?"

"Sir"—she moved closer and spoke quietly—"there was a problem. He's going to be detained until—"

"What? Detained? What for?"

Shirley tapped her acrylic nails against the counter. "Sir, please calm down. They are bringing him now."

"I am calm; this *is* me calm, madam. You don't want to see me—upset." Paul clenched his hands into fists and dug his nails into his palms. Luckily, Papaji and his security entourage turned the corner at that moment and made their way toward Paul.

His father seemed to be a relic of the giant from Paul's memories. The cane he used now pulled his posture to the right. The beard that had been black and, on special occasions, wound up and glued tight against his jawline, was emancipated from the tyranny of beard fixer and flowed silver down his chest.

"Papaji?" Paul moved toward him.

"*Puttar*, they think I'm a jihadi!"

"Sir, keep your voice down," the officer said between his gritted teeth.

Onlookers whirled around to stare.

"That's my father! Where are you taking him?" Paul jogged alongside them. "Wait!"

The group walked into the airport security office. The police officer closed the door, then turned toward Paul.

"Your father made some peculiar statements on the plane to another passenger. We have to take him in for a background check and questioning."

"What did he say?" Paul felt his family surround him.

"A lady he was sitting next to asked him if he was an Arab."

Paul felt his face drop miles.

"He used profanities, then threatened to show her his sword to prove he wasn't."

"You must be mistaken. He's an old man; he doesn't know what he's saying. Clearly he's senile."

"We found a large knife in his suitcase. He checked it in India, but still, we're living in crazy times."

"Knives are ceremonial to our culture, sir; they are not to be used to fight. They are for show."

"Bad time to say anything aboard a plane."

"You should talk to that lady who started the whole thing. She's ignorant. He was only trying to prove he was a Sikh, the furthest thing from a jihadi terrorist."

"Details." The officer used his tongue to pick out an invisible fragment of food in his incisor.

Paul hated the ignorance he'd experienced since September 11. People assumed the turban he wore was related to the head covering the mullahs wore in the Middle East. He'd read about a few attacks against Sikhs, one of the victims an owner of a liquor store, clubbed by an imbecile who was never caught. Stupidity is more dangerous than intelligence, he thought.

Maija moved toward the policeman. "Listen, if he hasn't done anything wrong, hasn't violated any law, I suggest you release him now before I call my lawyer and best friend, who's a reporter for the *Daily Mirror*. She'd be happy to write a headline in tomorrow's paper and launch a full investigation into this matter." Maija's eyes flashed steel, an attribute Paul adored about his wife.

Within moments, Papaji was out of the security office and staring, weary-eyed, at his American family. He shook his head and mumbled, "*Mané Sikh han*." He looked at Paul and smiled, all teeth.

"It's been too long, *puttar*." He held his hand out to Paul, and Paul took it.

"So who do we have here?" Papaji said in English, with an

intimidating tone, and looked from Maija to Isabella to Vic. He shook Maija's hand as if she were made of glass and nodded pleasantly at her.

Isabella walked up to him and said, "Hello, Papaji."

He seemed taken aback by her directness, but instead of showing surprise, he said, "Hello, *potrí*."

When his eyes rested on Vic, something in him seemed to change. He went to him and said, "You must be Varunesh Singh. Let me look at you." Papaji ran his eyes across Vic's form as though he were searching for something. He seemed to be making note of his height and weight. He perused his face and paused, as though the world he'd once known as flat was now round. Papaji bent down closer to look Vic in the eye. "Oh," was all he said as he gently ran his huge thumbs across Vic's bushy eyebrows, then pointed to his own tufty brows.

"Nice to meet you, my grandson." His accent was thick across the English words he struggled to find.

The air around Paul seemed to get heavier; he used his pointer finger to loosen his shirt collar. Something in the air stung his eyes, and he wiped them with his handkerchief.

"Papaji, let's get out of here before they change their mind about us. Let's go." He turned to Vic, tossed him the keys to the Cutlass Supreme and said, "Get the car, *puttar*; bring it round."

Vic looked shocked. "But I've never driven."

"Nonsense, go!"

Vic did not hesitate a second time. When he brought the car, Paul saw that Vic's arms were stretched to their limit, gripping the wheel at ten and two as if his life depended on the completion of the task. He drove too close to the curb and slid one tire up onto the sidewalk. Maija had to show him where the parking brake was.

"Good-looking boy," Papaji whispered to Paul in Punjabi. "Good he follows *Khalsa.*"

Maija asked Papaji to sit in the front as Paul would drive home, but he insisted on the backseat, next to the kids.

As they drove home, Paul looked at his father's reflection in the rearview mirror. Papaji was taking in the scenery, and Paul imagined he was probably looking for monkeys in the trees or for signs of snakes in the tall grasses.

ON THE WING

Watching

Posted on October 9

Watching is patience magnified. If you are fortunate enough to see a butterfly's spectacular flight, you have to resist the desire to run after it; if you do, you will look like a fool. Let her come to you; she's coy. The most successful watching occurs when you catch her off-guard, while she's devouring her lunch, a decaying piece of fruit, or slurping flower nectar or a salty puddle of water. Her eyes are poor. Butterflies and moths are beautiful to our dingy world, but imagine what they look like to one another. They see ultraviolet colors, colors beyond the spectrum of our eyes. They are also nearsighted. The flowers stand out to them like flashing landing pads awaiting their arrival. The vegetation absorbs ultraviolet light, making them stand out. Their predators—birds, reptiles—can't see UV light, so this is their secret language. Because of her poor sight, it is easy to get close to her while she consumes her liquid diet. Her utensil of choice: a straw-like proboscis. I heard about a Postman butterfly, which got its name from its fixed flower route. From flower to flower, they drink the same nectar every day of their short lives. What a spectacular creature of habit.

Or, if you are even luckier, you will see a chrysalis freshly opened and the young adult, new to the world, pumping its blood through its wings readying for its first flight. The chrysalis tears open gently, the adult butterfly breaks free of the shell, and it veins expand the little sails. Its damp wings are like the curled lips of a clamshell. You feel honored to see its transformation. Change takes time. She zips her proboscis together like two sides of a straw, if she's lucky to have the ability to eat. Some, like the Atlas moth, are born without mouths. It seems an odd product of nature, an adult emerging after such a process only to lay eggs and die three days later. It is so ephemeral. A watcher bearing witness is graced.

But where are they? The answer is: everywhere. If it's cool, they rest beneath branches, warming their bodies. If it's warm, they are flitting low above grasses, flowers, trees, and puddles. When one catches your eye, it's because you showed patience to nature, and she is offered as a gift. They are the fairies in our world, pixies in the human realm. Their stained-glass windows so brilliant and whimsical we can't help but remember that this is what matters. You hold your breath and forget where you were rushing off to mere moments before. They are the sirens of the world we used to live in, the one we could live in.

If you get the chance to meet a butterfly in the wild when it's consuming a meal, you can look closely at its eyes, two orbs of glass with worlds inside. The light refracting through its opaque wings. Or, the edge of its hind leg fringed with tears and nibbles from battles lost. Look even closer at her almost imperceptible scales, each a different-colored sequin. Or observe how it carries on the wind, higher and higher, coasting on a mini current, then dives like a nervous debutante, shy at her first dance. They are nature in its moving state; it's only when you are quiet that she will reveal herself to you. Or perhaps she is watching you with her false eyespot when she is in prayer. To see her in flight is a gift—to see them in a glass case, drained of life, is like visiting the skeleton of a once-pretty girl.

Sightings

Here is a list of my butterfly sightings by memory, so they might not be accurate, and I do not have the exact dates, only the seasons. This list is far from complete, but a start is a start.

Elfin: Large black eyes lined in white, smaller than most leaves. Its scales glitter purple and green across its dusty brown wings.

Blue Copper: Iridescent on forewings: open grassy field. I almost got it confused with a blue, but it is much larger.

Eastern Tailed-Blue: It was a blue in size (tiny) and had two commas of orange on the edge of its wing and tufty tails the size of raindrops on the edge of its hind wing. It was drinking from a daisy-looking flower in the flats.

Spicebush Swallowtail: This is the largest butterfly I've seen, spanning the length of my hand relaxed. It has green tones on brown/black wings and bright yellow shades on the edges of the wings. It was drinking from a spicebush.

Little Yellow: The difference between a sulphur and a Yellow is their antennae. Yellows' antennae are black and white, while sulphurs' are pink.

Common Sootywing: It was like its name, dark in complexion. The wings were soft black/brown and flecked with white spots. It sat like skippers do, wings spread back, easily mistaken by the untrained eye for a moth.

Unnamed Blue: I still have yet to identify the invertebrate I found not too long ago, in a ravine in a suburban area. It is a blue, tiny in size, with white circles lined in black near its hind wing. Wings are fringed with white, and there is a deep brownish tone under the violet blue color (the left and right are different colors). To me, it looks like a mutant.

To my present plight, I wonder if anyone has anything further to offer. I still haven't been able to determine an identity for my finding. I wonder if, perhaps, the creature is not a product of nature but a creation of man's doing. A Frankenstein butterfly.

2 COMMENTS

You should get the Peterson's Guide; it's comprehensive. Also, don't forget that the environment could be responsible for affecting the butterfly. I know it sounds wild, but it's possible. Have you looked into environmental causes? —BF Girl NY

Thanks, BF Girl! I will get the book and look into external effects. —Vic

Papaji

Days later, during breakfast, Papaji looked at the backyard, through the kitchen window from the comfort of the dining table. His gaze had intent, as though sight itself was something he'd discovered only recently. He watched how the rain fell downward from heaven, as it usually did, but somehow the force of its landing seemed to pull the ground upward with each heavy drop. The raindrops' recoil splattered mud on the side of the house; gutters bloated with leaves and muck; muddy craters opened in the earth; grass became flooded rice fields; oak leaves not yet ready to fall spun across a large puddle in the backyard. Low areas under trees turned into seas, and bubbles rose to the surface and burst like translucent bombs.

His eyes meandered over the empty plates his daughter-in-law had placed on the table, and he hoped her *anddá* wouldn't be as hard and rubbery as the eggs that Tata, the cook, made for him in the flat in Delhi—those grayish-yellow balls of clay. Tata didn't know the first thing about food preparation, and in Papaji's mind he should have been either shot or relegated to the realm of tea preparation alone. Maija looked nothing like an Indian woman, with her wild hair and blue jeans. He wondered what Paul saw in her. But when she placed the perfectly jiggly eggs—like two cheerful breasts—in front of him, he couldn't help but purse his lips and offer a small nod.

It had been raining for five days straight since his arrival. He told the family that each day of rain represented a different member of the Singh household. No one seemed to understand what he meant, but they all nodded their heads and smiled at the breakfast table when he said this. He repeated his statement once more in his thick Punjabi accent, this time with his right pointer finger extended high above his scrambled eggs: "Each day is for *ik* person. Isabella has the first day, okay? Vic has the second and so on. My day is today." Much to his delight, they responded with smiles of agreement. He would have a good time while he was here.

"But who will have tomorrow?" Isabella asked with scrambled eggs in her mouth.

"If it rains tomorrow and the next, we will have a visitor," he said. And his American family seemed satisfied with this answer.

Home. So this was where his remaining family lived. Papaji had seen many homes, so many walls over his life, though he longed for only one home. That home, lost so very long ago during the great fissure that forced him south into India, was truly gone forever. It represented a time when the evil in the world was merely fiction in a cautionary tale, buried in a dusty book out of reach. Innocence, on some level, he'd left in the mortar between the walls, in the tiled floor, and with his family's worldly possessions. He'd left his innocence in the memories of his wife and first son, still pure before their journey. Home, home, home. His longing drove him, on occasion, mad. It became a phantom that haunted him like the ghost of a deceased loved one. It whispered in his ear and became embedded in his flesh.

Papaji was not comfortable in this house. He'd noticed Paul hadn't looked him in the eyes since he arrived. Not once. It had been a long time since he'd seen his son. He hoped that they would come together now, as they should have long ago. He'd imagined time and again as he planned this trip that they would talk about politics and

India and farming, as they should have done when Paul was a child. Papaji had crafted scenes of their reunion that consisted of tears and apologies. Perhaps he dreamed this scenario so often that he thought it was a true possibility.

He hoped Paul would come around. Paul could be working too hard, or maybe he wasn't eating well, he thought. Perhaps it was depression from the rain that made him so angry. Papaji himself always experienced a bout of sadness during the annual monsoon downpour in India. The village celebrated when it began because it put an end to the dry season; young and old would run out into the pelting rain and let the shower clean the dust from their clothes. After a week of merciless rain, the roads would become flooded, mudslides would commence, and the same village would curse the skies for their inexorable fury. From dry to wet, content to misery, the interconnectivity between humankind and nature was evident to Papaji. Since he arrived, he had been looking forward to taking a short walk in the woods to get a closer look at the trees and the wildlife, but because of the constant downpour he could only stare at the few trees gathered in the backyard through the fogged-up windows. One of them would have to give: Paul, himself, or the weather.

It was dark all the time in Cobalt. What a sad place. The clouds seemed to push down closer and closer to the ground each day, leaving pockets of mist and fog in nooks and crevices around hills and curbs. It was an altogether messy sort of rain.

"Pea soup, *hánji*," Paul said as he flicked an angry hand at the outside.

Papaji peered down at the soil through the thick, double-paned glass. This American earth wasn't made for the monsoon. It was not sturdy or porous enough. The soil flipped and flopped like over-whipped egg whites and deflated and farted when the air ran out of it. Papaji's Indian earth was different, stronger. Sure, their floods and torrential storms sunk their cities and villages, but they always rose again like a forgotten Atlantis. Here in Cobalt, the streets and drains didn't suck the water; they seemed to pour the water back into the streets with garbage from underneath. He'd seen this phenomenon through the front window in the living room. The drain on Peregrine Court was coughing up murky waters like an old man clearing his lungs. The concrete might cave in, and the trees might lift up and out of the ground on their own and walk away, roots in tow. Over-watered land with no irrigation and a town on the verge of being swallowed by its own bowels—what civil engineer built this place? No care for details, no planning for the future. Whoever it was, he was a *goonda* and should be run out of town with nothing but his under *kaccha*.

"A monsoon so late?" he asked. He used a pencil he'd found next to the kitchen computer to scratch his scalp under his white turban. Vic began to explain the differences between this rainstorm and the monsoon Papaji was familiar with in the Punjab, but in the middle of his treatise, he stopped talking altogether. Papaji caught sight of Paul's clenched jaw and squinting eyes.

"If your *puttar* wants to tell me how the world works, that's fine, Ikpaul." He glared at Paul.

"He's a smart boy, Papaji." Paul looked down at his plate.

"If he takes after you, I think not," Papaji mumbled and turned away from his son. He felt terrible the moment the words exited his mouth. Though Papaji tried to be civil, he found it difficult to change his old ways. He'd hated what his son represented for so long that he'd forgotten what it was like to see him as a person.

In Papaji's mind, there was an ongoing discussion: a *here* and a *there*. *Here* things were new and strange. He looked forward to viewing the American soaps like *The Young and the Restless* and *General Hospital*; they came highly recommended by his cousin.

He liked the voice of Tanya Earhart, Channel 9's meteorologist. He hoped to find out why Paul came and stayed in America. And he was somewhat cheerful about the possibility that he would be under the care of a good doctor soon for his leg and foot pain.

There, on the other hand—in India—life was familiar. The noises, smells, and overall congestion set him at ease. But the flat that stored all the Singh family's aging relatives, from Uncle Chand, whose stomach problems left a foul odor surrounding him, to Massy Sukminder, whose joints were almost completely locked straight, made him feel old. He wasn't dying like they were; he just had an old injury. His foot and leg throbbed daily. Shocking pain shot up and down his limbs with lightning precision. His son rather than his daughter would help. Girls left home to worry about their husband's relatives, but sons were always there for their fathers. Paul: his American son. He looked at Paul and his family. Even though they were Americanized and half-Latvian and mostly wore glasses, they looked like a good family.

Paul turned the TV on. The small box in plastic wood paneling sat on a lazy Susan so it could turn toward the living room or kitchen. The morning news was on, and weather forecasters were having a ball with their time in the limelight—the only ones who were giddy about the gloom. Tanya Earhart, the heart-faced meteorologist, set aside a few more minutes during every hourly newscast to update the quantity of rainfall. There were three inches so far. Tanya made good use of her extra time to teach the public some meteorological vocabulary. *Virga*, they all learned, was the term for rain that falls and evaporates before it lands. Papaji had seen virga many times but never knew the word for the streaks of clouds that hung halfway across the sky. Papaji watched very closely when Tanya spoke. Her long hair was teased for height, her lips glossy like two rows of pomegranate seeds. He felt that learning English was important, so he repeated the word under his breath, *veergha*, and made a note to attempt to use the word sometime in the near future.

After breakfast he moved to a love seat in the living room, where he sipped his small cup of tea and nibbled on a cheese puff. His feet, bare and calloused, sat atop a pouf while he waited for the package to arrive with his life savings. He had bundled the rupees and a few other important things, wrapped them in plastic, and placed the bundle in a small box, also wrapped in brown paper and secured with almost an entire roll of packaging tape. He'd insured the package and sent it with the highest priority the post office in India offered, which was the speed post international rate.

Papaji's exercise was a slow walk to the mailbox on the sidewalk, twenty feet or so from the house. He opened an umbrella, wrapped himself in his brown wool cardigan, slid on his worn leather sandals, and shuffled to the curb. He leaned to the left ever so slightly to keep his weight lifted from his aching limb. He opened the aluminum mailbox and brought in the bills, junk mail, and some important-looking notices from the Publishers Clearing House and left them in the catchall in the foyer.

It was probably the humid air that made his joints swell like small balloons, but still he tried to smile when Maija brought him another cup of tea with two aspirin *tink-tinking* on the side of the saucer. The sky continued to threaten to downpour. If it wasn't raining, it was about to; if it finished raining, the sky would sigh relief and expose a grayish blue. The sun and all its effects were just becoming memories tucked away in a different dimension.

As Papaji sipped his tea, Vic sat beside him. Papaji looked at him closely and saw his fairly new clothes, sneakers, and jacket and thought how expensive these clothes must have been.

"Things are easy here, for you all, I mean. No farm, everything inside, safe, secure."

"Did you need a shotgun? I mean, for protection and stuff?" Vic asked with wide eyes.

The old man sat deeper into the couch. "In the Punjab you needed to be ready for, what's the word? *Dacoits* and *budmash*."

"What's that?"

"They rob you in your sleep and kidnap the women. Very bad men, *bahut kharáb*."

"Thieves? Did you learn how to fight, Papaji?

"Yes, we had to protect ourselves."

"Was there a *da*—?"

"*Dacoit*."

"Was there a *dacoit* in your village?"

"Not just any *dacoit*—the most terrible in all the land. His name was Harzarah Singh. Some said when he was very young he drank the blood of a viper and filled with evil. I just think it was greed, and he was *págal*, crazy." Papaji wound his pointer finger at his temple. "But even Harzarah Singh could not rival the chaos that came with the Partition. It claimed even the sharpest men."

Papaji took another sip of tea. "See, I grew up there, *potrá,* my father moved to Rawalpindi before I was born, and Bebbeji's family was from the area. It wasn't easy to just go go go. That's why I stayed. No one knew if this, this Partition, would come or if we could return once India was separated from Pakistan. I couldn't leave our home unprotected. I sent Bebbeji and Kamal to the village long before. There they met with other family members who also were going to rebuild. I stayed alone."

He put down his tea. "I locked up the valuables we had in one room. We gathered, the ones who stayed, and watched over each other. My friend and neighbor, Aaqib, said he would watch over the house and told me to go. But I couldn't."

"Why did you have to go? Why didn't he?"

"That, *potrá*, is a good question. The one country was divided into two: one for Muslims, the other for Hindus and Sikhs and whoever else. The politicians, you know. So, everyone was instructed that there was a date when this change of the border would be made. Some left long before to avoid any difficulty. Your grandmother. The rest were left to fend for themselves. One can't imagine the poison in people, until such a thing..."

Papaji's mind wandered as he struggled to find the words. In the winter of 1946, he'd packed up his wife, Anjana, and son Kamal, and sent them with one bullock and as much wheat flour as it could carry along with a few other Sikh families heading south toward Amritsar. He'd watched Anjana walk over the hill with Kamal in her arms until he couldn't see them anymore. From there, he'd expected them to continue onto a Punjab village outside of Jullundur, their ancestral land. There was no telling what trouble they would encounter along the way. He had to trust the men of the other families, who were like brothers and uncles to him, to protect his wife and son in his absence. He had to have faith that they would be allowed back into their family's village. Papaji's father's family had moved from Punjab to the rural village north of Rawalpindi when they had received the land at a good price from the British. The land, it turned out, was more difficult to cultivate than promised. But in the end, it was a fine village with strong and intelligent people, and the wheat, with a little encouragement, sprouted from the ground every year. His father and mother had both passed away from typhoid fever, and his other relatives remained in Southern Punjab. That had left Papaji as the sole inheritor of the land on which he was standing. But what good was this land without his wife and son? His gaze had followed the horizon as far as the next mountain.

And now, a dark cloud covered Papaji, and he became quiet.

"What was it like?" Vic's voice brought him into the present.

"At first, calm. Many left, so we thought it wouldn't be so bad. Then came the riots, and in the middle of the night the window shattered. Big sound. My shotgun—I kept it under the bed—was next to me. I took up the gun and went to search the house. Someone had thrown a brick through the window. Then I heard the screams. A pack of thieves was running through the city, burning wherever they heard a non-Muslim lived."

Papaji paused and used his cloth handkerchief to wipe his eyes and upper lip. He replaced his glasses and then twirled both sides of his moustache simultaneously toward the sky with his thumbs.

"What happened with your friend?"

Papaji frowned.

"Did you ever see him again?"

"That's another story altogether. Another time."

"How did you find Bebbeji?"

"It took months. I walked at night only. The darkness kept us safe. Many others were also going to the new border. So we walked in a large group; the more the better, in case we ran into—"

"You walked for months? How many miles?"

"I don't know. Do you have a map, or a globe?"

Vic left the room and returned with an atlas of the world, which he spread over the coffee table. He flipped to the page with India and the surrounding countries. Papaji leaned over the map, squinted his eyes, and pointed a finger at the lower portion of Pakistan.

"There is where we started." He pushed his finger down about five hundred miles into India. "There is where I ended."

"You must have been very tired. What did you do for food? It seems impossible to be able to travel that far, on foot!"

"Yes, but I survived. Vic, there is much to say, too much for now." He laughed and shook his head. "I am tired. Please, I will sleep." He pulled the throw blanket over his legs and closed his eyes.

Within moments, he was snoring and dreaming.

Papaji dreamt of the rough roads, the regional checkpoints, and those who would try to benefit from the movement of refugees. There were many thieves, and their traveling group had to stand guard day and night. He'd taken comfort in the fact that not many dared to cause trouble with his people; the Sikhs were strong and known as fierce fighters. The travelers had taken shotguns and their *kirpans*. Their strength could also make them a target, for if they were defeated and word spread, it would surely destroy the morale of other groups also en route. At least his cousin, Maddan Singh, also accompanied the group. He was a learned man who had a legal background and relations with the Temple Committee in Amritsar that protected the *gurdwárá* and oversaw land ownership in the Punjab. He would know what to do if they encountered difficulty. Papaji now regretted staying as long as he did to guard their land and animals from thieves and squatters. He'd originally thought it would be only a year at most and had hoped to send for Anjana and Kamal as soon as the political heat disseminated. But he never set foot in that home again.

Vic

Vic was feeling bold. He asked Papaji about the old house, the war, the lifestyle they'd all had before the Partition, and then the farm they bought with the reparations after. As Vic watched the old man stroke the edges of his beard, hesitate with his finger at the tip of his nose, and search his thoughts before answering, he saw something that gave him pause. At that moment, Vic realized that he looked just like his grandfather except for the long, white beard and the deep creases around his eyes and mouth. He had the nose. He had the bushy eyebrows. He wore the glasses. Papaji was a glimpse into Vic's future. Learning about his family's past quenched more than Vic's bookish need for information; Vic began to feel less like a single star in the sky and more like a part of a constellation.

Perhaps this was the reason for the changes he'd experienced lately. Regardless, Vic felt mighty. He'd challenged his science teacher on his answer to last week's extra credit equation. He complimented his mother's cooking by telling her that she "should have been a chef" and that "we are lucky to eat such excellent meals." A well of strength was growing inside Vic. He was collecting information; knowledge was his spinach. Secrets made him feel powerful, and Vic relished his secret world. When he passed his reflection in the hallway mirror, he realized that he had grown at least an inch.

All week, he had been starting his days with thirty pushups and a jog around the block.

Vic put on his rain poncho and backpack and went into the dreary early morning without his sister. She would take the bus to school later; he said he needed the walk, and no one questioned him. The construction on Main Street had come to a screeching halt because of the rain. The great sinkhole from which they were removing debris was flooded and, like a geyser, spewed dirty water back onto the earth's surface. As Vic passed, a few men were busy setting up pipes to drain the hole.

The morning was silent and heavy. The oppressive weather insulated the town as Vic's sneakers splashed along Main Street. He crossed Glenwood then made his way through the thick forest, up one hill, then another. The bog was quicksand under his sneakers, and he grew irritated each time he had to shake his foot free of the earth's suction. At the forest line ahead, the brilliant white bark of a series of birches stood out against the gloom. Vic saw a glimmer of blue on a slick tree's bark—a butterfly like the one he'd found earlier, but this one was even more mutated. One of its wings was a stump, and the other was wrinkled though open. Its body had not fully metamorphosed during the chrysalis stage, and the thorax still looked like a caterpillar's, green and wormlike. The proboscis was missing, too. He watched it try to move, but he knew it wouldn't survive, not like this. He extracted his tweezers and gently lifted the insect into a tin. It fell against the metal, and Vic watched as it died. He would have to give it a good inspection when he returned home later. What a tragedy, he thought. A life not given a chance to live.

When he lifted the collection of branches, skillfully twisted into a covering at the base of the birch, he felt a chill of air on his face. The edges of the hole were damp, but the inside walls were not. He lowered himself slowly into the square shaft, rung by rung.

Vic had grown bolder each time he'd descended the ladder into the hole. Once he'd overcome the anxiety of having twenty feet of earth above his head, he was amazed by his secret presence within the hill of his village. The area directly below the surface entry was quite comfortable, nest-like. The lantern, hanging on a hook, was bright enough. Vic had brought a few more things: a can opener, small camping torch, some Band-Aids, a change of clothes, and a bottle of rubbing alcohol.

He had ventured quite far through the tunnel. Holding his lantern, Vic yelled his full name, Varunesh Dzintar Singh, down the shaft, and listened for the echo's reply. It took a long time, and the names fumbled over one another. But he had not walked the entire length. Time was of the essence now, as Vic knew he'd have to end his underground adventure if he saw signs of the rain seeping into the mine.

He put on his backpack and proceeded to move slowly through the tunnel. It went downward at a slight angle for quite some time, and his sneakers lacked adequate traction, which made for a slippery journey. Vic thought he heard something; he swore it was a bat, but then he remembered he'd just finished reading *Batman: Year One* by Frank Miller, and he told himself the noise was probably a beam creaking or water dripping.

The thought that the entire structure could crumble on him hadn't crossed Vic's mind until now. Suddenly he regretted not leaving a note at the surface in case he went missing. But he was here now, and everything seemed stable so far.

The farther he went, the thicker the air became. Vic's eyes watered, but he didn't wipe them because he didn't want to slip. As he continued slowly into the darkness, lit only by his lantern, Vic paused and turned to look how far he had come, but darkness consumed his wake.

He thought about Hansel and Gretel and their trail of crumbs through the forest, and he felt he should mark his path for the return journey. His mother's folktales had made quite an impression on him—when he was very young, she had told him her own version of Hansel and Gretel, and her Latvian adaptation was more gruesome than the one the Brothers Grimm had recorded. In his mother's version, the two children were lost forever in the forest, even after they escaped the witch's oven. The cloying smell increased the farther he went.

The tunnel continued downward, leveled out, then continued downward some more. It turned slightly to the left, then to the right. At times Vic felt as though the walls were closing in around him. Time seemed different in the mine. Without the marker of the sun or a clock to tell him exactly how many minutes were passing, Vic felt as though he'd been in the mine for hours, maybe even days. His senses were heightened as well. Sounds were louder in the tunnel: The dripping and creaking noises stood out against the silence. His feet became more sensitive to the type of ground on which he was walking. His sense of smell sharpened with the sweet air, and he felt the air's damp heaviness build.

Then Vic saw something shiny in the distance. The lamp offered only enough light to illuminate a few feet in front of him, so he continued forward carefully with his arm extended. The ground became slick, and he grabbed at the wall to support his sliding sneakers—but he slipped and fell into a large pool of icy water. His scream filled the tunnel. Once he realized the pool was only a few feet deep, he stood up.

Vic looked ahead to see how far the pool of water went. He picked up the lantern, thankful that it was waterproof, and swung it forward. A brick wall up ahead, haphazardly constructed, ran from below the water to the ceiling.

He knew he needed to dry off if he was ever going to make it to school, and he was thankful he had a change of clothes back at the entryway with the rest of his new stash in case he got stuck in the mine or caught in the rain. He would have to change into his PE sneakers when he reached school.

Vic hoisted himself out of the water and made his way back to the mine's entrance. Once there, he changed into a dry pair of pants and a clean sweatshirt. When he ascended the ladder and entered the peculiar morning light, he realized there wasn't a great contrast between the underground and the aboveground worlds. The eerie sky was uncannily oppressive and claustrophobic, too, not a liberating reentry into the land of fresh air. Vic took off running, his shoes making a sloppy sound as he flew down the hills and into Cobalt.

The second late bell rang just as Vic entered his science classroom, breathless from the jog. Mr. Drew smirked and pointed at the clock. "Singh, you are a lucky man. One second later, and you'd end up in detention lockout."

Mr. Drew closed the door to the classroom, and it automatically locked. Just at that moment, Joe Balestrieri arrived and kicked the door. Vic was glad to see him locked out of the classroom like an animal. Joe did this almost every day, as he'd rather sit in detention than learn anything. Mr. Drew ignored Joe and said, "Okay, people, turn to page one hundred in your textbooks. Today we are going to begin to memorize the periodic table of elements."

Vic's feet were still wet, as he hadn't had a chance to trade his soggy sneakers for the dry ones in his gym locker. His frozen feet were beginning to smell; he tried to ignore the stench of his pre-ripened, sweat-upon shoes as Mr. Drew began his lecture. He just hoped that Katie, sitting at the desk to his right, couldn't smell him. When she smiled at him, he forgot his chilly feet but couldn't manage to return the expression. He burped instead. It was a strange reflex over which he had no control.

Katie laughed and turned to her friend. This type of embarrassment was not unfamiliar to Vic. His neurological system understood chemical compounds, physical pain, and differential equations. It did not, however, behave properly around girls. In the past, he'd drooled, burped, and almost farted once (thankfully the gas bubble was thwarted) while interacting with a female. He'd even stuttered while talking to Nurse McClasky, whose pockmarked face and broad shoulders made her look manly.

But he felt different today, bold, confident, and strong. Ah, he thought, Katie really does smell like peppermint. He wondered if she had freckles all over her body or just on the apples of her cheeks. He noticed a butterfly she'd drawn in black marker on the front of her binder, and this gave him even more courage. He swallowed and said, "Hey."

"Yeah?" Katie turned toward him slightly.

"I want to join yearbook."

"Yeah, sure." She smiled.

"Okay?" He smiled back.

"Okay." She wrote something in her notebook and tore it off, handing it to him. It was her e-mail address, and underneath she'd written: *E-mail me!* ☺ He nodded coolly, though his heart skipped a beat.

The more elements his teacher recited, the more Vic thought of his unidentified little blue. He'd requested Peterson's *Field Guide to Eastern Butterflies* from the local library, but it hadn't helped his search. Cobalt had some blue butterflies but nothing that looked as odd as the one he'd found. Blues were a sensitive group that relied on very specific vegetation for their food. The Silvery Blue and Plebejus Blue lived in the area during the spring and looked similar to his tiny find, but their markings and overall coloring were very different. He would return to the butterflies as soon as he could to listen to what they were trying to tell him.

Paul

Paul couldn't believe his eyes. Adelaide had called earlier to let him know they'd printed his "excellent" letter to the editor, but she hadn't said that they'd printed the whole thing. It took up the entire Letter to the Editor section, and they'd even given it a title: "The Voice of Reason," by Paul Singh. It couldn't have come at a better time. He used the largest magnet to hang it on the front of the refrigerator, then backed up a few feet to appraise it from a distance.

He could hear his father reciting his prayers, the *Japji Sahib*, from his bedroom. The harmonious sound offered a sonic frequency to the air in the house. Paul remembered how his skin would tingle from the vibrations of the early morning prayers at the *gurdwárá*. *Ik Onkar. Satnam. Karta purakh. Nirbhao. Nirvair. Akal murat. Ajuni. Saibhang. Gur prasad. Jap. Ad sach, jugad sach. Hai be sach. Nanak, hosi be sach.* These lines brought Paul home. They invoked the idea that stayed with him regarding truth being god, being everything. Paul paused in the hall outside of his father's door and let the nostalgia wash over him; this made the hole in the center of his being more prominent.

Paul's favorite lines were at the end of the prayer: *Pavan guru pari pita maataa dharat mahatt.* Air is guru, water the father, the earth the great mother of all. He had recited small prayers in his own mind and had bowed before the micro-altar he'd made on the dresser with his copy of the *Japji Sahib* and an image of Guru Nanak on a slick, well-worn card. What would his father think of how little he'd passed to his children in terms of language and meaning? As his father recited the end of the prayer, Paul went back to the kitchen and waited for him to emerge.

"Good morning, Papaji. Did you rest well?" Paul spoke in Punjabi.

"*Sat sri akal.* Yes, yes, fine." Papaji was dressed in his white *kurta pajama,* and though his head had the *fiftee,* he hadn't wrapped his full turban. He did however, have a piece of cotton fabric tied around his chin and head, the *tatha.* To an outsider it would have seemed he had a toothache, but Paul knew he was fixing his beard in place with Welldone beard-fixing solution. The long hair had been twisted along his jaw, transforming his persona to a manicured arrangement of hair with a swirling moustache twisted to curved points. Kamal had taught Paul how to do this long before he had enough facial hair to try it.

"I came home for lunch. Are you hungry? I was going to make myself something."

Papaji ticked his head back and forth in an affirmative and cast his gaze out the window at the hazy sun peeking through the high clouds. He unbound his *tatha.*

Though Paul was hoping to find a few leftovers in the refrigerator, something from last night's dinner perhaps, he found a treasure instead: a stack of Tupperware containers, each labeled with the contents and the time to set in the microwave. Maija, you are wonderful, he thought. She'd made a chicken yogurt curry, basmati rice, and *daal*, and she'd sliced cucumbers, carrots, and onions and tossed them with cilantro. There was even a small container of pecan bars.

Paul washed his hands, emptied the food into more attractive serving dishes, and heated them. He and his father ate in silence. Paul thought Maija's curry was delicious, but he could barely remember the taste of his mother's chicken to draw a comparison. He began to doubt his taste buds and lifted the hot serving dish. He'd forgotten to use a potholder and burned his hand—and the smell of chicken curry and his father's beard fixer, along with the searing pain on his skin combined in some unearthly way and sent him on a journey into the past.

He remembered screams, gurgling sounds, his body flushed with heat. The tile floor was cold under his bare legs. He was a small child; the counter was so far above his head as he searched for the source of his pain. Tears flooded his eyes.

Oh, my God. Help! Someone help! Bebbeji picked Paul up and poured cold water over his body.

An old man came into the kitchen. *Just leave him, Anjana, he's going to cause more problems.*

No, I can't.

It wasn't your fault, what happened, but a husband won't see it that way if he finds out, and you will be left alone on the streets. Finish it!

Uncle, he's my child. I don't care what you say. Oh, God, what have I done?

Forever the past will haunt you through his existence.

As Paul reentered the present, the scarred skin on his side felt unusually tight. He looked around the room for something to secure his place in the world—he felt it was about to fall apart.

"Do you cook, also? American men cook, nah?" Papaji wiped his beard with a cloth napkin.

"No, Papaji, but I grill and make tea. Maija's cooking is much better than anything I could make. It's good, right?"

"First class. Very tasty. She cooks like a *sardarni*. Do you come home every day for lunch?"

"No, only sometimes." Paul put water on for tea and glanced at his letter to the editor on the fridge. "I was published. The newspaper here, look." He handed the piece to his father.

Papaji cleaned his glasses and squinted at the page. "'The Voice of Reason' is very important sounding." He began to read the letter aloud, struggling through the words in English.

Paul was impressed. His father's English was better than he'd remembered, perhaps due to spending time in New Delhi. In the city people moved from Hindi to English to Punjabi to Urdu depending on to whom they were speaking. Paul said, "It's about the construction."

But his father lifted his finger and continued to read, with his pointer underlining every word. It took several minutes; Paul made tea, drank his, and reheated his father's by the time Papaji lowered his glasses to the tip of his nose and said in Punjabi, "When can I see the station?"

"Soon."

"Terrible. Construction. We should learn about the soil."

"Yes."

"Never heard of this sinkhole business."

"Me either."

"No one in my family is a writer."

Paul's heart sank. He took the scrap of newspaper from Papaji and returned it to its place on the fridge. "My family enjoys reading and writing."

"Son, I am an old man."

Paul's jaw clenched as he tossed the plates into the dishwasher.

"I have to get back." Paul spoke in English. "I'll see you at dinner." He picked up the remote control and showed his father how to flip through channels.

"Ikpaul—thank you," Papaji said as Paul closed the door behind him softly.

Isabella

Night fell on Peregrine Court with the heaviness of a dark winter curtain, and Isabella was far from sleep. The speed at which the digital clock progressed felt unnaturally slow to Isabella, who had recently begun to cultivate a deep disdain for her insomnia's loneliness. The blood-red numbers mocked her as they changed to midnight.

As she sat up in her twin bed, eyes open wide as windows, she marveled at how her brother's presence just beyond the duct-taped line on the carpet and past the sheet hanging from the ceiling was absolutely no comfort to her at all. In fact, Vic's sleep sounds were so contented that his presence sharpened her hyper-vigilance. This was not the first time Isabella had lost sleep. Night terrors filled with all the horrors of hell had managed her nights from age six through twelve. Doctors chalked it up to an active imagination and hormones. When the nightmares ceased to torment her, she didn't bother to question why; she simply became a heavy sleeper, as though she were making up for lost dreamtime.

As of late, however, a new and curious sensation came upon her when night fell and darkness crept into every corner of the house. She had seen things in her room. At first, she thought her eyes were tricking her because these moments usually occurred during the dim twilight. Then she wondered if perhaps the figures and swaying shadows were images that she glimpsed between her waking and dreaming states. Yet when she could find no other options within her logical mind, Isabella conceded that her insomnia *could* be supernaturally influenced—and that's as much as she was willing to admit.

"I don't believe in ghosts," she said aloud. Perhaps she could convince herself of this, or at least prevent the revenant from taking completely corporeal form in the corner of her room. Believing and witnessing were two totally different things for Isabella. She had been aware of her mother's clairvoyance since she was a child. Before she was five years old, she knew her mother could do things that other kids' mothers could not. For example, when they'd once driven to the grocery store, an outing Isabella rarely missed as a child, the traffic had slowed as they passed a massive car accident on the expressway. Three small cars and a semi had been tangled into a mortal mess. Isabella watched as the EMTs and firemen tried to revive the victims, but her mother told her to close her eyes. *They're already dead, darling. But don't worry. It was very quick, and they look happy now.* Sometimes her mother saw the future, sometimes the past. Isabella had always feared a similar fissure in reality would occur in her life. The present was complicated enough for Isabella without having to deal with potential futures and unsettled, demanding pasts.

"I don't believe in you," she whispered, even though it sounded ridiculous to her. This time she directed her words at the closet, where she could see the faint outline of a tall man becoming clearer. She heard Vic turn over in his bed but knew he was too far taken by sleep to wake. She was glad he was a heavy sleeper; if he woke and couldn't see what tormented her, she would feel more isolated.

The closet door swung open, and the almost-there man reached inside. He looked as though he'd been dipped in bleach and stripped of all his color. Isabella sat up on her knees, letting her comforter slip from her fingers. It seemed as though the man was pushing aside the hangers in the closet. The spirit separated her clothes from Vic's and opened up a large gap, as though he were making room for something.

"What are you doing?" she whispered, but he didn't seem to hear her. The man crossed a line when he took her favorite black-and-yellow sweater off the hanger and tossed it to the floor.

"Hey!" As soon as she stood, bare feet chilly on the carpet, her confidence vanished. The figure turned toward her and smiled. The grin seemed strangely familiar. His eyes, too, were more visible, dark blue and piercing.

"Mine *mazmeita*, making room for the next visitor. Not much time, *mazmeita*. She will be here soon."

"Who are you? Who is coming?"

He ignored her, then became increasingly transparent until there was nothing left but the room as it had been before his visit. The hangers had returned to the same disarray as before.

Each time something like this happened—like a few weeks ago when she'd seen a round woman sitting in her desk chair knitting—Isabella entered a state of disbelief for at least a half hour. This time, she went to the kitchen because there was no use trying to get to sleep with her stomach tied in knots. It was a relief to see a small light already on in the kitchen and her mother sitting over a large bowl of ice cream, flipping the pages of a photo album.

"Oh, Queen Isabella, what are you doing up so late?" her mother asked.

"I couldn't sleep again."

"Here, sweetie, I'll get you some ice cream." She stood, retrieved another bowl from the cupboard, and scooped ice cream into a bowl for Isabella.

"Mama?" Isabella began, with a cold bite of rocky road in her mouth. "I think there was a man in my room, just now."

"I know, my darling. It's my fault."

"What do you mean?"

"It's making sense now. I haven't called your Oma in almost a month. Uncle Janis was always looking out for her." Her mother slid an old picture toward her. The edges were curled and brittle. The three people in the photo were smiling, though the sun was in their eyes. Two young women, with their hair curled in 1930s fashion and dressed in blouses and skirts, sat atop a boulder before a thick forest. A man in suspenders, with his woolen pants pulled above his belly button, stood alongside them. He held a cane in his hand and wore a hat firmly on his head. It was the same man who'd appeared in Isabella's room.

"This is Janis," her mother said, "and there is Oma when she was very young. And this is her sister, Alvina. Janis was much older than Oma, you know. I never met him." Her mother stroked her hair. "But he has visited me in spirit form since I can remember."

"This is too weird. Make it stop."

"I know, sweetie. Eat some more ice cream. Did he say anything to you?"

Isabella nodded. "He said he was making room for a visitor."

"He came to me tonight, too, you see. But I tried to ignore him. I should call Ma tomorrow morning and make sure everything's okay. I think she's coming here."

Isabella's bottom lip trembled. "Oma's coming?"

"Now, listen carefully. The only way to stop this nonsense is to ignore it completely. They lose interest if they feel they don't have an audience."

"Okay."

This connection to her mother was something she'd never felt before. Likeness, Isabella thought, was wonderfully comfortable.

"C'mon, let me tuck you in."

Isabella finished her ice cream and let her mom lead her back into her bedroom. Her mother slid the comforter up to her chin and patted her cheek. "Don't worry, honey. It won't last, okay?"

With those words Isabella found herself drifting off, finally.

Maija

Maija returned to the kitchen and to the photos. She removed a small black-and-white portrait of her mother from the sheer plastic sleeve. It had been taken when Oma was in her twenties. She flipped it over and it read: *Hermione, augusts 40.*

How like doorways, Maija thought, are these pieces of paper into the past. She envied her mother's porcelain skin and sharply drawn red lips, which echoed the elegance of the forties. Oma's hair was jet black and pulled into tight curls. Her eyes were focused gently on something off camera; her mouth was just about to turn into a smile. She was looking toward the future. This day had to be a happy one. World War II had just begun; the Nazis and Soviets had yet to sign their ironic Friendship and Non-Aggression Treaty, and Germany had yet to invade Poland. When the photo was taken, her mother's future was still filled with unlimited possibilities. Her soft gaze carried dreams of a farmhouse, beautiful horses, a family, a husband, and a daughter. Maija wondered if her mother knew that her portrait would travel so far, from Latvia to Germany and back again, through refugee camps, through DP camps in Poland, along war-ridden roads of the countryside, on to Cleveland, until its journey ended here on top of a wood-veneer kitchen table in New York State. Oma wasn't more than a short flight away; she still lived in that small apartment in Cleveland. But this picture was a world away.

Maija sighed. She'd been born after the war but had the weight of her parents' past on her shoulders. Maija did not carry history in the same manner that many children of war families did; in her dreams, she relived much of the torture and torment that her mother had experienced during World War II quite literally. Maija knew that Oma wasn't well. She knew, for the past few years since Oma's best friend passed away, that her mother should move in with them. And now, the dreams she'd been having of Latvia made it seem as if Oma was downloading her memories into Maija's mind for safekeeping, which could mean she was nearing her end.

Maija would wait until it was a decent hour, perhaps six or seven, to call her. It was still quite dark, but this night she wasn't going to sleep. Her mind was too full of the past for her to relax. She browsed the photos to pass the time and came upon a series of landscapes of Riga. She looked closer.

In 1967, when Maija was a little girl and her psychic abilities were surfacing through dreams of her past lives and deaths, Oma had taken her to the Riga Circus. It was an effective distraction outing. The pair stayed with Oma's sister Alvina's family. There were animals: dogs, seals, even a giraffe and an elephant. The clowns ran around the circle, lighting and juggling fireworks and throwing them at one another. There were even trapeze artists swinging in the air, dressed in silver costumes. She remembered the maestro himself, Cris Katkevics, wielding his staff and top hat, commanding the attention of all performers and audience members alike. Maija's memories swirled around her; she even smelled candy, sickeningly sweet.

After the main event—a series of scenes from fairy tales acted out by clowns, animals, and acrobats—Oma had taken her to Madam Blatvskavia to have her palm read. Maija's small hands pushed aside layers and layers of faux silk curtains of baroque design—the deeper she went into the tent, the stronger the perfume of frankincense and myrrh. When they came to the innermost center of the small tent, they encountered a velvet-covered table with various objects: leaves, string, crystals, a tambourine, and coins of different sizes. Madam Blatvskavia was sitting with her back to them but spoke gently in a Romany accent.

Have a seat, please.

Oma pushed Maija into the small chair and kept her hands, like weights, on her shoulders. In Maija's memory, Oma had been young then; she had curls in her dark brown hair and wore a handmade teal sweater with an orange stripe through its center. Three brass buttons the size of baby's fists clasped the sweater together. Oma's hands were hot, almost burning. Maija couldn't have been older than eleven or twelve at the time. Oma dropped a coin on the table. Madam turned around slowly and told Maija she must close her eyes and concentrate on believing in what will occur. *I don't convince, I just show what is what.*

I already believe, she whispered. At least she'd thought she believed; she'd been witnessing strange goings-on since she was a toddler. Her dreams were filled with other people's lives, and sometimes the dreams were so visceral she woke feeling like another person completely. She'd been terrified and hadn't slept for years. It hadn't been until Oma found Maija crouching under a chair, shaking and crying because she'd just seen dead Aunt Charlotte in the bathroom putting curlers in her hair, that Oma told her it was all very normal.

You are my daughter, are you not? she'd said. *It skips generations. I don't have it, but I knew you would.* Oma had dried her tears and made Maija peppermint tea with chamomile flowers that spun across the top like sea stars.

Oma's eyes, the shade of ancient ice, had calmed Maija. When her mother looked at her, the vastness embraced her and she felt as if she were falling forward. It was exhilarating—chilly and comforting, clear and all encompassing, Oma's eyes were a contradiction. The week prior to coming to the circus, Maija had seen her own death. It must have been from a past life, Oma reassured her scientifically, and she must have crossed that age when her previous death occurred. Yet it had been a terrible sight in Maija's mind's eye. She was a little girl sleeping in an eighteenth-century dressing gown; lace and uncombed cotton tickled her back. She was on a farm. A man came into her bedroom at night and strangled her. The act seemed so meaningless and terrifying. Now here she was, in Madam Blatvskavia's tent, awaiting her first real reading to see beyond a doubt about her ability.

Maija closed her eyelids tightly. She heard the skin of a small drum tap-tap-tapping, then she heard something falling onto the drum, like rain. *Open.* Maija, peeking, saw that Madam had dropped dried beans into the center.

They are all telling me the same thing. The beans rested on the right side of the drum. *You have the gift, but need to control it.* Madam poked at a few of the beans that were close to the rim. *The trees speak to you the most. Listen to them. I see changes in your future. Continents shift, perhaps a journey.* She grabbed Maija's hand forcefully.

Oma glared at her. *Careful with her hands. They are important, neh?*

I am careful.

Madam traced Maija's palm with her fingers. *There's something about a dark man. Someone dark. I don't know when or who.*

Yes, yes, we are done now.

Wait. I see great riches in your future...

Then Oma had grabbed Maija's arm and dragged her from the tent. *That woman's greedy. Dark man! Ha! You know she's a fake. Shame. She used to be so good. She's probably a Jew.*

That was that. They stopped by Alfonse's bakery for cake afterward and walked to Aunt Alvina's flat in Old Riga, where they would spend the night. The winter night was biting. Oma asked if she'd understood what happened, and Maija nodded her head in the cold wind as they walked on the cobblestone path.

Now, sitting in her kitchen, Maija realized she didn't want to become like Madam Blatvskavia; she wanted a normal life. She needed to sort out her memories from the ones that were coming from her mother.

The sky was just showing the first signs of morning. The backyard glistened with dew as the sun tinted the clouds pink. It was only five but she picked up the phone. "Hallo, Ma? It's me. *Labrīt*."

"*Meita*, what is wrong? Why are you calling so early?" Oma sounded frantic. Maija could hear her trying to sit up in bed.

"I thought you might be awake."

"Mine old bones don't need much rest."

"How are you feeling, Ma?" Maija looked out the kitchen window.

"Still kicking, neh?"

"Ma, I have to ask you something, and I want you to answer truthfully, okay?"

"Okay."

"Doesn't it get lonely there?"

"Everyone is gone, yes, but what can you do? You want I should worry about za dead, neh?"

"No, Ma." She thought about how she'd been worried about the dead as long as she could remember. "How are your eyes?"

"Fine, fine, darlink. I can still find my way around."

In her heart, Maija knew that her mother's eyes were beginning to weaken. The idea of Oma helpless and alone without a soul near to help her was too much for her to bear. She knew her mother. She wasn't one to ask for help.

"I want you to move in with us." The sentence fell out of her mouth and surprised even Maija. "Or at least come for a long visit. I work too much and need your help to watch the kids."

"Maija, please. I have mine little garden behind za apartments. I have mine Shoprite down za street."

"Listen, it could be temporary. Both Paul and I work so much. I am afraid that the children will forget their heritage." Maija knew this would motivate her mother.

"Isn't their Opa there, now?" She heard Oma clear her throat—a sure sign she was wavering.

"Yes, but he's not Latvian."

"Ah, well, good for him."

"Ma, they need their Oma. I need you." Maija bit her lip, and then said, "You can cultivate your own garden in the backyard. It would be wonderful to grow food here, with you. Maybe we can get some chickens for eggs." Maija thought about how she missed working with her hands and getting soil under her fingernails. She had been a farmer but hadn't had the chance to toil in the earth in years. She missed feeling connected to earth and to her mother.

"Really, neh? Vie big?"

"As big as you like."

"Okay, I will think on it."

"Good. I will send you a ticket—when you decide, of course. Paul's father was born the same year as Papa, you know."

"Really? Can you manage?" Though Maija knew she meant *imagine*, she'd grown used to her mother's approximation of the English language.

"Just needs a little surgery on his foot, and he will be able to keep up with you."

They said their goodbyes and hung up. Maija wondered how

she'd tell Paul that she'd invited her mother into their home. She could try to make the case that she was ill just like his father. Perhaps that would be enough. Paul couldn't say no. After all, family is family.

Papaji

Papaji received his package amid a thunderstorm. The mail carrier, covered in a plastic rain tarp that matched her dark-blue uniform, ducked into their cul-de-sac a half hour later than usual and gloomily placed a large pile of mail in the box. When Papaji saw the package the size of a check box, wrapped in several layers of brown paper and twine, an orb of stress in the guise of acid dissipated in his gut. He opened the box, called to his family, and lifted the stack of money from the wrappings like a treasure.

The proud grandfather smacked his son on the back and smiled. "You have a good doctor for me? One you would trust with your father's limb?"

"Yes, Papaji, we have a good medical group," Paul answered.

Papaji listened nervously from the doorway while Paul arranged his appointment. He heard his son offer Dr. Bhalla, the podiatrist, a discount on his gas for the entire year if it got him an appointment sooner. Paul handed the Kwicki Fill receipt to Papaji that read: *Dr. Bhalla's gasoline discount, 20% off, one entire year*. The doctor was Indian, probably Hindu, but the same subcontinent nonetheless. Papaji couldn't ask for more.

When they arrived at Dr. Bhalla's office, during a respite from the rain, the parking lot was flooded, so Paul dropped Papaji off near the entrance to the medical arts building. He waited for his son under the overhang and thought about how he still hadn't had the chance to wander around town or look for monkeys in the forest.

Papaji's romantic impression of the rain was dying, and a severe dislike for the wet stuff had begun to sprout. He was, however, enjoying spending time with his son at the station. To make amends for nature's cruel deluge, Paul had set up a sturdy chair and side table outside the convenience store as Papaji's lookout. He spent a great deal of time there in his white *kurta pajama*, with his red turban and long white beard, peering curiously at passersby and examining the construction site on Main Street. He knew his posture was powerful; knees spread, he held his cane between them among the layers of white cotton fabric. People slowed their walking or driving to stare back at him, and he'd smile and wave, sometimes with his cane in his hand, sometimes just with his large outstretched palm.

Though the rains forced the construction workers to stop digging, some workers came during those brief hours of hazy sun to drain the water from the hole or check on their abandoned equipment. Papaji befriended the men who were dressed in their orange vests and hard hats. He'd bring them sodas from the station.

Draining, achchhá? he'd say.

The men would nod and then drop a hose into the hole.

What's going on down there that's so special? He'd practiced this question many times before asking it. But he'd grown used to the answer.

Dunno, just following orders. They tell us to dig, and we dig. 'S not my job to know why.

To distract him, the men would sometimes let him direct traffic. There were plenty of pylons to force the cars around their huge mess, but if two cars attempted to pass at the same time, the STOP sign would be necessary to notify which could go first. Papaji loved spinning the sign and holding it up high and proud to cars. He'd even hold it up to Paul, in the store, who'd cover his eyes with his hands and shake his head. He'd sometimes get the idea behind the STOP sign confused with the come hither wave, and he'd end up asking a car to both stop and go, which would end in screeching brakes and him handing back the sign to Charlie and returning to his station. But he loved those moments when he could control his surroundings with a flick of his wrist.

His son would ask if he'd found anything out about what they were doing and why, but he never learned a thing. He'd looked deep into the hole many times, and the layers of asphalt and concrete and brick surprised him the most. Brick under all that garbage? Knowing there was something aesthetically pleasing under the asphalt made the hole in the ground even more of a puzzling eyesore. Maybe once his foot was fixed and he could walk with confidence, he could take a better look at the dig and its surrounding area.

They'd been waiting in the doctor's office for fifteen minutes before he heard, "Mr. Harbans Singh? The doctor will see you now."

"Yes, yes, coming." Paul helped him from the chair.

Papaji had been looking forward to this appointment. He'd been haunted by his foot pain for decades. The throbbing nerves almost defined him: He was the man with the cane. As he walked into the doctor's exam room, his heart took a fearful leap into his throat. He rested calmly onto the cold, crunchy paper that Isabella had warned him about.

The nurse took his blood pressure and left without a word. Paul paced like an animal in the ten-by-ten-foot room. Three jolly knocks on the door preceded Dr. Bhalla's entrance. He was a small man with a wide nose and pleasant grin. His balding head shone beneath the few hairs he'd convinced with hair gel to lay patiently across his forehead.

"*Namaste*," Dr. Bhalla said with palms pressed. He spoke in Hindi.

"*Sat sri akal*," Papaji said and bowed back. Though Papaji understood a great deal of English and Hindi, he felt the need to make communication difficult. He wanted to get his money's worth from this expensive visit.

"So, you've come a long way. How can I help you?" The little doctor sat on his stool and sank even further toward the earth.

Papaji spoke in Punjabi to Paul. "Tell him my foot has hurt for fifty-four years. Tell him."

"That long? You remember exactly when it started?" Paul asked.

"There are some things one cannot forget. Tell him," Papaji whispered in Punjabi.

"Dr. Bhalla, my father has been experiencing pain in his foot and leg for a very long time."

Papaji pointed to his foot.

"All right. Let's take a look." The doctor wheeled closer and asked if he could take off Papaji's sock and slipper. "Everything, please."

Papaji pretended to not understand and looked to Paul for advice. "Your sock, take it off."

"Ask him if he's a specialist. Ask."

"Are you a specialist?"

"Podiatrist, yes, sir."

The game continued: The doctor would speak to Papaji, Papaji would act as though he couldn't understand a syllable, and then Paul would translate and respond for him. Everyone played his role: aging patient, doctor, and loving son. It was a game of medical badminton; no one was rushed or anxious, simply using the lightest flick of their racket to toss the shuttlecock to the next person. Papaji slowed the whole process down; for him and his foot, this was more than just a checkup—it was an opportunity for liberation, and he wanted everyone to work hard for the payoff.

Dr. Bhalla crouched closer to Papaji's exposed foot and grinned. "The patient's foot is size twelve, maybe thirteen," he said as though he were making a mental note. He used a metal pointer in the shape of a skeletal foot to manipulate and poke the underside of Papaji's arch, the edges of his littlest toe, the crevasse between his ankle and Achilles. Every once in a while, Papaji grunted to make sure the doctor knew his poking and prodding was very uncomfortable. When the doctor came upon the small swollen bulges attempting to surface from between his third and fourth toe, Papaji made a hissing sound.

"Mr. Singh, we need to get some X-rays, okay?"

"X-ray, *achchhá?*"

"Okay. Okay."

"Go downstairs to radiology, and when you return, let my nurse know you are back. It'll only take ten minutes or so."

"*Hánji.*" Though he responded to the good doctor, he never looked at him, not even during the inspection. It was as though he was exposing something too difficult for Papaji to address.

A while later the three men stood around the X-ray of Papaji's foot. The film, shades of gray and white, floated low against the fluorescent panel. It was strange for Papaji to see inside so deep, as though skin and muscle were meaningless and so easily penetrated. They crouched around the doctor as he traced his metal pointer along the different areas of Papaji's projected foot.

"I believe this is a mass of scar tissue, probably from a traumatic injury. And this here"—his voice was almost too joyful for it to be bad news that he was delivering—"is potentially the largest neuroma I have seen since college. And that one was on a cadaver." He chuckled.

Paul looked down at Dr. Bhalla and scowled. "What's this neuroma?"

"Two nerves that grow together and make one larger one. Most of the pain is probably from that. But I'm not done. This area of the foot, here, is the flattest arch I have ever seen."

Both Paul and Papaji looked at the good doctor with their mouths open wide.

"Sir, I think you have several different problems here working together to cause your pain and discomfort. It will be a fairly short procedure with a quick recovery. You can walk with crutches immediately afterward, and then using a cane would be advised."

"No crutches," Papaji said in English. "Never crutches."

"Okay, that would be fine. But you would be advised to stay off of it for at least a week."

They nodded in unison. The old man's eyes welled with tears, but no drop grew bold enough to exit. Dr. Bhalla gave him a cortisone injection to stop some of the swelling, and a prescription for Vicodin that he could take for pain from the pinched nerves. The shot wasn't so bad because he sprayed liquid nitrogen to freeze the area before the needle went in. They made the appointment to return for the procedure.

Vic

Vic scoured the menu at Friendly's for an appetizing item. He was having a difficult time finding something without meat. The photographs of hamburgers, all of which he'd tried at one time or another, seemed fleshier than usual. He felt nauseous and suddenly claustrophobic in the red vinyl booth that grew subtly a few degrees warmer. The burgundy-checkered tablecloths, busy carpeted floor, and booths lining the restaurant's walls were almost full.

His grandfather, who was sitting beside him, seemed delighted by the brightly colored menu. His joy, Vic assumed, was most likely due to his recent diagnosis and treatment plan. His father, mother, and Isabella sat across from them and were already set with their usual orders. As Vic observed his family, he felt at once close to and far away from them, as though a single pane of glass was between them and he stood on one side, alone. This was his new perspective.

When the waitress came to take their orders, each Singh opted for either a cheeseburger or a hamburger, until they reached Vic. "I'll have the mushroom and Swiss with a veggie patty. I'd like to substitute fries for a side salad, please."

His words fell like an atom bomb on the entire table.

"He means *ham*-burger," his father said, as though stretching out the words would make it sound meatier.

"No. Veggie burger. Papa, I know what I mean."

His father's eyebrows rose, like a drawbridge, as high as they could reach, then slammed down around his eyes, shadowing his cheekbones. "For an appetizer, fine, but for your main dish you will have meat."

"I won't eat meat even if you make me order it. So, logically, if you want me to eat, you'll let me order what I want." He turned to the waitress. "Veggie patty, mushroom, Swiss, side salad." The words were a directive. Energy surged through his body. Was this what being a man was like? he wondered.

"What's this about?" His father appeared to half appreciate and half despise his son's new spirit. Vic took a sip of water and chewed on a pile of ice as if it were jerky. The two were locked in a staring war.

"Vic's gone veggie." Isabella chuckled, then coughed when their mother delivered a punishing glare. Vic's eyebrows rose, as did his father's.

"You should have meat or else you won't grow, Vic. You'll stay as short as you are today," his father said.

"I'm only an inch shorter than you, and I still have time to grow."

"What?"

"I measured. I've grown."

His father looked at the pile of fries the waitress placed on the table. "You cannot stop eating eggs. That's where the line is drawn."

The corner of Vic's mouth curved. "If you make it free range eggs, it's a deal." He sat back in the booth. Paul nodded. The heat disseminated.

"So, Papaji, it went well today?" his mother asked the old man.

"First class. Dr. Bhalla will perform the procedure next week," he said. "Procedure, not operation. It will be easy to recover that way."

"Good, good."

Vic noticed that his mother was relieved—he assumed because the conflict had passed. He saw that she was attempting to diffuse the tension and wondered why she did this so often. She ran from discomfort so fast that half of life could be missed. Discomfort, Vic thought, was a way of understanding your beliefs and philosophies. If you constantly ran, how would you grow? But then Vic remembered that she was different, special, and the life she experienced was through the eyes of a seer. She felt more lives than just her own. He'd never considered this before, because she was just Mama to him, and being Mama came with certain accepted difficulties. She would be the one to do the hard jobs in the house, like take the stray dog Izzy had kept in the garage secretly for a week to the animal hospital to be put down because it had a tumor-ridden belly. Stuff like that.

"Then you'll be running marathons." His mother smiled.

"*Neyji*, no running for me. I never liked to run. But a good walk will be nice. It's been a long time since I've strolled without a destination."

"Too bad it's raining. There are some great views from the hills of old Cobalt. I've walked there a few times," his mother said before eating a fry.

"The last walk I ever took was the longest walk of my life. My feet did the best they could. But now it is their time. Imagine, if you can"—he looked Vic—"this change. For no reason that you can see—no earthquake cracked the land, no lightning struck, no flood—but still you are forced to walk hundreds of miles. All of your life—what you called home, job, friends, and family history—all erased."

The waitress brought the rest of their food. "You know, Kamal went ahead with your mother." Papaji focused on his son directly.

"*Ji*, please."

"Memories are important, Paul," Papaji said.

"I don't want to talk about it."

"It? It? Your brother is not *it*."

"Enough." His father put his hands on the table and pushed himself to standing.

"Your brother is dead, but he still deserves to be in our memory. He was a good boy; you were a good boy." Papaji stood as well, though his body took longer to extend. The two men paused inches away from each other.

Vic observed his father as a scientist might observe his subject. In an attempt to be as unbiased as possible, he pushed away his preconceived notions about his father and studied his appearance, deciding that anyone would assume he was a hardworking and successful man, with his starched shirt, worn soft around the edges of the collar. As his father exchanged words with Papaji, he noticed his father's demeanor had darkened, as if a secret he'd hoped was lost had now surfaced. Whatever it was, he seemed powerless against it.

His father appeared to shrink. "I don't remember." Then he walked away from the table with Papaji right behind, hobbling with his cane. The pair exited to the parking lot, and Vic followed just far enough back so as to not disturb them. He stood within earshot just outside the Friendly's door, leaning against the wall so they could not see him.

"No? Well, you were young. Kamal's death—"

Vic had never heard anything about an uncle. He leaned forward to look at them.

"It was my fault, *puttar*," Papaji said.

"Papaji, you came all this way—for what? Why did you come here, of all places?" Vic's father turned toward the old man.

"Son, I am old."

His father threw his hands in the air. "And what? We are all getting older."

"Let it go, *puttar*, just let it go." Vic watched Papaji move close to his father, then pause as though an invisible barrier pushed against him. He frowned, then placed his large hand on his son's shoulder.

"I can't."

The two men stood still in the middle of the rain-dampened parking lot. Silence held them both. Vic watched Papaji make a motion to speak, but he stopped himself, struggled, inhaled, then seemed to find courage.

"Son, please don't be like me. Don't waste this."

"Waste what?"

"Your life."

Vic watched his father pause as though he was caught in a sudden downpour without an umbrella. Papaji looked at his son as though hopeful that his words affected him. But then Vic saw his father turn away. He walked quickly toward Vic, and Papaji followed. Vic ducked back inside, pretending that he'd just emerged from the restroom. Then they all returned to the table.

"So, Isabella, how is the play?" his mother was asking.

Isabella looked at her with disbelief and did not answer. Their mother placed her hand on her husband, who had sat beside her, and he softened. One touch, and she'd quelled the fury that was soaring.

Papaji wiped his eyes with his handkerchief and turned his attention to the burger the waitress had placed in front of him. "Ahh, fit for a king."

Vic's father turned his eyes toward the floor, and his mother shifted in her seat as though she was struggling. "My mother's coming tomorrow. Oma's coming."

"What?" his father said.

"Can she stay for a while?" Isabella asked.

"Yes, she will stay with us, for a short time."

"Why?" His father turned his anger on his wife.

"She needs us now. She is alone in Cleveland, in her small

apartment. Her friends have passed away. It's not right. She shouldn't be alone. Family should never be alone."

"Yes, but we don't have room."

"I could room with her, you know. I don't mind," Isabella said.

"And I could stay with Papaji," Vic offered.

"Not now," Paul grumbled.

Vic smiled at his mother, though he was certain she did not know why. Amazing, he thought, how you could slot someone into a category and so quickly they could prove you wrong. He was delighted she had made such a large decision for the household without consultation.

"Yes, darling. She's coming tomorrow. Her flight is tomorrow. That's that."

ON THE WING

Desire

Posted on October 17

How is it possible to reconcile killing a creature one loves? I read an article about a rare insect smuggler—yes, they exist—who was finally caught in a sting operation (pun intended). In his possession they found several Queen Alexandra's Birdwings, Atlas moths, and Rhino beetles. He had agreed to sell them to an undercover FBI agent for $10,000 total, and had, over the previous 25 years, stolen, smuggled, and sold thousands of endangered and nearly extinct insects. He only got 3-6 years and a $50,000 fine that he could pay by selling an insect or two. For a holocaust, only 3-6 years? The man should be locked up for life, jabbed with a pin in his midsection. If only the afterlife is how Dante imagined it.

The images printed in the paper of the Japanese smuggler are ridiculous. His face is always turned toward the hidden camera, as though he'd like to be captured. Perhaps that was at the center of his motivation—the pursuer desiring pursuit. In further investigation of this character, the FBI agent who courageously tossed this fiend in jail talks about how he felt the man was sexually attracted to him. Keep in mind the agent was a happily married man, though this did offer a particular kind of power in his undercover sting. In a way, the smuggler was caught by the one he desired. This desire or obsession for a thing is nothing like love. It is selfish. Love is selfless—at least how I imagine love to be.

The objects of desire for the obscenely rich are odd. Does the desire drive the market, or vice versa? A man attempted to board an airplane carrying forty snakes and rare caimans in a briefcase. A woman in Australia wore a specially designed apron with twelve pockets in which she stashed bags of rare and endangered fish. The items were worth tens of thousands of dollars. A man was caught with his own ark of animals: four exotic birds, fifty rare orchids, and a pair of pygmy monkeys no larger than his thumbs. Now, my question is: Is money at the bottom of desire? The man, by the way, hid the baby pygmy monkeys in his pants. When does life become a product like this? Perhaps we've already crossed lines allowing for the patenting of life. That was the tipping point.

Do we care so little for the lives of others? Or are we in denial about the act of extinction—not natural extinction but the one that we speed toward because of our carelessness? Perhaps someone should make the case that the loss of these small creatures that few worry about is going to ultimately affect our planet on a large scale—then maybe they would listen and not build another strip mall with the same junk food on every corner. Butterflies are the second largest pollinators next to bees. A butterfly's habitat goes under a strip mall. No more butterfly. No more pollinators to bring your crops into fruit. No butterflies, no food. Worried yet?

I am disturbed by the guidebooks I've found in the library. Each of them illustrates in detail how to capture and kill butterflies and moths. They say to use gas or put it in the freezer and describe the death clinically, as though you're hanging a picture on a wall. While I understand the scientific process has value, I still do not believe that repetition of such deaths, whether mammalian or insect, are really necessary. I can observe the butterfly by luring it close with sugar or sweat, and view photographs of its cross section. The hundreds of companies that sell butterflies in frames, in jewelry, or alive through toy kits are fraudulent. They say they have clearance from customs, but insect trade is not regulated, as it should be. People care little for the insects of this world, yet their disappearance will have direct effects on our ecosystem. Yes, it's true that it is more difficult to observe and photograph or draw the wild butterfly and moth, but if you really love them, then that's what you'll do. If one hundred people kill hundreds of butterflies, well, you get the picture.

I dream of seeing these butterflies during my life. But some of them are endangered and now so rare; it is likely that they will become extinct within fifty years if they aren't properly cared for.

White Witch/Ghost Moth (Brazil): One of the largest

moths in the world. Its wings spread like a birdwing and are white. 31 cm

Paris Peacock (India-Asia/Australia): It has a large black form like a swallowtail with iridescent green dots across its wings: a sea of green stars on a blanket of black night. 8-10 cm

Rosy Maple Moth (Eastern U.S.): Its comb-shaped antennae are like antlers on its head, and its body is fuzzy like a baby bear's to keep its body warm in flight. It is bright pink and yellow, like it escaped the Skittles factory. 32-44 mm

American Snout (South U.S.): An eater of the hackberries, this butterfly has a nose like a trunk, and near the end of its third migratory flight, when it dies en masse, it can leave the South covered in corpses. 3.5-5 cm

Chestnut Leafwing (one small area in Texas): It looks like dead organic matter, a leaf with a hole in its side. None look exactly alike, which helps it camouflage itself in a dense forest. 5.7-7 cm

Long-Tailed Skipper (Southeast and Southwest U.S.): Its body is mostly chocolate brown with long coattails; the center of its body, from thorax to center of the forewings, is peacock blue. 4.5-6 cm

Monarch (migration in California): I want to go to California to see the Monarch migration as they stop in the eucalyptus forest outside of Santa Barbara. Surely, there can't be a more spectacular sight in the world. 9.4 to 10.5 cm

Pygmy Blue (Western U.S.): This is the smallest butterfly in the world, and though there are micro-moths that are even smaller, I'd like to see it. Its whitish, brownish, grayish coloring gives it a pixie appearance. 1.2-2 cm

Queen Alexandra's Birdwing (Papua New Guinea): This beautiful butterfly has been killed in the wild for its size. It is the largest butterfly in the world, and endangered. +31 cm

Atlas moth (Southeast Asia): This is one of the largest moths in the world. Because so many are being caught and killed and framed like dead flowers, their numbers are dwindling. Don't believe websites that say they've collected only dead insects, or they've been cleared by customs. They are all liars. 25–30 cm

I am sad to write that I still don't have a name for my blues. Perhaps I should temporarily name it the Singh Blue.

1 COMMENT

I just thought of something. Could your bf be a hybrid? I've read about a rare thing where insects and some crustaceans can be born with both male and female parts. It's like a one in a million chance, but you never know. A gynandromorph? —BF Girl NY

Isabella

She smelled of roses. Not the kind that could be found in a plastic-wrapped bouquet in Price Chopper, or the perfectly closed ones in a corsage on the wrist of a prom queen, or even the kind sitting singly in a skinny vase atop a table in an Italian restaurant. No, Isabella thought, those flowers were imposters. They were criminals that failed to capture the freshness of the rose. *She* smelled like the wild kind, tangled along an old fence in a working farm in Pennsylvania. Isabella had seen them on a school field trip a few years earlier. Those pink buds were small and splayed open, which completely exposed their yellow centers for little insects to drink. They were sweet like clover and musky like honey. Oma's abundant bosom, which Isabella was pressed against in a loving hug, smelled just like that.

"Zoh good to see you, Isabella!" Oma's accent was as thick as it had always been.

Isabella attempted to respond, but Oma's breasts muffled all sound.

"I hope you don't mind—I already moved into your room, neh? It's a nice room."

"Izzy, why don't you go put your backpack down?" Her mother nodded toward the hallway.

She did as asked, and as soon as she opened the door to her bedroom, she found herself in a Latvian culture museum. Her dresser was draped with a lace cloth, atop which were a few pieces of amber sitting like mushrooms waiting to be found. Isabella picked up a large piece and held it to the lamp. Inside, she saw a winged insect. Its body was translucent yet seemed as though it might awaken from its slumber and fly away. Strange, she thought, how this piece of tree sap was like a time capsule. Isabella smiled when she noticed a miniature Latvian flag, a rectangle of burgundy with a stripe of white bisecting the center, standing tall in a jar of dry rose buds beside Oma's bedside lamp. On the ground beside her knitted slippers was a pile of carefully folded Latvian newspapers, each appearing to have been read and reread. The largest basket she'd ever seen was at the foot of Oma's bed, with slippers and gloves and all sorts of knitted goods in the vibrant colors of her country, with Latvian flair like pompoms and tassels, flowing over the edges. Remarkable, Isabella thought, how Oma could transport her entire home, country included, in a single suitcase.

Isabella was glad Oma was her new roommate. Vic had stored all of his dirty laundry under his bed, which made his room smell ripe. Each of Oma's possessions, from her small suitcase to the stack of books and letters, smelled quite nice indeed. Isabella appraised the room and had to resist the temptation to rummage through her grandmother's things. She was, of course, inclined to collect, perhaps even borrow or steal, so this battle was already one she was destined to lose at some point. It took Isabella only seconds to decide that the most interesting item her grandmother had brought into their room was the small wooden box on the shelf above her bed. Isabella knew that boxes held the most important secrets. It was very tempting, but she could not risk angering her mother or grandmother. So she set out to memorize her lines for tomorrow's rehearsal.

The living room was vacant. Papa and Papaji were conducting training exercises with Vic in the backyard. Isabella seized the opportunity to claim the good couch in the living room. She opened her copy of the play, but she couldn't concentrate: All she could think of was Michelle. How Michelle had been so great in rehearsal as Samantha. How the on-stage lighting made her hair a halo of blonde. How badly she'd wanted to be an actor.

Isabella had received an e-mail from Michelle a few days earlier, and all it had said was that she was going to be staying in the city permanently. She had been diagnosed with leukemia, but they thought she might have a chance. A chance? Isabella hadn't been able to process this information. Michelle sent her new address and asked for gossip to distract her. She asked for letters and e-mail instead of phone calls because she was in treatment and sleeping a lot. Isabella responded with a play-by-play of the recent events in her life. She told Michelle she was saving up bus fare for the ride into the city as soon as the play was finished.

Isabella tried to return to the script, to take her mind off Michelle, at least for now. She felt so helpless, knowing there was nothing she could do and being unable to visit until the play was finished. Forcing herself to turn back to her script, she flipped the pages to the second act, which was more interesting than the first, mostly about the personal pre-war lives of the individuals who were locked away in the windowless bunker waiting out the first week of World War III's nuclear catastrophe. This next section was more about the current situation: how the four individuals were managing the day-to-day survival in the bunker, the smell of the space, what they had to eat, and so forth. It was strange to Isabella to think of how people would change under this type of stress: leaders under the threat of nuclear fallout. Her character, the daughter of the President, had little to do with her father's position or with anything at all political before the first bomb was released. Now she was the central figure. Through their present outlooks, the audience would finally learn of the terrifying circumstances that released the hounds of hell.

According to the script, the whole world was at war, which began when Pakistan tested a series of advanced weaponry on New Delhi. In retaliation, India responded with a barrage of nuclear bombs aimed at Islamabad, Karachi, and Peshawar, killing nearly a million people. Then Russia invaded China and Iran, and a month later the United Nations and the Allies attempted to quiet the approaching apocalypse through diplomacy and offerings to the warring countries. But the Taliban got their hands on a warhead and hijacked a plane and hit Washington, D.C., and the sole survivors were those who had made it into this bunker, many stories underground.

Isabella sank into the comfortable couch as she read. The names of the foreign countries felt so far away, but when she read about a nuclear warhead destroying an American city not far from the one in which she lived, she felt sick to her stomach. Her character's role in the second act was as the linchpin of sanity in the dim light of the underground. The Vice President's nerves were beginning to fray, and the guilt was consuming him bit by bit. The plot was deepening; however, Isabella still felt the play was inauthentic. Perforating the dialogue was glorified gunfire, tape recordings of fake bomb sounds, and wailing air-raid sirens—*1,001 Cries* seemed more like a platform for experimental sound engineering than a high school theater production. She rolled her eyes when she read a stage direction that signaled a flurry of earthquake-like rumbles. Isabella thought Tewks might employ some music students to set up their xylophones and drums offstage.

As she read on, her stomach turned, but this time it wasn't nerves. Her face went hot, then cold sweat spread across her back. She ran to the bathroom and vomited. This, whatever it was, was not going away. What, exactly, was happening to her? As she stared into the bathroom mirror she made note of the dark circles under her eyes and the dehydrated skin on her cheeks.

Her mother and grandmother were kneading dough in the kitchen when she entered. Oma was as round as she had remembered her from a few Christmases earlier. Her sharp blue eyes appeared less clear, though, as though cataracts were taking hold. Wrapped around her robust waist was an apron made of raw cotton.

"Zoh, *mazmeita*, vie is your play?" She looked up from her large pile of dumplings.

"Fine, Oma." She sighed.

"Michelle will be proud of you," her mother said. "As soon as we can, we'll visit her family."

"You'll come, too?"

"Of course, Izzy. They need our support. She can beat this."

Oma looked at Isabella, and her gaze hit the rear of her skull. "You are looking at mine eyes, neh? I know. There are Cadillacs. What can you do?"

"Cataracts, Oma, not Cadillacs."

"What's za play about? A nice holiday play, neh? Santa Claus, or Rudolph?"

Isabella sat in one of the stools at the counter. "That's the thing. It's not a happy play at all. It's quite sad, actually, about a Third World War."

At hearing this, Oma placed her dumpling atop the large pile and pressed her hand against her chest. "Why such a horrible play? Nobody want to hear about za Rushkies, Jews, and Germans."

"The director is quite the piece of work, too. Treats us like children but expects us to know how to act already."

"Maija, darlink, is this true? World War III? Who would take pleasure in such things? It is madness."

"Ma, it's just a play. What can we do now? These children know nothing of the past." Her mother continued forming the bits of dough into round balls.

"Yes, we do, Mama. I know about the wars and stuff. The world is full of dictators, fallen empires, and bombs waiting to go off. Blah, blah, blah."

"Izjah, do not take these things zoh lightly." Oma turned her back to both of them.

"Why don't you go clean your room, Izzy? Make sure it's neat and tidy." Maija said this without looking up.

Great, she thought. Oma had only been in their house for a day, and Isabella had already managed to be sent to her room twice. She shrugged and rolled her eyes for dramatic effect, then entered the tempting boundaries of her bedroom. This, she thought, could end badly.

The next day, the rain washed the world of any color and lulled the population of Cobalt into a state of sleepiness. Isabella had succumbed to the gloom. Even her teachers were dragging. Mrs. Stein yawned uncontrollably throughout English class. She assigned quiet reading time, something Isabella noticed she was doing more and more lately. Isabella looked up from her copy of *The Scarlett Letter* and sighed. Three students were sleeping, their heads against their textbooks; one was already drooling. The humdrum was interrupted by an aide who entered the classroom and handed Mrs. Stein a note. Mrs. Stein looked at Isabella over the thick edge of her reading glasses and gestured for her to approach her large wooden desk. This wasn't the first time Isabella felt anxious butterflies bouncing against her insides, but it was the first time a teacher induced this sort of fear.

"Isabella, let's speak in the hall, okay? Best bring your things. Yes, your jacket, too."

"Yes, Mrs. Stein."

When they were outside and the door had closed, the teacher cleared her throat and said, "Mrs. Cohen wants to see you in her office."

"Why?"

"She didn't say. But one thing to keep in mind, Isabella, is that this is not the time to lie. Be truthful and answer all their questions, all right?"

"Okay. I have nothing to hide."

Isabella took the note and walked very slowly to the main office. She felt nauseous and took a sip of water from the drinking fountain. When she arrived, two people were waiting for her: Mrs. Cohen, the principal, sitting behind her desk, and Mr. Douglas, the assistant principal, who was pacing.

"Hello," Isabella said. "Mrs. Stein told me to come right away."

"Yes, Isabella, please sit down." The tension in the room was not promising; Mrs. Cohen was small in stature, but her voice was deep and commanding. "We have a few questions for you."

Mr. Douglas opened a large box: her entire collection from her locker. "What exactly are you planning on doing with all of these?"

Mrs. Cohen picked up a knife and several nails and pieces of glass from a jar.

"Nothing. I just collect things, Mrs. Cohen. I swear—ask Mrs. Stein. Why did you go through my locker? That's my personal property." She raised her voice not because she was angry, but because she felt if she spoke louder they would actually believe her.

"How do you explain these things?" Mrs. Cohen shook her head. "A knife? Isabella, we are so disappointed in you. This is not the direction we thought you would follow. I am not sure you should be the lead in the play. You aren't a good representative of Cobalt High. Not anymore."

"The knife isn't mine. I swear. Please." The knife *was* hers, but she didn't see the harm in having collected a dangerous object and contained it in her locker. She may have prevented an injury to someone else, for all she knew. The real issue was: They had invaded her privacy. Who would have tipped them off to her stash? Isabella thought about Tracy. She wondered if Tracy wanted her role so badly that she would divulge her ex-friend's habits to the higher-ups. When they were young, Tracy also collected things, though her collections turned toward more materialistic items rather than found objects. It had to be her.

"I am going to call your parents. Someone should pick you up. Knives aren't allowed here. No weapons of any sort."

"No, please. I—ouch." Her stomach began to ache as it had before, but this time the pain was so great she thought she might faint.

Mrs. Cohen picked up the receiver. "Please wait outside."

Isabella moved to a chair in the hall, sat down, and rested her face in her hands. Both her parents were at work; maybe no one would answer the phone. She wished she'd moved her collection to a place where no one would find it.

Mrs. Cohen didn't come out of her office, and as the minutes passed by, Isabella assumed she was still trying to reach someone at home. Then she saw Oma at the front doors of the school.

Oma was wearing her yellow raincoat, rain hat, and galoshes, and she held a walking stick in one hand and a tin of sorts in the other. She looked like an obstinate lemon hurrying across the linoleum floor. When she saw Isabella sitting there on the chair, she nodded, took off her rain hat, and continued into the principal's office. The door closed firmly behind her. Isabella heard loud voices within, a mix of Latvian, German, and bad English. In only a few minutes, Oma reemerged without the tin, smiling brightly, with Mrs. Cohen at her side.

"Thank you for coming down on such short notice, um…"

"Hermione, but everyone calls me Oma. Yes, it is good you called. I wanted to see za school where mine grandchildren come, neh?" Oma grinned at Isabella.

"Yes, all right then, Oma." Mrs. Cohen appeared to be in a much better mood.

Isabella was still dumbfounded at seeing the effects of her grandmother's persuasion, and they walked through the fog side by side for two whole blocks before speaking. Water sounds surrounded them as they went; the rainwater drip-drip-dripped off of trees and ran through gutters. Oma slowed her pace and straightened her rain hat. She appeared to relax, as though the weight of authority she'd carried into the principal's office had finally evaporated from her shoulders.

"Oma?"

"Yes?"

"You believe me, right? I didn't do anything wrong."

"Of course, darlink."

"Oma?"

"Yes?"

"How'd you do it?"

"Do what, darlink?"

"How'd you handle Mrs. Cohen?"

"I've handled much worse."

"Oh."

"You want to know a secret? Always bring a gift."

Oma

Papaji and Oma were like oil and water: mustard oil from the Punjab and spring water from Mežuļi. Not only did their languages separate them, so did their genders. They were grandparents, yes, but not husband and wife. This fact was difficult for the receptionist at the podiatrist's office to understand. Oma tried to explain over and over again, failingly, why she was going to wait for Mr. Singh when he woke up from the surgery.

"Nonsense," Oma said as she returned to her chair in the pastel-colored waiting room.

"It's okay, Ma. She's just not that bright," Maija whispered as she filled in Papaji's paperwork.

"She called me Mrs. Singh." Oma laughed and shook her head.

"It's a good name, Mini." Papaji smiled.

The day before, Oma and Papaji had spent time alone together. The house emptied: Maija to work, Vic and Isabella to school, Paul to the station. The stillness returned once the garage door closed and the last youthful member of the Singh tribe exited. The quiet was palpable. Oma turned on a fan over the stove in the kitchen to disrupt the silence. Papaji appeared to assume that she was going to cook, so he turned his chair in the living room to watch.

He smiled.

She smiled back.

She saw his curiosity; even after his substantial breakfast of cereal, pancakes, and eggs she knew he could still eat. Oma was a chef. She was trained in all the pastry ways of Latvia and Europe—from blintzes to *piragis*, cottage cheese cake to Alexander cake, she knew it all. She'd seen this look before in her husband's face, God rest his soul. Heinrich Georg Rainier Mazur died so long ago, his death was part of another portion of time, dog-eared in a history book. He was tall; part German, part Latvian; and together they'd had a child. But when history shifted again, he was drafted into World War II at the bitter end of the bloodshed. He was taken to the Eastern front, and it was there he was injured. As she whisked eggs together, Papaji had asked about her husband.

He died long ago.

Papaji pressed his hand against his chest and seemed to search for words. *You know, I don't know what to call you. The children call you Oma, and your daughter calls you Ma, but you aren't my grandmother or mother.*

She felt her broad cheeks tinting pink. *Hermione*. She pressed her hand to her chest.

Mini?

She nodded, though the irony was not lost even on her. She was short, but not small by any means; with an ironic nickname like Mini, she'd have to be as round and plump as she was. But whatever he managed to call her would be fine.

First class, you can call me Harbans.

Hairbuns? Harry? Okay.

And with that, they'd become formally acquainted with each other.

When Maija handed the paperwork to the receptionist, she asked her to call the pharmacy when they were ready to be picked up.

"Good luck, Papaji. I will see you in a few hours," Maija called as she rushed out the door. A gust of cool damp wind flowed through the waiting room.

The synthesizers and electric drums of the Muzak created an atmosphere of plastic comfort. Oma opened her large purse and retrieved a long piece of yarn, connecting it to her crocheting needles through a series of complicated knots. She quickly went to work on her project and within a few minutes she had a postage stamp–sized piece of orange, purple, and blue fuzz dangling from the two silver needles.

"*Ki halle?* What is that?" Papaji asked.

"A *zeķe*, a sock for you. It will help your heel heal. Don't worry, I will make two." She smirked and continued to twist the needles around each other as she hummed softly.

"Mr. Singh? We can take you back now."

The two exchanged a glance, and Papaji followed the nurse through the double doors. Oma was happy to wait, content to knit him a pair of warm wool socks that would keep the moisture away from his injured extremity. She wiped her eyes with a crumpled tissue. Perhaps she would have to go to the eye doctor, as her eyes were becoming dimmer by the day. She wondered how long it would take for her to write down all of the things she had seen in her life if she were to lose her sight.

She closed her eyes and found that she could still feel the warmth of the Latvian sun across her face. She could hear the whistling chick-adee and smell the layers of pine needles and leaves decomposing under her feet. Four out of five of her senses were extraordinarily precise. Her eyelids pressed tighter over the cataracts as she imag-ined the feeling of her porch in Jelgava. It had been decades since she'd visited Latvia. One thing she hadn't counted on during the slow process of encroaching blindness was that the memories she'd managed to bury would begin to bubble up to the surface. Then again, she wore history around her neck. Oma's amber necklace was a relic of the sunken forest off the coast of the Baltic Sea. Some said a flood had dragged the forest under the water tens of thousands of years ago. Others said the wicked were punished in a flood and the amber, as it washed onto the shore, was a reminder—the blood of the trees petrified. The ancient sap contained flecks of flora, plant memories. She'd worn the one-inch round beads about her neck since the day her grandmother had given them to her, removing the resin reliquaries only to shower. As soon as she'd dress in one of her handmade outfits—poly-blend pants with a blouse and the sea-green sweater with an orange stripe through the center—she'd put her necklace back on. Familiarity was important to Oma. Her eyes, they'd told her, would soon be useless decorations on her face. The worst part about it was that the doctors described in specific detail the different stages she would experience. First, blurring would occur in the center of her vision. The right eye would go, and then the left. Her peripheral vision would become the only reliable perspective from which she could see the world. Once, when she'd cut her hand on a knife that she thought was a spoon, she realized that squinting no longer worked. She'd felt the floor of her small apartment under her bare feet as she always had, but her own reflection was blurring. At least she had seen Latvia's independence and the rise of the Museum of Occupation alongside the Daugava River. She had been relieved when Maija asked her to move in.

She continued to knit, and by the time she made a complete pair of extra-large multicolored socks, the receptionist mumbled, "He is out of surgery and will be ready to go home in a few minutes. It went well."

"But of course it went well." Oma smiled.

As the nurse dialed Maija to pick them both up, Oma retrieved her small tin of raspberry Bon Bons from her sweater pocket and offered her a few. The double doors opened, and an orderly wheeled Papaji into the waiting room.

"You're still here, *ji*," Papaji whispered sleepily.

"Of course, neh? Where else would I be?"

Maija

Maija's eyes searched for a glimmer of the natural world outside the confines of Jones Drugs. She leaned on the counter as though it were the edge of her cage. Reconnecting with her mother had revived her longing for the outdoors. Searching for fresh air or natural light was not such an easy task, as not only was she trapped in the rear of the store, but the drive-through window was now bricked up. Her eyes searched for a hint of diffused sunlight. Her irises reached beyond the line of disgruntled drug-hungry customers; above the aisle stocked with Ron Popeil products, *As Seen on TV*; past the glaring brand names in the adult diaper section, which offered a false sense of dignity to those who suffered from incontinence (Poise, Certainty, Serenity, and Depends). Maija's eyes watched eagerly as a teenager entered through the revolving door and let in a rush of cool air. This wisp of fresh air, traveling on miraculous wings, graced Maija's cheek, and she shivered.

Riding on the back of that gift of fresh air was the scent of the ground outside, wet and musky from the decomposing leaves and drain overflow. Maija knew she would have to get outside if only for a moment. The phone rang, seemingly at a slightly higher pitch than usual. Tom and Shandy were both dealing with customers, so Maija lifted the receiver and pressed line three.

The line was quiet. Then she realized *she* was the one expected to offer a greeting.

"Uh, hallo."

"Is this Jones Drugs?"

"Yes, yes, of course."

"Who answers a phone at a business like that?"

Maija knew the voice. It sounded pink and glittery even over the phone. Maija disguised her voice the best she could by making it as deep as possible.

"Can I help you?" she grumbled.

"This is Eleanora Finch. I have a request about my prescription. Is there a chance someone could deliver the medicine to my home?"

"Deliver?" She coughed.

"Yes, to our home."

"We don't usually—"

"It's important," Eleanora said.

"Fine." Maija coughed again. "I don't see why not."

"You should be happy to have an errand to run. The gate code is our address." And she hung up the phone.

Three very clear thoughts simultaneously waltzed through Maija's mind. The first was most disconcerting: Eleanora was alive and had lived long past her vision. Maija had never been one for *schadenfreude*, but now, and for only one single second, she actually wished Eleanora had smacked her perfect little head on the floor of her shower and had been ushered toward unconsciousness. The second thought was strangely exhilarating: Perhaps the note she scribbled on the back of the PTA membership form had somehow altered the path toward her demise. The third and most pressing thought was that she had just agreed to deliver a prescription to the Finch residence, and she had the code to the gate that led directly into the Heights. Now she could inspect that haunted community to find out exactly what was going on out there.

Without looking directly into Tom's eyes, Maija simply said, "I have a very important delivery for Mrs. Finch," as she grabbed the small white bag and left the store. He must have filled the prescription earlier. What a guy, she thought. He actually could do his job when he had to.

As soon as she sat down in the car she rolled down the windows and took a deep breath. It didn't matter that the sky was mere moments from raining again; the cool air revived her completely. She drove toward the Heights and expected the surroundings to be somewhat familiar. However, everything appeared foreign and curious. The shadows from the storm clouds above painted the road a dark ominous black; the center trees that lined the road appeared gnarled; thick fog obfuscated the view of the village below, making the Heights feel separate from the rest of earth, unaffected by the goings-on in Cobalt. Maija was climbing the Jacob's ladder that connected the Flats to the Heights. As she drove, she heard a little inner voice inside her head whisper, *Just turn around*, but still she climbed. Within minutes she found herself face-to-face with that dominating wrought iron gate.

Maija was reaching through her open window to type in the code on the keypad when it began to rain. The cold water chilled her bare arm, and goose bumps sprouted instantaneously. After driving through the gate, she rolled up the window and put the car in park as the rain blinded her, the downpour eliminating all visibility. What was she going to do when she arrived, anyway? Ask Eleanora if she'd slipped in her blue-tiled shower? Or ask if she'd been taking her medicine? She'd been so focused on the gate, the Heights, and Eleanora's vitality that she'd completely forgotten to look at the drugs she was delivering. There were three bottles inside the bag: a broad antibiotic, a narcotic pain reliever, and an anti-nausea medication.

These medications spelled out infection, but of what kind, Maija had no idea. They were too broad to deduce a specific problem. As she slipped the bottles back into the bag, she noticed that the letter E that she'd assumed was in front of the last name was actually a T. Tracy? Isabella's former friend?

A car behind her screeched past, startling her from her realization. She noticed it was an expensive car; she'd never seen it before in town.

She began driving again. The roads were eerie and empty. Her windshield wipers worked overtime. Every house was white with black or dark-green trim. Two windows, like eyes, looked out from beside each double front door in the neighborhood, which made it seem as if the houses were watching one another. Smoke billowed from a few chimneys here and there, but otherwise there were no signs of life. She turned left on the first street, then made a right. Nestled at the very rear of a cul-de-sac, at the very top of the Heights development, was the Finch house.

Maija parked near the mailbox and turned off the engine. There was a new Mercedes in the driveway. The windows, covered by sheer curtains, glowed. She grabbed the umbrella from the backseat and opened the door. During her mad dash to the house, she managed to avoid all but one very large puddle, which covered her trousers in chilly water. The doorbell was a gargoyle with a glowing orange button inside its mouth. Strange choice of décor, she thought as she pressed the button firmly. A complicated series of notes rang emptily through the house. She heard a series of beeping sounds, then a click as the door swung open. Maija stood eye-to-eye with Eleanora.

"Yes?"

"I brought Tracy's medicine from the pharmacy. They said you requested a delivery?" Maija held the bag out before her. "I thought I could help."

"Oh, thank you."

Maija took a moment to absorb the décor. Beautiful marble tiles lined the floors. A wide spiral staircase spun to the second floor. She looked to her right and saw an extensive security system panel.

"How's Tracy? Is she feeling okay?"

"Oh, sure. It's just the flu or something." Eleanora seemed nervous.

"Good, good. Um…" She knew she had little time. "And how are you feeling?"

"What?" Eleanora pressed her hand to her chest and held her breath.

There was a noise on the staircase, and Maija saw a man staring down at her. He was short but still seemed to suck up all the light in the hall—Mr. Finch. He never looked cheery. He wore a rain-soaked jacket, and his damp hair fell in his face.

"Fine, I'm fine." Eleanora took the bag from Maija's hand and stretched a smile across her face.

"Mom? Who is it?" Tracy came out as well. She wore a tank top with pajama bottoms, and her face seemed flushed with fever. Maija could see a bandage sticking out from the edge of her armpit. "What's *she* doing here?"

"Tracy, why don't you go back to bed? The doctor said that you just need to rest."

"I'm done resting. I've slept for, like, four hours already."

"Tracy, go to bed, now." Mr. Finch's voice was tinny and sharp. Tracy didn't budge.

Maija edged closer to the door; her visit was about to end, and she hadn't unearthed any information out about Eleanora. She looked inside along the wall, desperate to find another conversation topic that could carry her a little longer.

"Wow." Maija eyed the large security panel. "What a, um, thorough security system."

"Yeah, Mom's paranoid since she got some weird letter. Now she thinks someone wants to kill her."

"Tracy! Shush!" Eleanora turned to Maija. "All right then, have a *nice* day." Eleanora put her hand on the door.

"Would you mind if I use your restroom? The rain, you know..." Maija looked expectantly at Eleanora.

"Okay, I guess." She looked at Maija's wet shoes. "It's just down the hall on the left."

Maija entered the house and immediately felt a cold draft. She knew Eleanora's eyes watched her as she walked down the hall and into the palatial powder room. The brushed nickel doorknob had been recently polished, and the lock that turned easily in her fingers was shaped like a human face, mouth wide and ready to consume. Beige tiles covered the room from floor to ceiling. Maija ran water in the sink and inspected the porcelain. The bathroom she wanted to peruse was upstairs, or at least she imagined it would be. What did it matter anyway? She felt silly. Did she really need validation, or some kind of physical proof to feel better about her vision? Maija turned off the water and went back to the foyer.

"Okay, then, bye."

Eleanora was still standing by open the front door.

Maija stepped out and then turned around to look at Eleanor. "If you have some time, I'd love to—" Then the front door closed abruptly, only a few inches from her face.

That was strange, Maija said to herself while jogging to her car. She could have at least asked me in for tea or the like on such a dreary day. So Eleanora was alive, but now her daughter was ill. She was hiding something. She definitely seemed afraid when Mr. Finch entered the picture. Well, who wouldn't be? He wasn't exactly a ray of sunshine. As Maija sat in the car and realized she'd have to drive directly to the doctor's office to pick up Papaji and Oma, she looked at her reflection in the rearview mirror and said aloud, "No more of this bullshit. No more psychic business."

Vic

As far back as he could remember, Vic had been a victim. He'd grown used to being teased by his peers at school. He'd even become accustomed to his father's gaze, which said volumes about how disappointed he was in him. Vic sometimes imagined that his father wondered, at times, if Vic had been switched at birth with a stronger, born-to-wrestle son. Most recently, since his father had seen the ultimate mark of weakness, the damn black eye and broken nose, Vic's training lessons had expanded to include strange variations of martial arts he was convinced his father had made up by combining Tae Bo and aerobic television workout programs with a genuine lack of knowledge of karate and kung fu. The addition of Vic's grandfather as an umpire—he actually wore a baseball cap instead of a turban when involved—made the fitness circus complete. Vic had hoped his grandfather would temper his father's increasingly rough-and tumble-exercises. But that was not the case. His father wanted to impress Papaji with his progeny's agility and backyard prowess. These sessions were more intensive than the ones that Papa held before Papaji came because, as it seemed to Vic, the two men fed off each other. The session had ceased to be centered on Vic at all and had morphed into a battle of masculinity between father and grandfather.

This day was no exception. Vic was embarrassed when Papa made him show Papaji how many pull-ups he could do while hanging on the lowest branch of a tree. But it was even more humiliating for Vic when he had to stand in the yoga tree position on one foot with his hands pressed together above his head to prove that he was as well-balanced as his father insisted he was. He made it almost two minutes in the position and would have made it longer if Papaji hadn't poked him gently in the side with a stick during the test. When his father instructed Vic to throw his knife at an old poster of Lee Van Cleef he'd tacked to the fence, his grandfather finally interrupted.

"Why would you want to damage such a wonderful poster? It's a classic."

"He's a villain." Papa shrugged, unpinned it, and gave the poster to the old man, who, later that evening, hung it on his bedroom wall like a schoolboy.

What Vic truly hated most about these sessions was that he was invisible during the process.

Papa grimaced and bent his knees. "Papaji, he needs to thicken up in the middle. That's where you get balance. You wrestle from the stomach!"

"Nah, *puttar*, you've got it all wrong. It's the legs that need work." He smacked Vic's knee. "Here and here—he needs to learn to turn quickly and defend all sides!"

Vic hated fighting. Of course, he didn't like being on the receiving end of a punch either, but the idea of intending to do damage to another individual, to break or bruise or cut someone, made him physically ill. He knew this was *his* problem; this was the reason every bully had targeted him specifically. They seemed to know he'd never retaliate, no matter how much confidence he was cultivating. He was quite certain his aversion to violence actually encouraged his father and grandfather. The less enthusiastic he was about learning how to bend an adversary's arm until it broke, the more they inundated him with terrible tales of the village life.

"*Puttar*," Papaji said to Papa as he inspected his knife, "your brother could throw a knife." The old man seemed to retreat into a memory, far from the present.

Vic watched his father's expression turn from joy to pain, as though someone had stuck a shard of glass in his chest. Vic had asked many times about his father's family, about other relatives he might have lingering in other parts of the world, but his father never offered an answer. He would turn away as though there hadn't been a question. Vic watched the distance between his father and grandfather expand until he realized the moment was ripe for his escape.

Papa mumbled something about snake wrangling and its similarities to disarming a *dacoit* as he took his knife back from his father.

"Knife throwing is not a talent," Papa said. "It's a circus act."

Vic excused himself to the bathroom and walked directly through the house and out the front door. He knew he'd only be free of the training session if he got lost. So he kept walking at a confident stride down Peregrine Court. He picked up the pace and turned to look behind him only when he arrived at the top of the community park on the edge of their small neighborhood. *Park* was a very generous term for the half-acre of grass, two benches, and stone-carved sign that read The Commons. A dry bench seemed as good a space as any that was *not* his backyard.

From this vantage point he could see the roofs of PMI's buildings peeking over the early autumn treetops. It looked like a self-contained space-age city. Vic went farther into the trees to get a better look, crossing the street and making his way into the thicket. The ground sucked at his feet and the air became heavy, moist. He looked up at the trees. Only dead or dying leaves clung to their branches. The forest was a skeleton army, petrified in its final charge. The branches were arms; the trunks were legs. He heard the wood creak as the wind picked up, and he moved backward to avoid a branch. It was then that he came upon another important discovery: an orange-and-brown butterfly with a touch of gray on the tips of its wings, sitting on a branch over his head.

Vic retrieved his new notebook from his back pocket. He had decided to begin a new one shortly after he'd witnessed his last notebook's cremation. He'd wrapped the replacement's cover in duct tape in hopes of making it fireproof. It was the Xerces Blue that inspired him to continue to record his surroundings. The idea that a butterfly could slip into extinction so easily troubled him deeply, and he decided that he would do his best to record what he saw and become a sort of lepidopteron watcher in his area.

Now, he used a dull pencil to sketch the orange-and-brown invertebrate as best he could. When he was done, it looked more like a manta ray than a butterfly, not in the vicinity of Nabokov's drawings, but his illustrations were improving. He felt honored to see it here—like this—yet he was also confused about its presence.

Vic continued to his fort, as it was the only place he could hide. He felt exposed and still too close to home to relax. The mine was safe, a space where he could be alone with his thoughts about the photo contest at school, butterflies, and Katie. It began to drizzle along his walk, but the dampness didn't bother him. A few times his sneakers got stuck in the mud, which made for uncomfortable walking, but in mere minutes he found himself at the birch tree that marked the entry into his underground fortress. He slowly lowered himself, rung by rung, into the darkness as he had tens of times before, but this time something smelled different. His nose was incredibly keen; perhaps its size did have at least one benefit. The air, he discovered, was thick with stale smoke that made him sneeze.

As he turned on the fluorescent lamp that sat on the last step, he realized the cause.

Cigarette butts, smoked to the very end of their filters, littered the ground around his feet. Someone had been here and had used his pristine sand floor as an ashtray. He froze. What if the smoker was still in the mine? What if he was watching him right now? He shuddered and picked up a butt to test the heat, but it was cold. The person or persons were long gone. A scramble of footprints turned this way and that in the sand. His supplies were rearranged on the shelf he'd built, and his extra clothes, some books and cans, and his shadow box were missing. He didn't care about the other things, but the butterflies were priceless. He curled his hands into fists and yelled. The thieves had left the lantern, which meant they were planning on returning. They'd also left a lighter with an iron cross carved into its plastic skin. As Vic climbed up and out once more, with lantern in hand and lighter in pocket, he felt defeated. He had a strange urge to destroy the ladder and fill the mine with earth so no one else could enter after him.

Paul

It was early in the morning, and rather than being curled up within the groove he'd created on his side of the bed, Paul was wide awake in his garage, alone. He was careful not to make any noise, though he could probably run the lawnmower without alarming the rest of the family as the garage was on the opposite side of the house from the bedrooms. It was chilly and quiet at this time of the morning; for Paul, it was the best time to be alone in his office with his research.

If there was one thing Paul could do better than anyone else in the house, he thought, it was keep secrets. Regardless of how much he wanted to tell his wife about the small makeshift office he had constructed in the garage, he didn't. He didn't tell her about the desk he'd made of particleboard, duct tape, and a few cinderblocks. He hid the fact that when he told everyone he was organizing the garage, he was actually stacking a precariously tall pile of empty boxes that provided wall-like cover from anyone who'd enter looking for a rake, tape, or a misplaced book. Paul's decision to construct an area of his own was born from necessity rather than genius. He needed a private place to think freely about the business the station was losing and the unpaid bills that were stacking up. The most recent notice that pushed him over the edge was from his auto repair inventory supplier. They'd stopped sending windshield wiper fluid, engine oil, and car tchotchkes. The tower of blue bottles had shrunk to nothing. Now they threatened to take his spare tire inventory, too, but said they'd wait a week on good faith. He didn't have the money. He couldn't pay. The station's business had continued to decline slowly, and if he didn't find a way to fix the traffic problem, he knew he would be forced to close and find other work. No one knew how bad it was. No one would know. He kept this secret closest to his chest.

This place in his garage didn't judge him. Here he could mull over his stolen maps for hours at a time without commentary, framed by an empty wall that wasn't afraid to bear the prick of several thumbtacked articles about Cobalt. Paul had managed to chart the entire web of Cobalt County's infrastructure, from gutter to sewer, bridge to river. How like a body a village was, he thought as he sat atop the thick tree-stump stool. The waterways were veins; the bridges were like joints connecting separate pieces of land.

Being a secret-keeper was the third item on his Life Goals List. The first item was the most important, and he hoped it was not just a dream: to find the cause of the construction and make it stop. Lists, in Paul's mind, were the only true literary art. Stories were for lazy people. Newspaper articles existed only to be drained of their information. Lists were active, forward thinking, organizing, helpful, and beautifully arranged. His list, a collection of oddly unrelated goals and dreams, was impaled upon a thumbtack against a wood beam to the left of his desk area. It read:

1. I will find the cause of the construction. I will have justice. When this one station is on track, I will open another station on Main Street.
2. Someday I will do something better than anyone else in the world. It might be small, like standing on one foot, or even just

becoming a city watchdog, but my name will be recorded on an award, and there I will live on forever.

3. I will become a first rate secret-keeper. I will store hoards of information and knowledge and try my hardest to overcome the overwhelming desire to share. But if I do share, I will choose my confidant wisely.
4. I will, one day, reclaim my ownership and discovery of the knot I created that is useful when hitching two water buffalo. The Singh Double Bend will be my first patent. The knot, Uncle Chand said, looked uncannily like the Harness Bend, but he was senile, obviously. It looks nothing like it. It will be one of my claims to fame, certainly.

The most important piece of research he'd conducted in his office had been connecting with a laboratory that was willing to run an 8260 test for petroleum on a water sample. Paul had changed his name to Clint Jones and made up a story about how he lived across from an auto repair shop and was worried that his water was contaminated. In reality, he needed to eliminate the nagging feeling that his gasoline was leaking into the groundwater of his town. If his station caused the hole, he wanted to know so he could fix it. The lab was willing to take a sample via the post and would have the chromatogram results in a week or so. The technician said she'd fax the results, and he'd given her the fax number at the station, which wasn't listed and therefore could continue to keep his identity anonymous. He knew the lab had no authority to report the results to the EPA or any government office; they just wanted the eighty bucks for running the test. Now he needed to get a few samples from inside the hole in the ground and mail them in as well. That information would tell him what was going on.

As he gazed lovingly at his secret lair, right under his family's noses, he realized, uncomfortably, that he wanted to share the beauty of his organizational ability with another set of eyes. He bit his lip, pressed his hands against his belly, and sighed. Secrets were a difficult business because they lived only in the mind of the keeper. His burden was growing with his stress, and he wondered if he alone could carry this task. Paul shuffled his feet nervously, then stood and paced the few feet he'd cleared behind the wall of empty cardboard. He opened the door to the house and peered down the hallway for a moment before he ducked back into the garage. What would the harm be in telling just one other person about his burrow and his research about the station? No, he thought, I need to keep my secret or else I won't be able to cross that one off the list. But perhaps there were secrets that shouldn't be kept, or maybe there were some secrets that could be kept by two people? Paul felt fine with this justification, and he amended the listed item with a final statement that incorporated the benefits of "healthy sharing."

"Son?" Paul jumped and dropped his pencil. Papaji was standing in the garage, with his Latvian socks on his feet and a puzzled expression on his face. "What is this?"

Paul pressed his forefinger to his lips. "Papaji? Oh, this is my office."

"*Hánji*. Why so early?"

"Couldn't sleep."

Papaji took in the whole operation.

"There is a matter we need to discuss," Paul said. "I need to show you something."

In a matter of moments Paul was going over the maps and diagrams of the city, trying to explain his theory about the disruptive digging across from the station.

"I think they are looking for something. That's why they keep flushing the water out from below. That's why they have the *badmásh* standing guard over the hole. See here?" He pointed to a map of the water system. "The pipes run right under the station."

"What would they be looking for, I wonder?"

"Did the workers ever tell you anything?" Paul asked.

"No, no, but they do look suspicious. I can tell when a man is lying—that's my gift."

Paul laughed and said, "Well, what were they lying about?"

"We should find out ourselves."

Paul and Papaji changed into working clothes. Paul helped Papaji slip his feet into an old pair of sneakers.

As Paul drove into town, he felt better than he had in years. He was a cowboy checking out the trouble at his station, and no one would stand in his way. Papaji was his sidekick who would back him up. The streets were completely empty. When they exited the car, he looked up at the early morning sky. The rain clouds had split and offered a glimpse of the still-starry sky above. They were lucky that the water had drained from the hole over the past two days.

Paul parked the car near the hole and asked his father to keep watch from the driver's seat. If something happened, or someone came, he told him to switch the headlights on bright. In Paul's fanny pack were several items: a small Maglite flashlight, a disposable camera with a flash, four empty sterile jars, and a few plastic baggies already labeled. On his feet were work boots. On his back was a black rain poncho. He wore a Yankees cap over his hair. In his pocket was his knife, freshly sharpened. He wished he had a rope ladder, but he only had a wooden one, which he dropped down, down, down, ten feet into the hole. He waved to Papaji, who was sitting in the car, key in the ignition, his hand on the headlight switch, ready to turn them on at a moment's notice.

Paul entered the hole with the flashlight in his teeth and his eyes agape, observing the different layers of earth as he went. First he saw asphalt and tar, then gray and cracked concrete. Brick and cobblestone came next. He imagined what this town would look like paved in hand-cut stone. The layer beneath was sand, then finally he came to brown soil. He'd thought the soil would have been black, but with the unnatural layers suffocating the earth, how could it breathe? He saw dismembered roots spear the rocks though no tree stood above.

When he reached the bottom of the ladder, he jumped into the cold water. It covered his calves and soaked into his jeans. With the flashlight still in his mouth, he unscrewed a jar and dipped it into the water, which smelled sweet and a little like chlorine, and then he filled a few baggies with samples of the soil. When he was all set, he inspected the sides of the hole. It was strange to be standing in a cross-section of the earth. He wondered what was below him. How far was it to the next layer of sedimentary rock, to the core? He remembered what they had told him when he bought the gas station. Leaking is inevitable, the inspector had said. That's why he'd installed a failsafe system. It was expensive, but he didn't want his gasoline to leak. Gasoline cost a lot, but most of all, Paul didn't want his business to harm the town he'd grown to love, even though the storms and freezing winters made it difficult to like. The forest here was lush. The ferns were plentiful. The rivers were full and content. They were growing fuller with all the rain. He rubbed his bare hand against the earth, then took the ladder in his hand and ascended, one rung at a time.

Papaji was sitting in the car. Paul half expected him to be in the station or driving the Cutlass in circles. At that image he laughed. He'd done it. He'd gone into the hole and gotten samples. It was still quiet. He waved to his father and began to pull the ladder from the earth's open mouth. A car was coming from the opposite direction. Papaji flashed the high beams at the car to blind the driver. Paul dropped the ladder on the asphalt and dove behind the side of his car. The other car passed them slowly. The headlights were bright and illuminated every imperfection of the road that Paul could see from under the car. Soon it was gone, and only the red rear lights shone in the darkness. He looked inside the blue whale and saw Papaji, like a manatee, spread flat against the seat. He tapped on the window.

"So?" Papaji asked.

"So," Paul answered and shook the bags full of samples. He looked over at his station and felt it looked different somehow. He squinted in the darkness and saw that the tire rack with his spare tire inventory was gone. A pink piece of paper was adhered to the door to the convenience store. They'd done it.

In less than three minutes they were back at home, and in only ten minutes Papaji was in his bed. Paul went back to the garage to work a little more. His nerves were shot; his hands were shaking. He knew if he didn't get to the bottom of this soon, he would be in financial ruin.

The following day, Paul mailed the samples to the Creative Services Laboratory, to the care of Mrs. Shari Lawrence in Mason City. The website said it would only take one week to process the samples—then he'd know what was really down there. That night Paul dreamed he'd slipped through his bed into the center of earth, and that the core resembled the village in India where he grew up.

ON THE WING

Endangered Karner Blue / G2 Imperiled Status

Posted on October 19

There is something strange afoot here in Cobalt, New York. I feel it. Every time I feel I am getting closer, the answers slip from my fingers. It seems as though someone does not want me to know more about the butterfly, or about the peculiar goings-on.

Though I will not disclose the location specifically—you will just have to take my word for it—I came across a hole in the earth that leads to a sort of collection of passageways under Cobalt. The surroundings around the mouth of what I will now call the mineshaft (for what else could it be?) is showing strange symptoms of poisoned earth. The last time I entered the hole, I spotted another one of these mutant butterflies. It was so close to death, having been born with an incomplete body, not fully metamorphosed. I don't know what to do about my findings, as they aren't really concrete. However, I feel that I've stumbled upon something. These two things have to be connected. Nothing in nature is coincidence.

As I was observing a few small whites flying playfully in a splash of sun—as they are always seeking warmth, being cold-blooded creatures and all—I realized how my eyes had longed to see a butterfly or anything flying in the air around town. When it is cold and cloudy, sometimes I will not see an insect at all, as they mostly hibernate. Butterflies in the area that are born from their chrysalis late in the year tend to go into suspended animation called *diapause* in order to survive the harsh cold. I've heard that butterflies in the Arctic do this in order to be there to pollinate the flowers in the springtime. I feel saddened at the end of a season. I do not look forward to the cold. The encroaching cold reminds me that I will not see many of my favorite sights for months. I take comfort in the thought that they will return when the sun strengthens. I can't imagine what it would be like for the ice to melt next spring and still not see them flying. Endangerment and extinction terrify me more than anything else.

The Karner Blue, *lycaeides melissa samuleis, Plebejus*, was named by the famous Vladimir Nabokov after the town in which he'd first identified it: Karner, New York. For a small creature, it has a lot of names. I've never seen one, not here—too far south from the Capitol district. But it is quite extraordinary even in photographs. The male's topside is a bright vibrant blue with pumpkin crescents; the female is a grayish brown. They both have a smattering of black spots circled in white. I am going to collect some photos to see if this Singh Blue could be a Karner gynandromorph.

Why is the Karner endangered? That's the question many lepidopterists are asking. Some believe its decline is correlated to the destruction of its main food source, the lupine. Others worry about the lack of canopy under which the females seek shelter and shade to deposit their eggs. Many agree with that one detail, whether the Karner prefers living in flowering lupine or not, whether it likes oak savannahs, old fields or pine barrens—they all believe it's habitat destruction that has caused its demise. Sometimes nature, too, makes creatures not fit for the environment.

I read about a moth in a museum in London that emerged from its cocoon as a gynandromorph. Half of its body was female and the other half male, though it wasn't as complete as a true hermaphrodite and lacked complete anatomy to actually reproduce as a male or female. It's amazing to see, but also, so sad. If this is a Karner gynandromorph, then nature is playing a cruel joke on us all. Instead of producing an endangered creature, she offers this newly emerged butterfly nothing. Without the ability to mate or lay eggs, its birth and death will not impact their already struggling species.

1 COMMENT

I agree; I am sorry. It's almost like a harsh message from the wild stating her time is almost over. —BF Girl NY

Maija

She sat up in bed, her fingers clutching the warm comforter that had cocooned her during the frosty and wet night. As her pounding heart maintained a dangerous rate, she caught her breath. The nightmare still lingered precariously on the edge of her waking mind. *Just a dream*. She exhaled and turned on the lamp. Three scenes replayed in her mind as the rest of the unintelligible dreamscape faded into the background: a sea of people dying from a plague, rising water consuming land, and finding her favorite slippers, which had slid under the living room couch. She'd missed the comfort they gave her aching feet after work. Maija turned toward Paul's half of the bed, smiling at this possibility. That was when she realized he wasn't there. The mattress was cold. The clock read four in the morning. The image of the plague returned.

She put on her robe and walked around the quiet house. She could hear her son's and daughter's familiar breathing sounds, Oma's light snore, and Papaji's grumbling. She walked through the kitchen, and when she turned into the living room, she noticed that the garage door was open a crack. She entered and saw a small glimmer of light behind the tall wall of boxes, and she followed it to Paul, discovering him inside some sort of rickety office, asleep atop the makeshift desk. His hair, without a turban, was mussed. Stunned, Maija took in the maps, charts, and lists hanging on the walls. For a split second she wondered if Paul had suffered a schizophrenic breakdown. She moved closer to read the headlines of the newspaper clippings: Water Main Down on Main Street, PMI's Doors Close as Unemployment Office Doors Open, Community Group Angry over Unexplained Construction. She knew he was upset about the construction on Main Street. Who wasn't?

Maija didn't know what to do. If she woke Paul, then he'd know she knew about his office—and she wanted him to confide in her naturally. But she couldn't leave him in the chilly garage. Maija tapped him on the shoulder, then scurried back into the house and into bed. Within a few minutes, Paul's cold body joined her under the covers, and all was as it should have been, or close to it.

Her nightmares, however, continued to pester her throughout her morning at Jones Drugs as she counted pills, controlled medicinal interactions, and served her customers their weekly cures. Seeing the plague victims' faces, covered in rashes and boils, was most difficult. Others, trapped in a flood, gasped for air as they swallowed more and more water, just as Eleanora had done in Maija's earlier visions. Her dream had been so real she could smell the sea and feel the sting of salt in her throat. At times like this, when Maija encountered something premonitory, she felt absolutely alone. She'd thought her mother's presence here in Cobalt would comfort her, but it hadn't. The dreams and visions remained solely her property, like a haunted house she couldn't sell.

With her doubt and fear building steadily, the pressures of work almost pushed Maija over the edge. Every phone line in the pharmacy lit up. Tom and Shandy did their parts, and Maija dove in as well.

"Hello, pharmacy."

"Maija, it's Eleanora. Could you deliver Tracy's prescriptions? It's just not possible for us to come in today." And she hung up without listening to Maija's response.

Maija took the opportunity to get out of the pharmacy, even if it was a drive to her least favorite development to visit her least favorite family.

As she drove up the hill to the Heights, Maija could see from this vantage point exactly how saturated the ground had become: Small streams leading nowhere ran down through the trees, and mud and soil that usually held trees firmly in the ground had turned into swamp, the roots defenseless. Peculiar how unprepared the ground had been for so much water—there was just too much. Sandbags were piled around the entryways into low-lying houses. Maija shook her head as her car fishtailed into a turn past the gate in the Heights.

The door into the Finch residence was open just a bit when she arrived. Peculiar, she thought. With security system and the paranoia she'd seen earlier, she never expected to walk right in through an open door.

"Hello?" she said to the quiet foyer.

The air inside was still. With the small white bag in her hand, filled with bottles of antibiotics and opiate painkillers, she went toward the kitchen, where she heard voices. She hid behind a wall and listened.

"The school called, Nora. Some kids have the flu," said a man, who Maija assumed was Herbert Finch.

"Tracy's not there. Why'd they call?" Eleanora said.

"They just went down the list. Still haven't traced the origins," Herbert responded.

"I wish Tracy only had the flu," Eleanora said.

"I do, too. But she's—"

"I don't want to talk about it." Maija heard Eleanora's heels tap across the tiled floor. "This is your fault. You couldn't pass up that deal, could you?"

"This again? You were with me during the development. You were there when I signed the deed. When I bought you that ring and those clothes, it didn't seem to bother you. But now you're mad? You're no better than me."

"Now our daughter has—"

"We don't know the cause. Not for sure."

"I know. I know because I am her mother."

"There you go again with that intuition crap."

As Maija listened, she looked around the spotless house. She saw not one single speck of dust and not one flower arrangement out of place. Suddenly she heard a voice behind her.

"Mrs. Singh?"

When she turned, she realized she should have known the face looking up at her, but it was a shade of whom she'd been, even a short time ago. Tracy's eyes were sunken into her skull, her blue eyes bluer because of the redness in them. Her hair was wet, as were her pajamas. "Dear Tracy, were you outside? In this mess?"

"I needed some air."

Eleanora and Herbert turned the corner.

"Tracy? Why are you wet? Were you in the park again? I told you not to go out there. You'll catch a cold!" Eleanora went to Tracy and wiped her face with a dishtowel.

"Yeah, whatever." Tracy shrugged off her mother and walked slowly up the stairs.

Maija handed the bag of medicine to Eleanora. "Here you go. Let me know if you have any questions." She walked toward the front door.

"Um, Maija…" Eleanora's voice cracked.

"Yes?" She turned.

"Nothing. Drive safe out there."

"Yes." Maija jogged to her car. This was too much. Tracy was ill. There was a flu outbreak at school. Eleanora blamed Herbert for something. How could he have caused Tracy's illness? That was impossible.

When she returned to the pharmacy, the phones were ringing off the hook.

"Pharmacy."

"Mrs. Singh, please."

"Speaking."

"This is Mrs. Cohen's secretary at Cobalt High."

Maija's heart sank, and she pressed the receiver closer to her ear. Mrs. Cohen's secretary requested that she or Paul, or even Oma, please retrieve both Vic and Isabella as both were "vomiting like there's no tomorrow." She said there was a flu outbreak at Cobalt High and almost half the students were green, turning green, or at the worst stage: pale as a sheet. That's the stage her children, as it turned out, had reached. As soon as Maija hung up the phone, the pit in her stomach grew. An epidemic was component number one of her apocalyptic nightmare.

Maija surveyed her surroundings and saw that Tom had already left on his mid-morning sandwich run to Wegmans, which meant she was manning the pill ship alone. She knew that Paul was busy at the station and she couldn't bother him. Oma and Papaji didn't have a car at the ready, not that they could drive with one almost blind and the other with only one foot. Maija grabbed her purse and keys and locked the register.

"Family emergency," Maija said to Shandy as she left.

Maija expected that the children would have been quarantined in an area in the high school, but when she arrived, she was surprised to see so many kids sitting in halls, slouched in chairs, lined up in the bathrooms. It was a catastrophe indeed. She found Vic and Isabella beside each other on the floor outside the nurse's office. It was dreadful for Maija to open the door and see their limp bodies.

"Izzy? Vic? Wake up." She lifted Isabella and Vic to standing and walked them to the car, driving home as fast as she could without jarring them.

Maija put them each to bed in Vic's room and placed trashcans on the floor beside each of them. She realized she was shaking only when she stepped into the kitchen and saw her mother and Papaji together. They were having tea and pound cake. The television was on, and Papaji was watching the local news.

"Harry, I think you have a crush on za weather girl," Oma said quietly.

"No, no, not true. She's just very intelligent."

"She has a weather vocabulary minute at za end of her section," Oma explained to Maija. "But she is looking pretty. I guess with za extra time she's getting because of za rains, they hired a makeup artist."

Papaji held up his hand to silence the chatter. "Shh!"

"Tanya Earhart here, and I've brought a guest with me, Professor Stuart March from Pierce College. He has an interesting perspective on the recent flooding we've seen in town. Professor?"

"See? She's intelligent and has smart friends." Papaji sat back and seemed to bask in the glow that emanated from Tanya's flushed cheeks and pink lips. Maija guessed he didn't hear a word Professor March said.

Maija went to the kitchen. Her mother followed.

"What's wrong, *meita?* It's obvious you are troubled, neh?"

"Yes, Ma." Maija sat on a stool. "It's a dream I had last night."

"What was it about? Maybe we can figure out what it means."

"It was terrible." Maija proceeded to describe the various scenes that still haunted her.

"Sounds like a nightmare, dear, nothing more. I've had them before."

"No! Don't you see? There's a flu epidemic at the school. It can't be a coincidence."

"Kids get sick all za time." Oma patted Maija's hand softly, but she shook it free. "Anyway, sounds like a normal dream, mit za slippers and all."

"Half of the Cobalt High students are ill. Something worse is going to happen." Maija leaned her face on her hands. "This virus is going to spread."

"Maija, what is happening?"

"I told you—"

"Not your dream. You really think that you can see things on such a scale? Why? Why would you be chosen to have such sight? It's unheard of."

"What would you know of it, Ma? You've never had to deal with this. You've never had visions come true."

"Haven't you been, well, off lately, neh? Your visions haven't all been true."

Maija looked at her mother and replied, "Yes, I know, but this one—"

"It's just not reasonable. You should get some rest, neh? Here, eat some cake."

Maija took the cake and tried to breathe.

An hour later, Maija checked on her children. The room was stuffy, so she opened the curtains and cracked a window to let in fresh air. She finally relaxed. Caring for her children made all the supernatural worries drift away. She sat on the edge of Vic's bed and patted his back gently. She was being silly; these kids just have the flu. You've seen it before, she reminded herself. They'll vomit all day and maybe even tomorrow, too, then they will sleep and wake refreshed though skinny. You'll feed them broth and rice, and soon they will be at school again.

"Mama?" Vic's back was to her.

"Mmm?"

He turned. "Mama, I don't feel good."

Maija's heart dropped. Vic's face was covered in large hives and a red prickly rash. He was going to vomit, so she got out of the way and directed him to the wastebasket she'd placed next to his bed. The worst thing she could do was react to how awful he looked. The swelling almost sealed his eyes shut, and the red rash seemed to be spreading down his neck and body.

"It's okay, Vic. Breathe, breathe." She rubbed his back. When he returned to sleep, she rose quietly and left.

The receiver shook in her hand as the receptionist at the family doctor's office put her on hold. Maija nodded to her mother, who was watching her from the living room couch.

"Yes, boils, I think. Hives, vomiting, rash, should I bring him in? Yes, he goes to Cobalt High. An outbreak? Of what? Just the flu? The flu doesn't look like this—his eyes are swollen shut. So, this is common? No, but you think that—well, how would you know? How long? Three days. Okay. Fine. Yes, yes, I'll do that. Thank you."

When she hung up, she felt better. At least there were others with the same symptoms. At least they weren't the only ones. She recalled the medicine that she'd delivered to Tracy Finch. It was an anti-nausea medicine, and she did look weak. Perhaps she was the source of this terrible outbreak. Leave it to a Finch to start something like a plague, Maija thought.

Paul

Paul felt the pistol in his pocket. The nearly frozen air surrounded him as he marched down Sycamore toward the station. He had no choice. It was his divine duty to protect his family from the ills of the world. For Paul, it all came back to the construction—the damn hole in the ground at the station. He had to make it stop, do something. They couldn't take the station from him bit by bit. Desperation surged through his body like a drug, each step propelled by the bills on his desk that already had gone to collection, the calls from unidentified numbers, the faces of his sick children, and his wife who still hadn't said a word, as though she'd already accepted doom as their fate. He'd prayed that morning when he turned the key in the lockbox hidden in the garage. He prayed for the first time in decades to Guru Gobind for guidance. This was war, and he needed his ancestors. He'd practiced at the shooting range, but he had never aimed the gun at a person—nor did he intend to. But waving it in someone's face, yes, he could do that. Scare the shit out of the person in charge, the son of a bitch. No problem. No problem.

His pace quickened as he approached the rear of the station. It was quiet, as if all the sound had been sucked out of the world and the only thing that existed was Paul and the few feet of air surrounding his body. He reached the front of the station and saw a customer waiting to fill up an old Plymouth. Paul looked out at the road to survey the mess, the thorn that had embedded so deeply in his side, and his breath escaped his lungs. The behemoth pile of debris, the gash in the earth into which he'd recently descended, the prehistoric machines, and the portable toilets—all were gone.

But where?

Disbelief consumed him, and he looked around as though someone were playing a terrible joke. Perhaps it was never there, he thought. Or perhaps it moved? Paul jogged to the center of the street and spun round slowly in an attempt to see what was no longer. The road was clear. He kneeled down and searched with his fingers. As his eyes adjusted he saw the seam where new asphalt met the old road. The difference was subtle. He stood and walked back a few steps.

The man with the Plymouth said, "Gone, eh? They musta fixed it."

Paul smiled. He unlocked the convenience store and put a sign on the gas pumps that read: 10% OFF GAS AND PURCHASES, TODAY ONLY. Within a few minutes, cars started to enter the station, not en masse, but a steady stream nonetheless. People bought cartons of cigarettes and six-packs of pop. They filled their tanks all the way instead of halfway. Mrs. Carmichael walked in, as usual, with her fistful of coins and a grin.

"Feeling generous today?"

He laughed with his eyes and nodded. The world was right again.

At the end of the day, Paul felt as though he had been terribly silly—aggressive even. He vowed to lock the gun back up in the garage as soon as he returned home. The city must have read his letters and the editorial piece. They had finally taken his pleas seriously. He cracked open a soda—something he'd never done before because it was an expense, after all—and he celebrated in the quiet buzzing of the store's fluorescent lights.

The archaic fax machine under the counter clicked on, and a few sheets of paper ran through. He put the soda down and retrieved the sheets. A letter from Creative Laboratories appeared in faded type:

Dear Clint:

Please find the following analysis of the sample. We felt it necessary to get these results to you as soon as possible. We made note of a high level of volatile organic compounds and other carcinogenic chemicals in the sample. It is important that you do not touch these materials with your bare skin or breathe the vapors from the surrounding areas. Please find the data results below.

Thanks,

Shari, Creative Laboratories

Paul's stomach dropped below his feet. He folded the fax three times and tucked the papers under his register. He washed his hands. In the mirror he saw a man with hollow eyes and a certain puffiness he'd never noticed before. He felt dizzy.

Paul locked the station and sat alone behind the counter, debating what to do. After an hour, no closer to a solution, he went home. Later, as he turned the key in his front door, he stopped. What would he do now? He just couldn't pretend that nothing had been discovered under the ground. It was his duty to keep exploring the ills in the earth. But when he pushed open the door and saw his sick children sitting together on the couch, beside the two aging relatives, and heard Maija in the kitchen preparing a leftover curry to which he knew she'd added broth and water in order to stretch it across this second meal, Paul found himself on a ledge between right and wrong. He wanted to protect his family from what lay underground, but if he did, the station would be in peril again, and he could not protect them if he had no livelihood. How could these two opposites overlap? Life was so fragile, and he needed to protect it. That's the only thing of which he was sure. Paul's mind stood on the edge, balancing between two rights and two wrongs.

During dinner he turned to Maija and said, "*Piyar*, the construction is done. They listened to my letters at last."

The reaction he received from his family was better than he'd imagined. Isabella and Vic both said "yay," Maija sighed, and Papaji grunted proudly.

After dinner, he and his father took their tea and sat together in the living room while the rest of the family cleaned up.

"So, *ji*, any news from the water people?"

Paul shook his head.

"That was some outing we had," Papaji said in Punjabi.

"Yes, yes, it was. It is secret that we went there. Never tell anyone what we did. Okay?" Paul responded in his native tongue.

"Of course, son, of course."

"Never."

Paul pursed his lips and attempted to steady his building fear with his relief. Later that night, when everyone was asleep, Paul drove to the station and retrieved ten three-gallon water jugs. When he returned to the house, he stashed some of them in the garage and took the rest to the kitchen. Papaji walked out of the bathroom and looked at him curiously. Paul smiled, said good night, and hoped Papaji hadn't seen him place the water beside the kitchen sink.

Isabella

Isabella looked at herself in the mirror and saw how much of a toll the illness had taken on her appearance. Her skin was yellowish. She'd lost weight, too. After two days, she was beginning to feel human again. She and her brother had survived the worst flu Cobalt had ever seen, and, in the safety of their quarantined bedroom, Vic and Isabella had made a pact to fake-vomit every few hours. They shook hands, even though Vic was uncomfortable touching his sister, and agreed to convince their mother that they weren't up to heading back into the halls. It worked; they got the rest of the week off from school.

When the flu charade was in full force, Isabella took advantage of their quarantine. No one dared enter their room because of the heaving sound effects. Her mother knocked occasionally to let them know about mealtimes, in case they were hungry, and to remind them about shower time. Cleanliness, Isabella knew, was one of her mother's first rules of a happy home. Between these two important visits, and with Vic sound asleep, Isabella managed to pillage her grandmother's things without being disturbed. The box filled with secrets sat under her bed. It was heavier than it looked, but she scurried back to the safety of her bed with it in her hands.

She tucked her bed sheets around it so she could cover it completely in case someone opened the door. The wood creaked when she lifted the lid, and the box exhaled a breath of rosewood and myrrh. She reached inside and pulled out a pile of well-worn letters. The first letter was written in a language Isabella hadn't seen before but assumed was Latvian. There were several Js, double Es and Zs, and accent marks above and below the letters like tails and ears. Her mother never shared her native tongue. Isabella wished she had learned Latvian, German, and Punjabi. Then maybe she could get a job with the United Nations as a translator and have an exciting life traveling around the world, listening in on top-secret conversations. She looked at the other letters, all of which were written in what Isabella took to be German and or even Russian. She traced the script with her fingers anyway, as though the meaning would come to her in time regardless of the language barrier. Names, however, were easier to recognize. She found the names Hermione, Heinrich, Olga, Alvina, and Otto. She was familiar with Hermione and Heinrich, her grandparents, and Alvina, but the rest meant nothing to her, not yet.

Beneath the stack of letters was a small pile of photographs of different sizes. The first one was, in Isabella's mind, the most beautiful image of a woman she'd ever seen. The woman's eyes were turned to the left of the camera. Her expression was mature, as though she'd seen a great deal of pain. Her short hair curled tightly against her scalp. Around her neck hung a large pendant, and though the photo was black and white, Isabella could see the stone's translucency. The woman's lips were sharply drawn and wore a dark lipstick. The curve of her porcelain cheeks was as lovely and round as a cherub's. Isabella turned the photo over in her hands and read as best she could: *Hermione, 2 februāris 1938, Katoju ielā, Rīgā.* Isabella knew that Oma was born in 1923; therefore, in this photo she would have been fifteen. Isabella sat back in her bed in awe. She was about the same age as her grandmother, frozen in the image.

She spent the rest of the day imagining the lives of those captured in the photos. Some photos appeared cheerful and seemed to have been taken during family gatherings. Others were during wartime; she knew this because of the presence of guns, uniforms, and grim expressions. One image in particular Isabella inspected closely: a handsome man standing alone beside a tree. He was smiling, but there were shadows behind his eyes as though he'd seen too much. Who was this man? Isabella's hand shook a little as she turned the photo over and read: *Heinrich, decembris 1944.* Was this an image of the grandfather she'd never known? She went to put the photos back inside the box when her hand grazed a raised piece of wood on the bottom.

She gave the small block of wood a push, and the entire bottom panel came free, exposing a hiding place. Isabella's heart pounded as she heard movement in the hallway just outside the door. She couldn't stop now; she was compelled by history. Under the panel were several items: a lady's watch, a large amber pendant, a string of amber beads, a pair of cufflinks, a fine gold chain with a modest Star of David hanging from it, and an enamel charm that looked like an eye. The eye seemed to speak its purpose just through its gaze. Isabella turned the Star of David over and over in her hand.

She heard a brisk knock at the door. Isabella stuffed the jewelry into the bottom panel, the photos back into the box, and covered the whole lot with the thickest part of her comforter. She stuffed the letters under her pillow—she would hide them in her shoebox later because she needed to know more about them. Her heart raced as the door opened. Her grandmother stood there, smelling of meatballs and cookies.

"Hallo, mine darlings. It's time for lunch. You must keep up your strength if you will get better, neh?"

Once Oma left, Isabella reconfigured the contents of the box so everything was as she'd found it, then placed it under her bed. She tapped Vic on the shoulder to wake him for lunch, but when he didn't move, she left him alone.

Isabella sat at the dining table beside Oma, who was already enjoying a dark brown slice of bread with hard cheese and a sliced apple. There was a steaming hot bowl of soup waiting for Isabella.

"This is *frikadelu zupa.* Meatballs and dill."

"Thank you." Isabella tasted the soup and felt instantly warmed. The small yet adequate meatballs were succulent, and the cream on top of the dilly clear broth made it rich but still fresh and light.

"Are you feeling better?" Oma looked pleased.

Isabella paused with a meatball in her mouth. She wanted to ask if Oma was Jewish, and if so, why she'd hid this all these years. If she was Jewish, that meant that Isabella was, too, at least in part. Suddenly, Isabella's history felt foreign to her, as if the disparate pieces of her identity had fallen to the floor and scattered like a detailed jigsaw puzzle. She wanted nothing more than to collect them and paste herself back together again. Instead, she swallowed and said, "A little, yes."

"Good, good." Oma did not take her eyes off Isabella. "Did you have a question, darlink?"

"No. Yes. What were you thinking about planting in the backyard?" Isabella knew how silly this sounded, as the backyard was more soupy than earthy, and Oma wouldn't be able to plant anything until spring, which was months away.

"Ah, yes, gardening. Do you like to garden, too?"

Isabella nodded. "Mama doesn't have much time to garden, but sometimes we do."

"What would you like to plant, then? We can plant almost anything here. Za soil is rich. When it's normal."

"Anything? Huh. I guess it would be nice to have some flowers. Something bright and humungous."

"Za dahlias. They would be nice. We can plant them in za summer. They will grow taller and taller until their flowers, like suns of red and purple, reach za sky, neh?"

"If it ever stops raining," Isabella said.

"We had everything in mine garden in Latvia. Za tomatoes tasted like springtime, and za lettuce vas a rich purple."

"Purple lettuce?"

"And za cucumbers and squash would feed a whole family. That is, unless za birds and animals ate them before we did."

Isabella finished her soup and nibbled on a lemon cookie. She felt full and brave and thought about the contents in the box. "Oma? What was Opa like?"

Oma's eyes sparkled. "Yes, Izjah, you never got za chance to meet him, neh? He vas tall and good-looking, when he smiled, you know."

Isabella knew the man in the photo had to be him. Was it his star as well? She lacked the courage to ask. "Do you miss Latvia?'

Oma didn't answer and instead cleaned the plates and poured two cups of tea without responding. When she returned to the dining table, she said, "Have I told you za story about za animals and za girl?"

Isabella shook her head no.

"Zoh, it vas a long, long time ago. I don't even know vie long. Mine little country is four thousand years old. Latvia vas made mit these tribal people, neh? And there vas always big war. They were too small to defend themselves. Invaders came always and slaved us. Then, one day za Germans came and took our land away and made us work in big farms. They owned za land, they stole za earth, za trees, za branches on za ground." Oma sipped her tea. "Zoh, there vas a girl whose father married a bad woman who already had her own daughter. Firewood vas scarce because za Germans took everything, neh? Za evil mother blew out all za fire in za house and sent za stepdaughter to za ogre's castle to get fire."

"So she sent her to die," Isabella said.

Oma nodded.

"On za way, za girl passed a cow that asked her, 'Oh, please will you milk me? Mine udders are zoh full.' So za girl milked za cow and went on her way. Then she came upon a sheep, whose hair vas to za ground. It said, 'Oh, pretty girl, won't you shear me? I am so hot.' So, za girl sheared za sheep. Then she found a horse tied too tight to za fence, neh? And za horse said, 'My owner tied me too tight; won't you un-tether me?' So she did."

"What a nice girl."

"Yes. Zoh, in za ogre's castle, za girl meets za ogre who licks his lips to eat her, when a mouse comes from za wall and says, 'Oh, girl, take this gold, neh? And run as fast as you can.' So she goes back through za forest. Za ogre was on her heels but za cow, horse, and sheep all told za ogre to go in different directions, so she got away."

"Phew." Isabella sighed.

Oma took a sip of tea and wiped her mouth with a handkerchief. "Well, za ugly stepmother thought dis was a good deal mit za gold, so she sent her real daughter to get more gold from za ogre za next night. She also met za cow, horse and sheep, but she did not help them. When she got to za castle, za ogre went to eat her and za mouse gave her za gold and told her to run. She ran as fast as she could, but za cow, sheep and horse told za ogre where to find her and—he ate her."

"Eww. That's terrible."

"Neh, za second real daughter deserved it. Nature is brutal. She will help when we help her. Well, sometimes, you know."

"What happened to the first girl?"

"She married a prince."

"Of course she did."

"Yes, he saw vie beautiful and kind and smart she vas, zoh he said, 'Now that is who I should marry,' neh?"

Isabella smiled at Oma and thought about the cautionary tale about the balance between nature and humankind. She looked outside and saw that the rain was clearing a bit; she could see the water running from the gutters toward the trees and bushes that were drowning.

"We won't be able to plant anything here for a while. The trees, the soil—it's all too wet." Isabella sighed.

"Okay, when you finish your cookie, help me mit something in za backyard, neh?"

Oma put on her yellow rain clothes and went outside. When she was finished eating, Isabella dressed warmly and followed. Oma was at the side of the house lifting small but hefty bags of sand. She'd built a row that was working hard to keep out the few inches of water that had built up and headed toward the backyard. Without asking, Isabella lifted a small bag and helped Oma complete the row.

"Now, maybe we can keep za ground healthy."

"Oma? Where did those bags come from?"

"I don't know, darlink. They were next to the garage. Maybe yours father brought them?"

Isabella wondered why her father would have bought sand bags but not place them properly. He seemed even more frazzled than usual lately. Earlier that day, she'd heard in a weather report that Cobalt and the tri-city area was set for a long ride with the storm and suggested blocking low-lying areas and keeping gutters clear.

"However they came, it's good they're here now."

Vic

Vic decided to use his illness vacation to conduct a sleep deprivation test; he wanted to see if he could transform into a nocturnal creature. The first night was the most difficult because, as he saw it, he went about it the wrong way: He began at a disadvantage, as his body was still healing from the trauma of the flu.

Vic truly missed the daylight as he sat alone on the couch, watching re-runs of *The Golden Girls*. In the shadow-filled room, he felt lonely as he winced at each punch line about Blanche's boyfriends and Rose's stupidity. It would have been easier if everyone else was nocturnal as well. He turned off the television and rested on the floor. He'd lost a bit of weight because of the flu, but he hoped to keep the muscle memory from all of his recent exercises. Yet he could only do ten sit-ups before collapsing, sleepy.

Vic went to the kitchen and drank a pot of old coffee and a flat cola he found in the rear of the refrigerator. He felt a surge of energy and did thirty push-ups and an eye test in which he used a cup to cover one eye, then tried to read *Time* magazine in the dark. He couldn't read very much at first, but then some words became clearer. Soon afterward, he vomited all of the caffeinated beverages and made a mental note to not drink so much coffee on an empty stomach. When the pink morning light shone through the curtains in the living room, Vic curled up with a multicolored blanket that Oma had knitted and watched the sunrise. The clouds had parted after the night's rain, and he decided that the reddish sky was the most brilliant thing he'd seen in weeks.

Vic made notes about his inability to fully transform into a nocturnal creature. He wrote that it was most likely due to the fact that the system in which he existed—with Oma's baking, Mama's cooking, Papa's bossing around—basically was filled with day life and therefore, it would be nearly impossible to change on his own. It was the system that gave the guidelines for such things, he thought, and no one walks alone.

Vic continued to test whether he could become a nocturnal creature over the next two days, but after exhaustion took him, he gave up and turned his attention back to the Karner Blue. It still seemed odd to Vic that he may have found a dead Karner, gynandromorph or not, in an environment that was not a suitable feeding ground, and so late in the season. Most guidebooks stated that the Karner flew from April through July, or September at the latest. Butterflies were insects that thrived on schedule and habit. They depended upon the environment to provide their eggs with a sturdy leaf on which to grow, a food source for the caterpillar once it hatched, and flowers or puddles in which they could feed once they were in flight. Alterations would occur when, say, the weather was extremely cold, which would signal a longer hibernation period for the butterfly in its pupa or adult state. Everything else in nature was on a schedule. What would need to happen in order for the Karner to appear so late in the year, in a habitat not useful for its feeding? The dead forest in which he'd found the butterfly was far from any legume or aster or clover or lupine, the Karner's favorite flowers. He'd read a little about a butterfly, the Xerces Blue, that sounded quite similar to his butterfly, but it was extinct.

He remembered an insect book he'd had when he was a boy, and he thought it might be in the garage, where all the other lost and in limbo items ended up. He went out to the garage and tiptoed around until he found a box with children's books. Memories washed over him in waves as he flipped through different books from his youth, like *Island of the Blue Dolphins, The Wind in the Willows,* and *The Boxcar Children*. He found the insect book, and it was more detailed than he'd remembered. When Vic turned to leave the garage, he spied his father's collection of maps and charts.

He'd known his father was up to something, but until that moment he wasn't sure what, exactly. As he looked at the maps, he found one map in particular that was very interesting. It illustrated the entire PMI campus when it had first been constructed: a sprawling creature that sucked up most of the natural space in Cobalt. Since the map had been printed, several buildings had closed and been leveled, and the beast's size had become a collection of empty streets and dead-end buildings.

Vic followed the map along Peregrine Court to Main Street, then along to his land. PMI had covered a great deal of the area. Even the inadequately small park, The Commons, had once been a paved part of PMI; the alterations had happened long before he'd been born. The place where he'd found the blue had once been PMI's. After PMI closed many arms of its company, they'd attempted to reconstruct the area to appear as though nothing industrial had happened before. Now the land comprised a sad forest and their neighborhood. Vic marveled at PMI's handiwork, how they must've boasted about their reintroduction of habitat that they'd previously bulldozed. What would cause a company to simply give up their land and buildings amid a boom? This was long before any corporation could receive a tax break for "green" purposes. What was below his neighborhood? What had made PMI run away from Cobalt? He wondered about his mine and whether the hollowed earth could hold the weight of the structures above. Perhaps, he thought, the mine was an even larger piece of the puzzle than he'd originally imagined. As he drifted to sleep, with the morning light peeking through a gap in the curtains, he dreamed of a butterfly caught in an underground maze being chased by the Minotaur.

Papaji

Papaji held one end of the navy fabric between his teeth and finished wrapping the rest around his head. He had tied his turban the same way his entire life. He'd wash the five yards of fabric, gauzy and light, then hang it between two trees. When it was dry, and slightly taut from starch, Anjana or Kamal would hold one end and he the other while he folded the fabric over and over again until it was only a few inches wide. He'd comb his long, wavy hair and twist it into a loose knot on the top of his head, then tie a *fiftee* around his head like a band to keep the hair in place. He'd wrap the fabric in artful layers, careful to overlap the seams just so, and use a thin piece of wood, like a pencil, to tuck in the loose edges of fabric. His father had taught him, and he'd taught Kamal. But he'd never taught Paul. Who had? he wondered. Paul's turbans looked just like his: Punjabi Sikh style, perfectly curved, not too big, not too short, in black, navy, or maroon. As Papaji tended to his long beard with beard fixer and comb, he acknowledged just how absent he'd been in his son's life. He wanted desperately to make up for the lost time. He felt deep in his gut that there was something Paul was keeping from him.

One of the clues he had was Paul's desk in the garage, which was in disarray. Piles of papers, sticky notes, and notebooks filled with abandoned and scratched-out drawings littered the place. More filtered water surrounded the area, as Paul had recently made it clear that his family would only drink bottled water as well as use it to prepare tea and meals. Papaji had grown used to bottled water because India's water was not reliable as far as bacterial overgrowth was concerned. But he'd always thought American water would be fine to drink, as it claimed to be from wells or aquifers or some pastoral spring somewhere never too far away.

With his new turban tied, the old man went to Paul's office. He opened drawers, shuffled through papers, and sorted piles. After a few paper cuts and one nasty puncture wound from a tack, he found a piece of paper with letterhead from Creative Laboratories.

Paul had received the results and lied.

The lab's 8260 test for petroleum found lighter hydrocarbons, and this report included the results on a full-chain 8270 for semivolatiles: It wasn't petroleum from the station leaking into the ground. The rest of the results were unfamiliar to Papaji, but Paul's notes on the page were written in Punjabi, which made very clear what they said. It must have taken his son hours to interpret the acronyms: TCE, VOC, ATSDR, EPA, CPF, and CREG, which in his notes read trichloroethylene, volatile organic compound, Agency for Toxic Substances and Disease Registry, Environmental Protection Agency, Cancer Potency Factor, Cancer Risk Evaluation Guide. Even as a civilian, without a chemical engineering background or scientific training, Papaji knew these words added up to something bad. The information sat heavy on his chest. He had to do something. For once, he had to help his son, who couldn't handle the situation on his own.

As Papaji sorted through Paul's notes and papers, he made a short list of the involved parties: the City of Cobalt, Kwicki Fill, the Finch family, and PMI. He crossed off the city because he knew they wouldn't be forthcoming. He suspected the last two were connected somehow; Paul had explained that the Finch family had been the last to own the land. Papaji looked in the phone book, then picked up the phone in the kitchen. He would get to the bottom of this once and for all.

"PMI, can I help you?" a woman's voice said.

"Hi, yes, I own a gas station in Cobalt. The one on Sycamore."

"Uh huh. Our plant closed there years ago, sir. We're only in Springfield now."

"Yes, can I speak to someone in planning or development? Or Mr. Finch?"

"We don't have that department here. Mr. Finch no longer works for us."

"Someone who has knowledge of the history of the land in Cobalt then?"

"I suggest you contact your historical society."

"Let me talk to the manager."

"One moment." The elevator music began.

Papaji found it difficult to sort his thoughts with the sound of an emotional clarinet streaming into his ear. What would he say to the manager? What could they do for him? He swallowed hard and reminded himself that he used to solve problems for the village: same problems, different village.

"Yeah, this is Marv."

"Mr. Marv, did you work at the Cobalt plant? See, I am the owner of the Kwicki Fill station on Sycamore, and—"

"Right next to the old plant? Sure, I remember it."

"There's been a dig here for some time now, right in the middle of Sycamore, and suddenly it stopped. I want to know the cause of the construction." Marv did not respond, but Papaji could hear a cigarette being lit. He continued, "See, I think PMI is behind the whole matter."

"Why would you think that, Mr.—"

"Singh."

"Mr. Singh. We are the largest employer in the area."

As soon as the answer to a question sounded arbitrary, Papaji knew they were heading nowhere. "Thank you for your time." He was now certain that PMI was involved somehow.

Papaji went to his room and slid his hand under the mattress. He pulled out the bundle in which he'd received his life savings. In the wrapping he located another object, hidden in a different layer of paper and fabric. He delicately unwrapped an ancient *kirpan* sheathed in bone. This knife had belonged to his great-grandfather, Sardar Ranjit Singh. Every male in his family at some point or another had held the handle, either wielding it as a weapon or holding it as a keeper of history. The blade was dull and could no longer slice through steel or flesh—or paper, for that matter. He'd given it to Kamal when he was old enough, but after he'd died in the accident, he'd taken it back as a token of his dead son.

Papaji retrieved his diamond whetstone from his room and opened the door to the backyard. He dusted the water off of a wrought iron chair that had been leaning against the table, in an out-of-service-for-the-season kind of fashion. He sat down, placed the diamond whetstone on the table, and slid the blade against the stone as though he were slicing a piece of the stone. He used even pressure as he slid the blade five times on one side, then five on the other. The vibrations took him back to the Punjab, to the last time he'd used the *kirpan*. It had been many years ago, when he was a young man during the Partition.

He'd already sent Anjana and Kamal ahead and was now protecting the *gurdwárá* in the village with many others. The threat of the attack had come suddenly. The entire village had gathered inside the *gurdwárá*'s walls. The fire started when a Muslim attacker threw a torch on the roof. Papaji could still taste the bitter air. After that, it was mere moments before the attackers broke windows and began to butcher nearly everyone. Papaji had managed to escape. He'd been one of the fortunate ones—until a gang of men armed with swords and pistols caught up to him along an empty farm road with nothing on it but fields of wheat. Two men aimed knives at him and held him tight. He was glad to see his good friend, Aaqib, in the group.

Brother, let me go. It's me.

Kneel. Accept Islam. Sardarji, this is your life. Just say the words, the leader of the group of *goondas* said. Aaqib did nothing.

Papaji was stone. Nothing had prepared him for such an impossible situation. On one hand, there was his life; on the other, death. Attached to his life was submission to a religion and turning his back on his ancestors. He'd grown up learning about the sacrifices that his gurus had made for their religious freedom. Denying these thugs their victory was the only option. He then thought of his wife and son, who were far away from the danger. How would they manage fatherless, widowed, and impoverished?

Kneel! A man with one bad eye drove his knife into Papaji's foot.

The pain was unbearable, and he fell the dusty ground. *Kill me, for there is no decision I will make for you.*

Cut his throat.

No, we should make him Muslim where it counts.

The group argued about what they should do with him. In the confusion, they did not see him take out his *kirpan*, nor did they see him grab the smallest man of the group, a boy of fourteen who was taunting him with a stick, and press his blade to his throat.

Drop your weapons, or I'll kill him.

They all turned.

One of them shook his pistol at him. *You won't do it. Look,* bhái, *he's too young to die.*

Too young to die, but old enough to murder and loot? You are insane. He spit and pressed the knife to the boy's throat. The boy winced. He knew he was no killer, and he let the boy go.

Aaqib went to him and said, *Just stay down,* bhái, *and kneel.*

But before he knew it, Aaqib hit him in the head with the butt of the gun, and he fell. They weren't murderers or thieves. It was the war that had poisoned everyone.

Papaji checked the blade for sharpness, and a drop of blood appeared on his pointer finger. He heard someone in the house, and then the sliding door opened. It was Paul, who pulled up a chair beside him.

"Ikpaul, I saw the results."

"What?"

"I called PMI. Didn't get anywhere."

"Why did you call them?"

"Someone had to."

"Papaji, this is not your business. You can't just come into my house after so many years and pretend that everything is okay. It's not okay." Paul stood and paced along the patio.

"*Puttar*, I haven't been a good father to you." Papaji looked at his son and felt as though he were seeing him for the first time. What had he done?

"It's fine, Papaji."

"No, it's not fine. I need to say some things, please. When I wasn't there to protect your mother during the long journey, I blamed myself. The war left me bitter. I could not move on from that, ever. I was weak. You—you are strong. You protect your family, your city, everything. You work hard to make sure that we are all safe. *Puttar*, I can learn from you."

Paul's lips parted just a touch, and after a large absence of words he said, "Thank you."

"We need to do something about the water."

"Yes, we do."

Papaji held out his *kirpan* to Paul. "This should have been yours years ago. To pass on to Vic, *samajhna?*"

Paul took the *kirpan* from Papaji's hands. The rain fell like gentle tears, as though nature were washing away their past regrets, cleansing both of them.

Maija

On an average day, somewhere between past and present, Maija's mind rested uncomfortably, as though at any moment a breeze might come to push her from the precipice of reality. Her perspective had too many elements to interpret. It was maddening: the visions and her lack of control over them, the conversation at the Finch home that didn't make sense, the conversations in her mind. This problem of neither here nor there became a larger and more persistent problem when she'd found a pile of letters neatly tucked away in Isabella's secret box beneath her bed.

Maija existed alone in an unusual space of uncertainty. The ways in which the past crept into her mind and others' futures she'd never truly understood. She'd always hated this part of herself, the one that made her different, with every inch of her being. She'd thought it was useless until, of course, she came across each and every letter her mother and father had written to each other over the year they'd been separated during the war. She realized her father's vision of the future had been as precarious as her own: Her father had been an unwilling participant in a vicious war, her mother a vulnerable yet strong woman who'd escaped an impossible situation with only her wits.

Maija read the first few letters with her back to the bedroom door, ready to stash the evidence of her tertiary snooping as soon as another person came home. Soon, the words cascaded over her and made her physical surroundings disappear.

Janvāris 45, Poznan

Dearest Heinrich:

Tonight I can only write about small things. If I think about sadness or the world around both of us, I will not be able to continue. The snow covers the city like a shroud on a corpse. Your package arrived yesterday. I am shocked it came at all. Poznan, bombed and gutted by German artillery, barely holds together for us the remaining survivors. There was no note inside your package, only cigarettes and money. These will help me leave this dangerous place. Thank you, my darling. This flat is the only one left standing, which means they will come soon and count the dead, then jail the rest. I am vulnerable—you know why. I only have to open my mouth and they know my religion and my country. I am growing worried that you have not received my letters, as the last was returned to me here in Posen. I pray that you are okay. Charlotte said the front collapsed and took with it many soldiers. I will leave tomorrow by train if they are still running. The Russians bombed the railway coming in and the Germans bombed the tracks leaving. I am caught between a hungry lion and a wolf. They say they will both meet soon. Whenever I feel cold and hungry, I think about the dinner we had together on our farm last spring. Do you remember the duck, the roasted vegetables, the bread and wine? My love, I hope that we can meet again after and make a new life together. Perhaps have the child we've always wanted. Though I am not sure if I want to bring a soul into a world that allows a hell like this unfold. When you think of me, think of how I love you. Think of how our love surpasses this nightmare. Think of the bench we sat on together in Riga along the Daugava River. You brought candies and carnations. It was that moment that I knew we would be married. When you slid your hand into mine, I fell in love with you forever. My dear heart, I will see you in this world or the next. I am going to move north and hope to slip past these devils. Look for me there. I pray for your safety.

Love eternal, your wife, Hermione

Maija sat with her heavy heart in her chest, her head in her hands. Their love, so clear here on the page, was something she'd never known.

Februāris 45, East Prussia

Dearest Mina,

I write this from a bed in the infirmary. I am on the Eastern front. The winter is hell. I was caught in a firefight. My foot—it's badly wounded. I write this in the dark, my darling. Another officer promised to get this to you. You see—I know they will try to execute me in the morning. I saw it. I heard them speaking in my mind. I know you might think it's crazy, but I know. I just know. They want to rid themselves of the injured. I am leaving here tonight, with my friend who is also injured. I don't know how far we will get in this winter, don't know if I'll ever set my eyes on your beauty again. I did see us together with a daughter, in a farm in a place untouched by this war. Perhaps it is also our future. What use is the future if we do nothing to change our path? If I survive this, if we survive, let's leave this insanity behind. I can only hope.

For now, forever, love, Heinrich

He had the sight. Maija had always resented the move to America. Resented her father for dying when she was so young. And now, she saw that his decision to uproot them all and move to America was based on a premonition, a promising future he'd seen. She knew her father had been wounded on the front, his foot nearly shot to pieces. But that was all she'd heard of the myth because Oma had never been very forthcoming with details, understandably. Through the letters, Maija learned that his companion did not survive. She learned she shared her father's sight. She learned that he was the one who wanted to come to America and never be forced to fight in another war against his will again.

Maija stood and vacuumed the room slowly, methodically, as though she were protecting each moment in the past. Oma's memories had become more vivid in her mind lately. If only her mother had the sight; perhaps it would have helped her find freedom sooner. Perhaps she could have avoided the DP camps and the fights, the terror and the hunger, the loss of all of her family members and most of her friends. How easy we move from the precarious past, Maija thought. How soon we forget. Now it made sense why Oma was so adamant about the past, her past, never forgetting—and yet how difficult it was for her to talk about it at all. Blindness would soon steal her vision. Maija alone would have to see for both of them.

She heard her mother return from her afternoon walk. "Ma? Want some tea?" she said as she went to the kitchen to prepare the water.

"Sure, mine darlink. Thank you."

It was over tea and black bread that Maija knew she had to enter territory that had been off limits her entire life.

"We don't talk. We never talk. Not about the hard things, Ma. I have been carrying them for so long. Things I don't understand. Things I need to understand. Ma, I need you to tell me, tell us."

"I don't want to talk about za past, neh? It's done."

"It's not done. Not for me. I see things. Useless things. And then I see things that are important. The past—your past, I think. But I don't know what it means. Please."

Oma pursed her lips and seemed to think hard about something before she spoke. "Is Izjah home?"

"Uh, yeah, I think so." Maija projected her motherly call to Isabella, and before long her daughter appeared.

"Izjah, sit down here, neh?"

Maija saw her daughter beside her mother, and for the first time saw the resemblance that rested in Isabella's well-defined lips and high cheekbones. There they sat, three women of three generations, all drinking the same tea. Was this the miracle she'd been waiting for?

"I know you have questions, Izjah. So, maybe you should ask them now. It's poison in your blood when you cannot speak your mind."

Maija watched her daughter find courage, then confidence. "Oma, are you Jewish?"

"Yes, Izjah. Yes, we are."

"Why did you hide it for so long?"

"I hid it from even myself, neh? Everyone died for this. Mine sisters, mine mother and father, even mine husband died eventually from za wounds, neh? Zoh, these things go deeper inside. Far under our skin and bones and in our blood. When we came to America, I decided it would be easier to keep hiding. It doesn't change my blood, neh?"

Isabella nodded carefully. Maija bit her lip and said, "Ma, why didn't you tell me Papa had the sight?"

Oma dabbed her eyes with a tissue.

Maija continued, "It would have been easier for me all along, knowing that I wasn't alone."

"He didn't want you to know. It vas za last thing he asked of me before he died. You were too young to remember. It wasn't cancer, darlink; he died of a full heart. He'd set out to bring us here. He set out to care for us. To have you. Once he did these things, he vas old. He vas full."

Maija reached out her hand across the table and held her mother's hand. For the first time in her life she, too, felt a full heart—but her head filled with questions.

Isabella

Isabella counted her steps as she walked down the busy hall toward the theater. Tewks had called an emergency rehearsal today, as he'd decided they were all far from prepared for opening day. He also wanted to speak with her before rehearsal. "One, two, three, four, five," she said under her breath. Maybe counting only worked when trying to sleep, not when avoiding nausea. "Six, seven, eight, nine," she said, and on ten she ran into the girl's bathroom.

Her clammy hands pushed open a stall, and she assumed the familiar and uncomfortable position in front of a toilet. The bathroom cleared out. Could she still be feeling the effects of the flu, or was this something more? When she was through, she rinsed her mouth at the sink and took a sip. The cool water felt good.

Tewks was going to fire her as soon as she walked into his office. Could a teacher fire a student? Isabella's mind raced. Her new interest in the play would fall flat because someone had set her up. When Mrs. Stein forced her to audition for the play, she would have taken any way out. But since her discovery of her grandmother's religious heritage, Isabella had renewed her interest in history. Her grandfather, Heinrich, fought in World Wars I and II. This was a statement she could recite, empty of empathy—a memorized slogan like, "I'm half Latvian and half Indian" or "Yes, my last name is Singh." She had no idea what it meant to fight in a war, hold a gun, kill a person, lose a family member, or immigrate to a foreign country on which all your hopes and dreams had been pinned.

Before she knew it, she was standing at the door to the theater. Rehearsals had been cancelled when the flu broke out, and this would be the first time she'd seen Tewks since she was called to the principal's office and told she didn't deserve the lead role. She thought of what Oma would do in this situation. Isabella took a deep breath in, then let it out. She puffed up her chest, made her eyes squint. She needed to bring a gift for Tewks. There was a snack machine in the hallway, and from her backpack she scrounged up fifty cents. The only thing that cost a mere fifty cents in the machine was a packet of multi-flavored Life Savers. It looked meager beside the large chocolate cupcakes and candy bars, but it would have to do. Armed with attitude and candy, she opened the door.

It was dark inside, and the silence was heavy in the already insulated theater. She was the first to arrive, so she went to Tewks's small office behind the stage to see if he was there. The door was open, but no one was inside. She hesitated for a few seconds with the doorknob in her sweaty hand, but instead of listening to doubt she pushed the door open completely.

"Mr. Tewkesbury? Hello?" she said to no one.

She'd never been inside his office before. It was warmly decorated, with an antique desk and comfortable-looking chairs. On the desk were photos and an old mug filled with lollipops and pens. The bookshelf held tons of books, and she picked up one and opened it, but before she could see if she recognized the title, she felt a hand on her shoulder.

"Miss Singh, looking for something?"

Isabella looked at her teacher and stuck out her fist with the Life Savers. He looked puzzled but took the candy and put it on his desk.

"I am glad you are here. We need to talk. Take a seat."

Isabella sat down. "Okay."

"The principal told me they found oddities in your locker." He seemed quietly angry.

"Oh, that stuff was mine. I keep things I find. It's like—like—" Isabella searched for a harmless hobby—"scrapbooking. Just like scrapbooking."

"Scrapbooking."

"Why did they think to search my locker for anything in the first place?"

"Someone mentioned you were holding dangerous materials in your locker."

"Who?"

"The note was anonymous."

"Someone wants me to get kicked out of the play. I didn't do anything wrong. Look, I'm telling the truth. Why can't you believe me?"

Tewks removed his scarf and closed the door to his office. "I do believe you. I feel better having spoken with you, Isabella. I think we can continue rehearsing for the play now, right here."

"Oh, but no one else is here."

"We can do a read-through together. The group is waiting outside in the theater. Did you bring your script?"

Isabella suddenly was uncomfortable. Tewks's chair stood between her and the door.

She stood. "I'm beginning to really like the play, Mr. Tewkesbury. It's pretty cool, you know."

He smiled but his expression did not change. "I'll play Erik's role, then, okay? Let's begin with the first act, scene two."

She didn't move. That was the scene where they kissed.

"Samantha? Scene two."

"I forgot my script."

"I should have another one here somewhere." He turned to his bookshelf.

"I am going to be sick." She wasn't sure if this was true, but she was sure a promise of vomit would derail his momentum.

"Aren't you feeling better? Remember what I told you, Isabella?" He moved closer. "Sometimes you just have to figure out a way to make do and not ruin the whole production." He raised his hand to her face. "Now, what do you look like without these glasses?"

He grabbed them from her face, and she became nearly blind and utterly vulnerable. His face blurred before her, and she clutched at the corner of her backpack to stay connected to something familiar.

"Give them back."

"Just a minute."

"Now. Please," she said firmly. She picked up her backpack, which was heavy with textbooks. She would swing it at him if he came any closer. If that didn't work, she would try to kick him in the crotch.

"No need to be snippy. I just thought you could use some one-on-one instruction with the director. Other students would be jealous. Plenty of others could have had that role, Isabella. I picked you." He handed her glasses to her.

She moved diagonally toward the door, and though he was standing before it, her quick movement forced him to get out of the way. She pushed the door open with the same force she'd used when she came in.

"Hey, Izzy! Hey!" Erik jogged up alongside her. "Where are you going?"

"Tewks is a jerk."

"Tell me something I don't know. What happened?" Erik held her arm gently, and they walked together along the hall to the exit and outside.

Isabella's eyes dampened.

"Hey, don't cry. Did he do something?" Erik puffed up his chest, then wiped her tears with the side of his hand. She looked up into his blue eyes. She realized that he was wearing cologne, and all she wanted to do was curl up against his chest and breathe.

"No. I don't know."

Erik bent down and said, "You wanna go get a milkshake?"

At that moment, Isabella fell in love.

Paul

Paul looked out the window of his Kwicki Fill and smiled. He selected disc two on the CD player under the counter and hummed along to Johnny Cash. He admired the rack of tires outside the window that had been returned on good faith, and the extra tower of engine oil they'd delivered along with it. It was cloudy, as always, but today he noticed the intricate edges outlining each cloud. All were unique—the way they moved, their density or thinness, their variegation of white tinted with smoke. The clouds danced like friends at times; other times they fought like enemies. They tugged, layered, and even weighed heavily on one another like siblings. He'd never observed this before. He'd only seen them as a vast carpet of gray. He watched one cumulus give way to a bright blue sky for a minute and watched another feathery cloud close the seam.

"Glorious," he said to himself and to the store. He was waiting for Papaji to pick him up. They were going to an appointment with the City of Cobalt, and Paul had to collect the research that he'd left at the station. Paul felt good about this plan. He would share the results from the water testing and tell them about the connections he had made between PMI and the quality of the water. They would be required to do something. He would bring the proof. As he bent toward the shelf where he kept his papers, the old knife in his pocket scuffed his leg, so he removed it and put it with his collection of defense tools under the counter.

"Too many *paranthas*," he whispered to his reflection in the window. His waistband was not forgiving, and he would have traded anything for the one-size-fits-all feeling of the *kurta pajama*; its waist was cinched by a fabric cord that could be adjusted to one's eating habits. You could hide your robustness, a full pregnancy, and many other secrets beneath the folds of the fabric. The extra inch or so in the waistband would come in handy, particularly after the wonderful *parantha* breakfast he had with his family that morning.

"Urrgh." He grumbled as the button slipped out of the eyelet of his slacks. He fastened the single button on his jacket and looked into the reflection in the window again. Not bad, he thought. His dark-brown suit and black turban looked quite regal. He looked intelligent, trustworthy, and ready for a meeting with Mrs. Donatella Mooney, a member of the city planning board, in downtown Cobalt. He placed his folder on the counter and straightened his turban, then wrote a sign and taped it to the inside of the glass door: TEMPORARILY CLOSED. WILL RE-OPEN TOMORROW. —PAUL SINGH, OWNER

It was a rare thing for Paul to close his convenience store for a whole day, but this was important business, and he wanted to be free in case other meetings followed. He fantasized about the praise he would receive from the city officials for uncovering strange goings-on across from his station. They'd nickname him The Watchdog, someone not to be messed with. They would give him one of those citizen awards and show the whole ceremony on the evening news. Maybe all the research would add up to something; maybe one of his life goals would be achieved.

He heard a car pull into the station and park along the side. In his rush he dropped his notes, and the papers scattered across the floor behind the counter. The bell rang on the door. "*Ik mint*,

Papaji," Paul said without looking up as he gathered his notes, drawings, and documents and slid them into the folder.

As he rose to his feet, something struck him with such force that his turban fell off and rolled across the floor. Stunned, Paul fumbled for the bat under the counter, but before he could grab it, he felt another strike against his skull, and his vision went black.

Vic

Vic looked at the forms on the clipboard. The words on the page may as well have been written in Akkadian. The nurse, whose breath was a gust of coffee, said his mother would have to read and sign them to the best of her ability as soon as possible. Vic took the forms with him into the hospital room, where he signed his mother's name on the line that read, "The patient or responsible party acknowledges responsibility for payment," and once more where it read, "The patient or responsible party understands hospital policies," though he hadn't actually read the small print in its entirety.

When Vic was through with the paperwork, he turned to his father, known to Cobalt County Hospital as the critical patient in Room 127. If Vic ignored the tube of oxygen in his father's nose, the IV in his hand, and the clip on his fingertip that monitored his heart, it was easier to imagine that his father was simply ensnared in a heavy slumber. But the fantasy was threadbare and dissolved as soon as Vic looked closely at his father's face. He dared not touch his cheek; from a distance he looked like a wax model of Paul Singh. The wax figure's left eye was bruised and swollen shut. Bandages heavy with brown blood were taped to his temple. It looked as though a special-effects artist had created two deep cuts on his now-shaved head and had used staples worthy of Frankenstein's monster to close the wounds.

Vic pulled the extra blanket over the sheet-covered silhouette of his father's knees. Seeing more of his body than necessary while he was a defenseless hostage of the hospital bed made Vic angry.

He swallowed, but his dry throat only scratched.

"Ma, do you think he's cold?"

His mother was sitting in a chair beside the bed, staring at Paul catatonically.

"Ma?"

"No," she whispered.

She'd been like that since she arrived. Her face was still, her breath shallow like his father's. His mother appeared to have retreated deep inside herself. She hadn't said a word more than two or three letters long. She was cryogenically frozen in her shock—a totally useless state, in Vic's eyes.

"I'll just take these to the nurse then," he said.

After he handed the papers to the nurse, he went into the waiting room to speak with the others. Isabella was still wearing her white sweater, the cuffs stained with Papa's blood.

"Iz, I'll trade you." He gave her his hooded sweatshirt. He put the bloody sweater in a plastic bag. The police, who'd stopped by earlier, might need it, he thought. Maybe he should call them again to see if they found who did this.

"Vic, we'll figure this out." Oma was confident and calm.

"Sure," he replied emptily. "It's getting late—you should all go home. I'll stay here with Mama and Papa. Izzy, call Adelaide to pick you all up, okay? Ask the nurse to use the phone. I'll call home if anything changes."

"I should stay with you, *potrá*." Papaji rested his large hand on Vic's shoulder.

"No, Papaji. There isn't room. Please take care of Izzy." He whispered the last part.

"He'll wake up soon. It's only a matter of time." Papaji nodded at Vic as he went back into the hospital room. "We'll be back in the morning."

Vic nodded back, though he knew that even if his father woke, it was possible he had brain damage. All he could think of was the conversation he'd had with him that morning at breakfast. Vic had come to the table without his head covering.

Papa? Vic had said.

Yes?

Don't get mad. Vic hid behind his large pile of potatoes.

What did you do with your hair? Paul had touched Vic's ponytail, free of his patka. Vic wore a bandana wrapped around his scalp.

I'm just trying something new. I'm sorry, it's not really—I mean, it's still clean and covered, right?

It looks foolish.

Just for today?

Vic saw the disappointment in his father's eyes. *The turban is very important, but what's more important is that you never cut your hair,* puttar. *Please, promise me*, Paul had said.

I promise, Papa.

Fine, for now.

Now, at the hospital, Vic felt helpless. The doctors had relieved the pressure around his father's brain as best they could by drilling a hole in his skull near one of the fractures and suctioning out the fluid. Now it was a waiting game.

The floor under Vic's feet blurred as he walked down the now-familiar hallway. As he passed a vending machine, he saw a bag of barbecue-flavored chips. His mother liked barbecue. She said they reminded her of summer. Vic fumbled with a wrinkled dollar that the machine rejected several times. His blood pressure skyrocketed. All he wanted was the silly bag of chips, and a thin pane of glass separated them from him. He curled his hand into a fist and put it straight through the glass, took the chips, and returned to Room 127. He placed the bag of chips carefully on his mother's lap. Blood rushed from his wrist.

A nurse who saw the event ran into the room.

"Sir, sir? Okay, we're going to have to look at that. Hold still, please, sir."

The words warbled in his ears. The nurse grabbed his willing hand and called for a doctor. Someone came in with a sterile sheet and tools. Vic looked at the purple and blue squiggly patterns on the hospital floor. He didn't respond to the prick of the needle that someone told him would numb the area, nor to the tugging on the skin on his wrist as the needle went back and forth. His mother had screamed only once when she looked at him, but other than that she hadn't made a sound. When the doctor finished repairing his wrist, with six stitches and a bandage, Vic swallowed a pill in a small paper cup. He picked up the chips that had fallen to the ground, sat in the other available chair, and ate them one at a time, succumbing to the artificially relaxed state.

~

Vic and Isabella had received a call from Papaji just as they were about to walk to school earlier that morning. The two of them had run to the station while their mother called the police.

Vic had pushed on the glass door, which opened easily enough. He'd made note of the sign. Time had moved strangely: He saw Papaji sitting behind the counter, desperately holding onto someone. Then he saw a man that looked like his father, except that he didn't wear a turban, and his head was caked with blood, his face badly bruised. Blood pooled on the floor around the side of his head, and his turban had unraveled across the floor. His suit, which had been nicely pressed only an hour ago, was crumpled.

Isabella cried and took his turban to him.

Get off him! His neck could be broken! Vic pulled his sister and Papaji carefully away. *Call 9-1-1.*

Isabella held the turban to her chest and cried. Her fingers had pressed into the puddle of blood. Vic picked up the receiver and dialed the number himself.

Hello? Um, my dad's not moving. There's blood on his face and the floor.

The voice on the other end of the phone said, *Sir, my name is Sue. What's your name*?

Vic.

Where are you?

Vic gave the address.

Is he breathing?

Vic put down the phone and went to his father. His body was warm, but he couldn't see his chest move. He leaned close to the floor and listened. He felt warm air.

He picked up the phone again. *Yes, I think he's breathing.*

Okay. I'm sending an ambulance right now. Vic, it's important that you don't move him, okay? Not until the EMTs stabilize his neck, okay?

Okay.

Vic, are you alone?

He stared at Isabella, who was hyperventilating, and Papaji, who was staring intently at Paul. *No, my sister and grandfather are here.*

Okay, Vic, are you safe where you are?

Yes, um, I think. What do I do? What should I do?

You did the right thing calling, Vic. It's important now to stay calm and wait for the ambulance. They should be there in five minutes. It's important that you stay on the phone with me until they arrive, okay, Vic?

Okay.

Vic looked at the floor, and when he saw his father's knife, he took it and stowed it under the counter. By the time the EMTs and police arrived, Isabella had run out of tears. Vic had met them near the gas pumps and tried his best to stay out of their way. He'd helped his sister and Papaji into the back of the ambulance before he entered. He held Isabella's hand the whole way and kept his gaze set firmly on his father, whose eyes were closed. In his lap he held his turban.

Isabella

After two days of seeing her mother suspended in time and space like a leaf petrified in amber, Isabella forced her to take a break from the hospital and go home to shower. For motivation, she told her she smelled.

"Like those towels that sit on the bottom of the bathroom floor molding away. It can't be good for Papa either. He's in a coma, but he can still smell and hear what's going on around him."

That got her home for an afternoon, at least, though Isabella hoped she would fall asleep and wake the following day. Adelaide, always the helpful friend, drove Isabella to and from the hospital on the successful retrieval mission.

Isabella felt like an orphan. The attacker had taken both her parents the day he walked into the Kwicki Fill. Her father's hospitalization and her mother's immobilizing distress left Isabella to question her role in their family. She'd defined so much of who she was against her mom, dad, and brother. Vic, as the eldest child, was supposed to be strong, sharp, and in control. Isabella, however, didn't have a clue what was expected of her, or what she could do to help. On TV when a tragedy struck a family, the characters separated into binary camps: those consumed by sadness and those who rose above their personal feelings to save the day. She wasn't a hero *or* a black hole of suffering. What was left for her?

The police had contacted them at home a few times for information they'd forgotten to record at the scene. They asked if Isabella or Vic had noticed any cars parked at the station when they'd arrived, or whether they could think of anyone their father had recently pissed off. The police didn't have any leads, but Papaji and Oma were working hard on the case. They wouldn't leave these things up to the authorities.

While her mother was napping, the four remaining members of the Singh/Mazur brood came together over tea and *piragis*. When Isabella sat down on the couch, she noticed that both her grandparents had lost about ten years. Oma's white fuzzies, as she referred to them, were curled tightly to her scalp, and her lips wore red lipstick. Papaji's long white beard was rolled neatly under his jawline; Isabella could see her father in his jaw. Because of her father's attack, routines such as grooming had gone out the window for the entire family—but her grandparents' fresh look meant business. They'd even brought notepads.

"Okay, zoh, there are some things that everyone should know. No secrets now, okay? It's important to flush them out into za open."

Isabella wondered to which secrets her grandmother was referring.

Papaji cleared his throat and said, "I've made an appointment with Mrs. Mooney, the woman we were on our way to meet. We think that's the best place to start. I have put together some of his notes along with a copy of test results Paul had kept in his top drawer in the garage. Maybe this lady knows what they mean."

"That's good you didn't give them to the police. I could take a look, you know." Vic was eager to be involved.

"Just leave it to us, neh? We don't know who did this, but we know they are willing to—" Oma paused when she looked at Isabella. "But you can help mit other things, Vic."

"Like what?"

Papaji said, "To begin, you are the man of the house temporarily. So it's important that you do the things that your father did for you before. That's how it is done in the Singh family."

"But I don't know—"

"You are doing just fine."

"What about me?" Isabella wanted to be a part of the family's restructuring. "I can do some stuff, too."

"Yes, Izjah, we need you to do za most important part of our investigation." Oma took a small sip of her tea. "You will keep up za appearance that we aren't looking into Paul's attack ourselves. You need to continue back to school and to rehearsal. This way, whoever's watching us now relaxes back into their normal routine."

"So," she said with a sigh, "you just want me to stay out of the way."

"No, you are much more important than that. *Potrí*, you are our representative to Cobalt."

"Whatever." Isabella didn't buy it. She felt as if they were talking to her like a child again.

"Iz, I get it. You see, when you go back to school, everyone will be asking you what happened. Think of your job as the PR person or something."

Isabella knew her position yielded the least power. "You're not coming?"

"I'll go back tomorrow."

She shrugged, went to her room, and shut the door quietly behind her. She listened to their voices whispering plans and ideas she knew they didn't think she could handle because she was too young, or too weak.

"It's not fair," she said aloud, hoping they would hear her. Isabella jumped into her bed face first and let the events of the recent past press her into the pillow. She missed her father. It was an awful thought, but it was a spot of light on a very dark cloud that she had been able to stay at home from school because of what happened. The kids at school would feel sorry for her. Tewks—well, she hadn't figured out what to do about him. Their awkward exchange had frightened her, until she realized he was all bluster and no punch. He was not threatening even when he was making threats. She knew the show would continue, and Tewks would probably pretend she had always been his favorite.

But now there was Erik, the real bright spot in her life; they had enjoyed a milkshake at the Burger Depot together. He called daily now to see how she was doing. He even offered to do all of her homework and anything else that would make her life easier. Isabella felt guilty for experiencing a blossoming in her heart when it was simultaneously breaking.

The door opened, and Oma's scent preceded her body into the bedroom. Isabella stayed motionless, with her face planted in her pillow. When Oma sat down on her bed, it creaked but still Isabella didn't stir. She felt Oma's hand on her back.

"Darlink, I know this is hard on you, especially you."

"I'm not weak." Her words were muted by the down surrounding her cheeks.

"No, no, you are a strong young woman. That's why it is difficult, you see."

Isabella turned to face her grandmother.

"It's because you are so strong, and there is not much we can do, that you are frustrated, neh? But Izjah, Rome vas not in one day built. We all have lots of work ahead of us, and it depends on our willingness to stick together that we will come out of this. Okay?"

Isabella smiled. "Yes, okay."

"Good. Good. We will stick together now. We will pray for Papa, neh?" Oma rose from the bed and retrieved a small book from her bedside table. She pulled the red silk ribbon that opened to a page, sat down on her own bed, and read.

"Oma?" Isabella sat up in bed.

"Mmm?"

"Are you—I mean, do you believe in God?"

Oma smiled. "Of course, darlink."

"Why?"

She put her book on her lap. "I have seen too many things that have cleared mine doubt."

"But do you think there's just one god for people of all religions?"

Oma looked at Isabella, puzzled. "I don't understand what you mean."

Isabella took a deep breath. "Does it matter if someone's Jewish or Christian or Sikh? Aren't they all praying to the same god?"

Oma shifted back and forth on her bed. She shook her head. "Jews and Christians and Sikhs are different, Izjah. They all believe different things."

"Do you think a person can change their belief, convert to something different?"

Oma straightened her sweater. Isabella knew she was making her grandmother uncomfortable, but she had to push now. The present circumstances changed what was appropriate and what was taboo. Oma appeared to experience a series of different emotions, from anger to frustration; then finally the furrow in her brow dissipated, and she arrived somewhere near peace. "Mine mother was Jewish. I am…"

Isabella smiled encouragingly.

"She died because of it. The SS took her and my father, and they killed them both. I still have her necklace, but that's all I have of her. They took my husband, too, your Opa. You never met him, but he vas a wonderful man, yes."

Isabella sat beside Oma and held her hand. She couldn't think of anything to say, so she listened.

"Za soldiers took him. I thought he'd been killed until his letter came. We were living in East Prussia, just left Latvia for za very last time. They drafted him against his will. We were always just one step from—he didn't want to fight for za Germans. But you did what you had to do, to stay alive." Oma had tears in her eyes. "We found each other after za war. Za Red Cross found me, brought him there after a year, neh? His foot vas split in two from shrapnel. We started from scratch—lived on a very small farm and worked for our meals." She smiled.

"Oh." Isabella pressed Oma's hand between hers.

"There are miracles, you know."

Isabella nodded.

"Darlink, be prepared. This will not be easy."

"Mom's acting like he's already dead."

"Shhh. I will talk mit her. You be strong for your Papa tomorrow, okay?"

Oma kissed Isabella's forehead, and the scent of rosewater escorted her to a safe place.

Oma

Oma found Maija's bed empty. The quilt was undisturbed, as it had been for days. She found her sleeping in the closet on a pile of Paul's shoes. Maija had wrapped herself in Paul's flannel robe and put a winter hat on her head.

"Darlink, get up." Oma's voice was clear, but Maija did not stir. "This is embarrassing." Oma bent over, bracing her back with her free hand, and tugged at her daughter's arm. "Please, *mieta*."

Maija rose like a ghost.

"Come, we will talk."

Oma led her to sit down on the bed.

"I know how this is awful. I do. What are you blaming yourself for? You didn't know this would happen, right?"

"No, of course not." Maija's voice was hoarse.

"Well, what are you doing, acting like all hope is lost? Forget yourself. Think of za children."

"He hasn't moved at all. And here I was just focused on these stupid visions."

"And now you're just focusing on yourself. Again! Zoh selfish, neh?"

"I could have done something to see this coming. Here I was watching Eleanora, not my family—"

Oma slapped Maija lightly across her round cheek, which turned her pale complexion flesh-colored again. Then she took off the winter hat, releasing Maija's disheveled curls, and pressed her face between both her hands.

"You need to snap out of this self-pity. There's no other option." She squeezed and spoke in Latvian. "We are all in this together. Now get showered and dressed and be the mother that your children need right now."

Hearing her mother tongue seemed to force Maija to reenter her body. She looked into her mother's piercing eyes and responded, "I don't know where I've been."

"Okay," Oma said.

"Ma." Maija tried to run her hand through her matted hair. "I thought that I was supposed to take care of *you*. I had a feeling your eyes were really going south. But you're here for me, us, I mean."

"Yes, I am here, darlink."

Downstairs, Oma found Harry watching television and organizing his notes. She sat beside him on the love seat. A newscaster was announcing the birth of a new sinkhole that had presented itself along the old factory road in the next town. The man stated that the hole was large enough to swallow a Volkswagen Beetle. When the camera cut to Harry's bona-fide weather goddess, Tanya, he began to pay closer attention. She stood outside in the rain on the weather deck with her guest and friend, Professor March. In their Channel 9 yellow raingear and Wellingtons, they stood in a puddle up to their shins and discussed the buoyancy of Noah's Ark. A small wooden model of the Ark—possibly made of toothpicks or cork or plywood; Oma couldn't tell—bobbed in the puddle.

Professor March cleared his throat and said, "This is a replica of the Ark. As you can see, it floats quite well here. So it is very probable that it made it through a storm quite like this one."

"I think we owe it to our viewers to observe this replica over time to see if it really withstands this storm. It doesn't look like the rain is going to be letting up anytime soon. In fact, another storm system is coming our way. Whaddya say, Professor?"

Shortly thereafter, the newest graphic appeared on the channel: a small picture window focused on the smallest Ark in the world, navigating its way through the puddle.

"What do you think, Harry? You want to bet me?"

"I am no gambler." He smiled. "Sure, okay, five rupees."

"Five rupees then. I think it will fall over."

"I know it will stay afloat."

They shook hands. Harry was still basking in the glow of his television darling.

Maija passed through the living room into the kitchen. "Coffee," she said, and poured beans into the grinder. As the high-pitched coffee grinder wailed, Oma watched the news continue with a daily run down of not-so-interesting events: the pre-holiday parade in the mall, the opening of a new ice cream store on First Street, and a man in an orange jumpsuit and shackles being marched into an armored vehicle. Harry also watched with interest.

The television reporter said, "Mr. Bozeman was convicted today of being the leader of a child pornography ring." The camera cut to a mug shot of Bozeman, his hair receding from his bloated, pale face. "The D.A. said there was enough evidence to put him away for three lifetimes, but that they would settle for one without parole. Bozeman's neighbors reported they had no idea such a monster lived next door. A terrifying story with a proper ending, I'd say. Back to you, Tanya."

Later, on the way downtown, Oma sat in the back seat and glimpsed her daughter's face in the rearview mirror. She saw that she'd joined the land of the living: Maija was clean, and she'd covered up the dark circles under her beautiful stormy eyes. She was in mourning; the pain was all too clear. It was understandable. This was the first trial they'd experienced as a family.

Maija pulled in near the front of the building and put the car in park. "Ma, Papaji, I don't think I'm up to this. I just need to get to the hospital. Then the pharmacy needs me this afternoon; I've used up all my sick days, and if we want to keep our health insurance—"

"Don't worry, darlink. We will take za bus home later. There's no telling how long za meeting might take."

Harry offered his arm to Oma, and together they walked up the stairs and entered the building. The woman she assumed was the secretary looked underfed and in desperate need of sunlight. There wasn't a visitor chair or even a dusty fake ficus. The only furniture that surrounded the thin woman was a desk, a phone, and an old computer.

"Can I help you?"

"We're here to meet mit Mrs. Mooney."

"Yes, she's right over there." The next office was more of the same, except it smelled like a cinnamon candle and had even less light.

"I am glad you both came, Mr. Singh, Mrs. Mazur. Please sit." Mrs. Mooney was as big as a young water buffalo. When she sat in the wood chair, Oma felt miniscule. "Can I get you some coffee or tea?"

"No, thank you." Oma thought of all the times poisons had been used to do away with a person in her home country.

"All right, well, first I have to tell you how sorry I am to hear about Paul. His accident was unfortunate."

"It was no accident, Mrs. Mooney," Harry said.

"My apologies. I meant attack. And please call me Donna."

"That's why we're here, Donna."

"I'm listening."

"Tell us about za meeting you scheduled with Paul. We know he was on his way here when it happened." Oma looked pleadingly at Mrs. Mooney.

"He first contacted me through a colleague. Bernice said he wanted to speak to someone who handled the construction on Main Street. I don't specifically handle it; I am on the board for city improvements and such. I agreed to meet with him."

"About za hole."

"Yes, there is still some debate over whether that hole was manmade or a sinkhole. We are investigating other alleged sinkhole possibilities in the area. With all this rain, anything is possible. There haven't been many sinkholes upstate—but plenty just miles away in Pennsylvania, so it's possible. Sinkholes happen when an imbalance occurs under the ground—either through construction, a change in the water table, or an external source."

"We've had all of the above."

"Exactly. The rain has reached record amounts, and then there is the construction in the Heights. A sinkhole was quite a possibility."

Oma rolled her eyes.

"He also said something about results, like water testing results. He sent a sample of the groundwater near the station to a private company, and he said he wanted to show it to me. I never got a chance to see it, so..." She reclined smugly in her office chair.

Harry pulled an envelope from his jacket pocket. "Here is a copy of the results. I would appreciate it if you would study them and have your science people also take a look and let us know what they mean. For Paul."

Mrs. Mooney took the envelope and opened it. She looked over the sheet. "We don't have a science person. But I can ask around, see what I can find."

"I would love for you to come to our home for dinner sometime. Perhaps the day after tomorrow? Mini here is an excellent cook."

"Mr. Singh, I don't know if that would be appropriate."

"Tea then, perhaps after you speak mit your colleague who can interpret za test?" Oma asked. "We could chat about it over tea?"

"Tea, okay. That should be fine."

"Good." Oma took one of Donna's business cards. "I'll call tomorrow just to see if you've found anything. And here's our number." She wrote it down for her on a scrap of paper.

ON THE WING

**"Water, water every where,
Nor any drop to drink."
—Coleridge**

Posted on October 30

A single droplet of water makes little sound. A cloudburst, however, makes a symphony. As I watch the rain falling from the Maple Street Bridge, I bask in the concert building around me. I stand under the cover of a large walnut tree and feel at once safe and terrified that it might collapse under the storm. From this location, I can see the creek below, a tributary to the Coquina. It churns like a vengeful river god. The flotsam and jetsam collect on the bloated banks: severed branches, aluminum cans, and plastic bags. As I watch these pieces cling to the bank, I can't help thinking that these seemingly insignificant objects of modernity will define us. Is this the Plastic Age?

Where do butterflies go when it rains? Their delicate wings, constructed of veins and scales, can't withstand the penetrating raindrop as it propels downward. Their wings can't fly waterlogged. They are in hiding under leaves, branches, shrubs, and bushes. I wonder where other living things like raccoons, beavers, and skunks are hiding. Are they clinging to grasses and trees? Have they washed away? Or did they already evacuate on their own ark? It is afternoon but already getting dark. The wind is blustering, whispering worrisome things in my ear. The darkness creeps in now, and I feel that this storm will never end.

The rain falls in sheets, and sometimes it comes at me sideways, drenching my legs. If you watch closely, the millions of droplets make divots in the creek's surface, even as it rushes past. The last light of the day highlights the falling water, giving it a milky sheen, somehow hopeful and blinding.

This rain has made the whole town of Cobalt sad. So many people mope about, disconnected and disinterested, as though the clouds shield them from the excitement. I wonder why the rain induces sadness. Are we solar powered? Perhaps it is due to a remnant from our evolutionary past and not being able to hunt or frolic about during a downpour. Perhaps we are inherently sad creatures, sensitive and partial to the opposite of what we have. I am not certain.

When I close my eyes, I hear a choir building. The leaves shake as the water droplets ricochet against everything like a mad weapon. It roars like an animal closing in on its prey. I take a step out from under the cover of the tree and open my arms wide to the rain, letting it take me as its own. There is something liberating about giving in completely.

After everything we make—the houses, roads, and walls we build—she still manages us. We can build a tall fence, but the rain still falls. We can roll up our windows and brace ourselves, but the roads are still slick. The world we've created, full of creature comforts, warmth, light, and food, is never as strong as her. That's a fact. There are things we can control and things that were never in our hands in the first place. It's hardest to define that line. To make it clear and come to terms with it.

1 COMMENT

True. I wonder, though, if we can work together? Maybe instead of working against Mother Nature? —BF Girl NY

Isabella

The tops of her sneakers were a creamy red, and the laces were white. Red sneakers didn't match many things, so Isabella decided they matched everything. It was a perfectly logical leap in her mind. Dresses, skirts, jeans, shorts—every outfit in her closet had been paired with these sneakers. After a while her mother had stopped making snide remarks and, Isabella hoped, also saw how they matched everything. They were a type of security blanket. And her first day returning to school after her father's attack wouldn't have been possible without them on her feet.

She kept her eyes focused on the way the laces crossed over and under and through the eyelet holes, and how her jean cuffs fell perfectly to the floor so only the tips of her shoes peeked out shyly. The halls of Cobalt high were segues through a hellish dimension, and if Isabella kept her attention on her feet, she would be able to avoid the piercing glares, ignore the rumor-mongering students, and make it to first period unscathed. Of course, the masses wouldn't allow her to pass so easily because she was marked as different.

"Hey, hey, you're Isabella, right? The girl whose dad was attacked?"

Isabella kept walking, but the body attached to the voice stepped in front of her like a wall of persistence. Regardless of how much she wanted to continue to class, Isabella stopped.

"Yeah, that's me," she said, hoping her response would be enough for her to pass.

"Do you think it was racial?"

The girl, Joslyn, was a writer for the school newspaper. She wore, from head to toe, an unflattering shade of brown that matched her long braids.

"What do you mean?"

"There are rumors that someone did it because they thought your dad was an Arab, not that Arabs should be attacked either, but Sikhs had nothing to do with 9/11, you know?"

"Haven't heard anything like that."

"Who do you think did it?"

"Who do *you* think did it?" She returned the question with ferocity.

"I think it's either a race crime or a crackhead. Except nothing was stolen, right? So, unless the crackhead was violent, it wouldn't make sense. They said the attacker's weapon was a blunt object, like a large glass bottle or a baseball bat, right?"

"I have to get to class."

"You gotta give me a statement for the paper. It's your responsibility." Joslyn had a large gap between her two front teeth that Isabella wanted to widen with her fist.

Katie, the redhead on the yearbook committee, stepped in front of Joslyn and pulled Isabella to safety. "Um, actually, Izzy promised to give me a statement first. She'll get to you later."

Katie led Isabella down the hall and blocked anyone who made a move toward them. Tewks passed by and waved enthusiastically. People she didn't even know gave Isabella a nod of recognition or sympathy. It was strange being famous for a tragedy. She wanted to be invisible, and for the first time in her life she longed for the dull walls of her history classroom.

"Thanks," she said to Katie.

"Yeah, no problem. Joss thinks she's already a professional journalist. It's hilarious."

"Did you want to ask me questions?"

"Nah—but I did want to see your brother. Is he around?"

"Somewhere."

"Can you tell him his photo won for the inside cover for this year's yearbook? He won a coupon and stuff." When Katie smiled, her freckled cheeks blushed. She showed Isabella the photo, a close-up of a blue butterfly set against the gray-brown bark of a tree.

Isabella hadn't known he'd entered a photo in the contest. "Cool, I'll tell him."

"And, um, you can ask him to e-mail me for the coupon."

"Sure. And thanks, Katie."

"Anytime."

As Isabella slid into her desk, she was happy to hear the bell ring and the teacher, Mrs. Saint Pharr, begin the quiet history lesson about the Civil War.

Maija

After the nurse checked Paul's vitals and left the room, Maija took off her shoes and curled up as best as she could beside her husband. His hospital bed was meant for only one body, but she turned on her side. As she stroked his cheek, she whispered into his ear all the things she thought he'd want to know.

"Izzy didn't want to go back to the play, but that's what you would've wanted. Vic is taking care of everyone; you'd be so proud. Your father and my mother are like a couple now. I am not okay. I can't lie. I need you to come back. Please come back. You've been gone for five days, Paul. It's not okay. You can't leave me alone."

She looked at her husband closely and searched for a muscle twitch or flutter of an eyelid that would signal his comprehension. His long eyelashes were closed; his breathing was steady; his hands lay at his sides as they had for days. She waited for her miracle, but it didn't come. She felt like a child foolishly waiting for a falling star, but she couldn't turn away because as soon as she did, a comet might fly past. Maija wondered what it was like to be in a coma. Did he dream? Could he hear her? Was he trapped and voiceless? She pressed her hands to his chest and closed her eyes.

Nothing.

"We are working hard on finding who did this to you. Oma and

Papaji have a plan, which means nothing will get it their way." Maija sat up and stroked her husband's forehead. She turned on the television and watched the news. The rains would be bad tonight, they said. Stay off the roads. When visiting hours were over, Maija went to the parking lot, ran to the car, and jumped in, soaking wet from the downpour.

The Cutlass handled the rain fine, but it felt like driving a boat, with its bald tires and huge frame. It was quite dark, and the streetlights only made it harder to see because the rain caught the light and ruined visibility. Maija's hands gripped the wheel as she drove. The Main Street sidewalk had washed out and was completely submerged. Somehow, in the darkness, Maija turned too early onto Maple and found herself on the long way home. The wind picked up, and the rain pelted her windshield as though determined to break through. Before she came to the Maple Street Bridge, which was a small creek overhang, she saw flashing lights and heard sirens. She braked, but the car skidded and fishtailed across the road before finally stopping mere inches from the police car.

A cop waved to her, and she rolled down her window. "Ma'am, you're gonna have to turn around, carefully. The bridge washed out. Sinkhole opened, we think. It took a huge part of the road with it."

Just then, another car came behind Maija, its headlights glaring. She covered her eyes against the light and then felt the jolt, which sent her body forward until the seatbelt abruptly stopped the forward trajectory. When the car stopped moving, she undid her seatbelt and got out, unhurt but shaking.

"You okay?" The other driver rolled his window down. "I'm so sorry."

"Please, get back into your car. It isn't safe here," the police officer yelled. Maija ducked past the cars, lights, and flares and jogged between the pylons. She looked down into the bloated creek.

Though it was dark, the flashing lights illuminated the crevasse and what was left of the bridge. She leaned in and saw a bumper of a car in the hole, sliding toward the dark water.

"Ma'am. Get out of there."

"Sorry. I just wanted to see."

"It could have been worse. No one inside the car. Just parked."

Maija doubled back to the hospital and drove a different route home. She was relieved when she made it home safely. But as she walked to bed, the ground beneath her feet felt unstable.

Vic

His father's knife was heavy, cold, and well worn, like a rock tumbled against a creek floor. Vic let his eyes wander across the handle, where elephants danced tail to tail. But the longer he looked, the more impossible it seemed that the image carved into the handle was actually a pachyderm. The married couple riding the elephant looked more like tufts of hair or humps. The elephants looked boxy, as though the metal worker's tool hadn't been sharp enough to create a precise picture. Had they really been elephants at one time in this knife's existence, and after too many hands touched it, they'd become squares with squiggly tails? Could he have simply thought they were elephants when he was young? He had a stuffed elephant toy someone had brought from India. It was decorated in beads and mirrors and smelled of mothballs. Maybe that's why he thought they were elephants. Maybe they never really were. Memories were so easily distorted.

He flicked open the blade and ran his finger softly down the edge. He accidentally drew blood. It was strange how sharp it still was. He'd seen his father sharpen it many times; Vic's earliest memories of his father sliding the blade against the leather strap or the knife sharpener occurred when he was too young to see above doorknobs or onto countertops. He closed the blade and put it back into the pocket of his cargo pants.

It was raining lightly, and Vic wore his camouflage rain slicker with the hood drawn tightly around his face. He was behind a wide hemlock about fifty feet from the entrance of the mineshaft. Vic looked through the binoculars at the cluster of birch that marked the entrance. The familiar tree trunks were now scarred with symbols and markings he couldn't make out from the distance. Why couldn't they have left the trees alone?

Vic saw that the hatch was clear and decided that he had to go now if he was ever going to find his shadow box. He felt it was still in the mine. He descended into the hole, and when he reached the bottom, he knew it was no longer his space in any sense. Vandals had spray painted the walls with graffiti; empty bottles of Krylon littered the ground. Vic ran his hands across the primordial doodles of stick men and profanities. One of them obviously had a thing for the word *shit* because there were at least twenty versions of this word written in various fonts: Old English, cursive, block, and even letters engulfed in flames. The cavemen stick figures were more imaginative. Thankfully these idiots wouldn't be representing the twenty-first century thousands of years from now. There's no way this mine would last that long.

Vic made his way through the dimly lit space and came upon a pile of garbage. Empty beer bottles, cans, magazines, and the remnants of his effects were piled carelessly in a corner. His heart sank when he saw the edge of his shadow box poking out from beneath a burned *Batman* comic book. He retrieved it, and, though the glass had red paintball splotches covering it, he was satisfied that the butterflies were still inside. And now that he had the box, he could take it and leave the mine.

Yet he didn't want to leave. Remembering the maps in his father's office, he realized he wanted to go a little further, to see what was behind that wall. He moved faster than he'd ever moved underground. He was confident and surefooted, and when he came to the water that he'd slipped in earlier, he walked across it without acknowledging the cold. He ran his hand across the wall and realized it was quite corroded. He pushed on it, and a few bricks fell in. He pushed it again and a part of the wall collapsed completely.

He swung the lantern into the hole. The air was stale, and he held his nose. There was a lot of water inside, as much as he was standing in, and lined up against the wall he saw an army of rusted black metal drums. The drums were corroding, and one had tipped to its side. They each had the unmistakable skull and crossbones right in plain sight. Now he knew there was something hidden below. He had no desire to get closer to the drums and moved back toward the exit.

About to leave the mine, shadow box in hand, he saw a clumsy silhouette descending the ladder. Vic hid behind the curve in the wall and watched. It was Joe.

Vic watched Joe jump off the last wrung, take a can of spray paint from his jacket pocket, and start on the only wall that hadn't been touched by his grime yet. Vic made out the words *Die Mother* and he assumed the next word that would complete the phrase. The sight of this made him angry. Something just snapped.

He went to Joe and, with the precision and viciousness of a predator, said, "Put the can down. Now."

Joe jumped back and looked at the can, as though considering what he should do with it. Then he turned to Vic and said, "You're on my turf."

"This isn't yours," Vic said.

"If I say it is, it is. Got it, loser? Get out of here before I break something else."

Vic knew that diplomacy wouldn't solve a thing. So, without pause, he curled his fist and slammed it into Joe's jaw as hard as he could. This made him drop the spray-paint can, and Joe let out a sound somewhere between a squeal and a yelp. Vic went in for another punch and made contact with Joe's nose.

"Leave."

Joe grabbed the ladder and climbed out quickly. Without his backup, Joe was just a bit of thunder without the lightning. Vic rubbed his hand, already sore from the punches. Retribution was his, but he didn't feel good for the blood that spilled.

Later that evening, before leaving to visit his father in the hospital, Vic went into the backyard with a small garden trowel. He dug a shallow grave under the oak, revealing rich black soil. The butterflies were like brittle dried flowers with antennae and legs. His hand trembled as he placed them in their grave. Their secrets died with them. He wanted to say a few words, as a close friend would say at a funeral, but he couldn't think of anything profound enough while he covered them with soil.

"Sorry," was all he could muster.

Their existence and deaths would remain a puzzle. Whether their names were Karner, Melissa, or even Xerces was irrelevant. Vic didn't want to jail them in a box. It was obvious now that these invertebrates did not belong here, and their presence was most likely the fault of his species. He decided to keep his blog going as long as he could as a way to connect with others with similar interests. One day, he hoped to visit the Presidio in San Francisco and see the Xerces habitat that had been destroyed.

Paul

Paul was trapped between a dream and his immovable body, and he wanted desperately to be either awake or unconscious. The coma held him hostage. His dreams and memories governed his mind. Over and over they played, never finishing, until finally, one time, the entire memory played clear through from beginning to end, and he began to understand the meaning.

It was a dusty day. Kamal, though he limped, was fast; Paul tried to stay close, but the high grasses closed behind his brother's back as he passed and made an impenetrable wall for eyes. His limp, a gift of the snakebite years earlier, gave him special powers. That's what the elders said. That's what Kamal told everyone. His dance with poison gave him immunity to other, less natural dangers.

The shotgun bounced against Kamal's broad shoulder as they led two bullocks to the last quarter of their land. The wooden plow had seen better days but still managed to cut the earth deep enough to sow seeds for the fall. Their family had one and a half hectares, which produced enough food to feed the Singh family and store some for the following year, but nothing more. There had been a drought in the village for the past few seasons, making the farmers anxious for the small harvest and even smaller meals. This, coupled with the pressure on Kamal and Paul to do all of the tasks Papaji used to do before his foot injury made it painful to walk, left the two brothers' friendship strained.

Here. Kamal handed Paul the shotgun. *You carry it.*

But Papaji never—

Time to learn. Can't rely on others to help you forever.

Paul lifted the heavy gun onto his shoulder and smiled to himself. They cut across the fields; the fall air was crisp and better to work in. Kamal led the huge bullocks to the rows they were going to sow. October was cool, the best month to sow the durum wheat. Kamal signaled to Paul to help him knot the harness on the bullocks so the plow would force a straight path that they would follow with seeds. Kamal lifted the harness and went in front of the bullocks to make certain they were secure.

Bhâí, *tie the double knot so they can't come loose,* Kamal yelled to his little brother. The shotgun was unwieldy. Paul shifted it to his other shoulder, and as he did so he lifted the rope, and the shotgun discharged.

He'd held it by the trigger. There'd been too many things in his hands. He'd felt rushed. The blast spooked the one-ton bullocks, and they ran in the direction they'd been aimed.

They trampled Kamal.

Paul's hand got caught in the rope, and he was pulled behind the beasts as they ran a frantic course.

Paul could not open his eyes; he felt his mother's hands carefully wipe his face with a damp cloth. She dressed him in white cotton *kaccha*, slid his *kara* back on his wrist, combed his hair with the *kangha* and wrapped a turban around his long hair.

It must be a miracle, he heard her say. *God has taken mercy on me today.*

Paul drifted back away. The next time he opened his eyes, he could hear the *bháíjis* playing their harmonium and tabla around the *Granth Sahib* while the readers took turns with the prayer. Then they all began to sing *Ardas,* and he knew what had happened.

All alone in the *haveli* he stood from his cot, wearing the clean white clothes meant for the recently deceased, and walked toward the voices like a phantom. Villagers stood in mournful angles around the dry funeral pyre and body. The holy men sang loudest with Papaji and Bebbeji. Paul stared at his brother's body.

His mother had prepared her dead son's body like she had his own. Paul learned later that Kamal's back had been broken like a stick, his body crushed.

An auntie pulled him to the front of the gathering and wiped his face—told him it was improper to cry. *The guru says, everyone wishes for a long life, and yet no one wishes to die. Shh, shh*, bachchá.

When the song was done, Papaji said a few words about his son's work ethic and strong heart. The words were sufficient. The dead needed help in their passing, the living needed help with the new absence. Papaji brought the oil lamp from inside the house and held it out to Paul.

You are now the oldest, the only. You must light the fire.

Paul stared blankly at the flame. He was too young to take the place of eldest. His head throbbed a silent blinding rhythm. Papaji took his son's hand and pulled it toward the flame. He couldn't light his brother on fire. It wasn't in him to do so, even if ceremony expected this of him. He held the lamp in his hand, balanced it between his forefinger and thumb, and bent close to his brother's face. It was foreign, stone, strangely cold and yellow. The beating Kamal had taken distorted all elements that were supposed to be his: His face was swollen and sunken at the same time, his body bent toward the left.

This is not my brother, Papaji. Where is Kamal?

He is gone, puttar. *My son is gone. It's not him anymore. Light the flame.*

Paul bent toward his brother's chest and listened for a heartbeat, but instead of a thump, his ear was greeted by questions. If the body was not his brother's, then where had he gone? An auntie prayed aloud, asking that Kamal be reincarnated into someone with faith. Perhaps his life would then be better the next time around. A claustrophobic weight pressed against Paul's heart. When he tipped the oil on the branches, he released the tears that the elders told him were inappropriate. If not now, when was it best to cry? he wondered.

The flames took time to catch, but when they did, everyone stepped back except for Paul, who watched his brother slowly burn to the ground. It took hours before he was no more than a skeleton in the cinder. Paul collected the ashes in an urn and poured his brother into the canal. He was eldest now, the only, but he knew he'd never fill his place. There had already been the heavy question of his origins that plagued his every move. He knew that when Papaji had sent his mother ahead, many months had passed before he reunited with her. She'd accepted Papaji's love tensely, and, less than nine months later, Paul was born.

Over time, Paul began to believe the look on his mother's face. She did not see him anymore, only the possibility of losing him. To her, he was vulnerability. It was her expression that Paul walked away from years later when the vacancy in her eyes became a vortex, a void.

He left before he lost himself in his empty reflection.

~

Each time he felt closer to the waking world, the hooks of unconsciousness would sink deep into his lids and pull straight down. It was a wicked battle, but Paul's will was strong. He opened his eyes, just slightly, at eight o'clock that evening. Paul was certain of two things: that he was still alive and that he was thirsty. His family was gathered around, and Isabella was the one who noticed. A half hour later, he smiled at the joyful faces surrounding his bed and moved his pinky finger just so. His return to life was going to be a slow process, but he was thankful to be back.

The doctors told him and Maija that there was no telling what memory he had, what he would regain, and what portions of his personality he might have lost forever. Paul was frightened by the idea of having lost his past, not because he was attached to memories but because he wouldn't know which memories he would have lost and which ones he might need to seek out. The situation was completely out of his control, but he recognized his family members and remembered his address, and the doctor said that was a good beginning.

When they took him home the first time, he wasn't strong enough to walk on his own. The therapeutic adjusting the nurses performed prevented sores from appearing on his body, but his muscles had begun to atrophy regardless. Vic and Papaji lifted him in his wheelchair across the front door stoop. He relaxed in the familiar surroundings, but his family still appeared tense.

"Maija, dear, why don't we make Paul's favorite meal tonight?" Oma looked at Paul for his reaction.

He smiled. "Roast chicken sounds delicious."

Maija and Oma exhaled and got to work.

He thought the eggshells on which his family was walking would drive him insane, but he kept it to himself, as he was thankful to be home. Instead, Paul read the expressions of those around him; he knew their eyes wouldn't be able to hide a thing. The look in Papaji's eyes was heartbreaking. Paul saw him cringe when he glanced at his injured head. The first time he went to the bathroom alone, he saw his reflection in the expansive mirror: Fluorescent light drew shadows under his eyes, they had shaved his head completely, and the massive ridges of staples on the side and top of his head shimmered like a metal mountain range. He was a monster.

They'd taken away his *kesh.* At least he still had his beard. No wonder his father looked defeated. He had been scalped. Paul felt a terrible sinking feeling in his chest and leaned against the counter as he stared into the face of the person who was not him.

At the breakfast table the next morning, the smell of bacon reminded him of something, but the idea was distant and difficult to grasp. The harder he tried to find the memory, the further it slipped away, so he chewed on a piece of toast. His family seemed happy to have him home, but they all were holding onto their tongues.

"What?" Paul asked, but it was more like a statement.

Maija pressed her lips together, and everyone except Vic looked away and mumbled their apologies.

"We want to know the last thing you remember, but we don't want to press you for information," Vic said.

"Oh, is that all? Well, that's easy." He smiled. "See, Papaji and I just got out of the hole on Main Street and someone pulled up to our car. That's when I was hit, right? The car hit me."

Their faces told him otherwise.

"That's not what happened, *puttar.*"

"It's okay, Papa," Isabella said. "This type of memory loss is natural for your injury. It can be temporary. We're just so happy you're home." She smiled.

"What happened? You have to tell me."

Maija cleared her throat. "You were attacked, darling. Someone attacked you in the station the morning you were going to meet with that woman in the city planning office."

"Oh, I see." His voice cracked.

That day, the occupational therapist visited. They worked together on things that he'd learned as a child but had lost somewhere between here and there. Tying his shoes, holding a pencil in his hand, and using a fork to eat were a few of the exercises on which they focused. These tasks came back to him very quickly, and he never had a hard time remembering his family members' names or anything like that. The therapist was confident that he would have a full recovery in time because he learned quickly, though he could not give a specific date.

"Time and hard work—that's what will make you better. I'll be back in a few days," he said as he left.

Later, he was in his bedroom when he heard a knock. "Can I come in?" It was Papaji.

"Yes, of course." Paul put down the photo album on the comforter. "Please, I was just looking."

"You are doing very well. You'll be back in no time." He spoke in Punjabi.

Paul nodded in reply and readjusted his oversized baseball cap. "It's hard to remember everything."

Papaji sat beside him on the bed and stared at his hands. "You were the first to come here all on your own. You are strong, and you have many people around that you can trust."

"I came to America because—"

"Ikpaul, let me tell you a story. Before you were born, I had a friend who was like a brother. He betrayed me, almost killed me. I changed that day. I lost my faith, and it took a long time for me to realize that in truth, my friend had saved my life."

"Papaji—"

"There was so much loss."

"I know, Papaji, your favorite son died and all you had was me." Paul turned away from his father.

"I failed everyone, but you especially. My fear paralyzed me, and Kamal's death was my fault. I should have worked the fields. You were too young."

Paul looked at his father.

"Paul, you are my son."

"But—"

"You are my son."

Papaji leaned closer to Paul and touched his shoulder with his hand.

Maija

Maija woke to raindrops thumping against her bedroom window. She could hear each droplet collide dully with the glass then slide down, as the window was the only obstacle in its path. She could hear the gutters rushing with water and knew that though it was only morning, a tremendous puddle had already formed and would soon burst and flood the tulip and daffodil bulbs that she'd left in the ground the previous year.

She pressed her eyes shut and listened to Paul's soft inhale and rushed exhale. His mouth, she imagined, was closed, and his thick eyelashes, like velvet fingers, were fanned across his high cheeks. His body was an ember against her back. He produced such heat during the night—a gift he attributed to his abundant chest hair—that Maija would only wear light nightgowns through the winter and in the summer she barely wore a stitch. Maija settled against his body and opened her eyes. He's here, she thought. I'm free.

She felt free of the unnecessary burden her sight had inflicted upon her in a series of images, voices, dreams—all of which she was forced by her curiosity and guilt to interpret. Now that Paul was awake from his coma and here in bed, she would not pay attention to silly otherworldly stammering even if it demanded her attention like a child threatening to fall to the ground and unleash a tantrum.

That was the promise she'd made when she'd prayed to the image of a faceless god: For Paul's safe return to consciousness, she would disconnect her cord to the supernatural and unplug her ear from the divine socket for good. She couldn't forget her part of the deal; second chances were a rare gift. She was now living solely in the present without having to worry about the lives of strangers. She was free. She hoped.

There was a knock on the bedroom door, and Vic and Isabella entered. Maija smiled at her children and put her finger to her lips; they were excited to see their father. Viewing Paul in his injured state at the station must have affected the children, but Maija knew they were strong enough. She just hoped that Vic would stay peaceful and Isabella wouldn't turn to drugs or boys to fill the void that fear had opened inside of her. Perhaps she would have to keep an eye on them both to make certain they adjusted. Vic pursed his lips when he saw his father's bare head and the gash-like wounds that he would carry with him the rest of his life.

"Hi, *puttar*." Paul opened his eyes and looked at his children.

Isabella took a seat on the edge of their bed, careful not to shake the mattress. Vic stood in the corner of the room, near the old armoire, with his arms crossed.

"How are you feeling?" Vic asked.

"Like a million bucks. How do I look?"

"Wonderful." Maija put her robe on and sat on the edge of the bed.

"Papa, I need to tell you what I found." Vic looked as if he'd put on weight, and his chest had broadened since she'd looked at him last. Vic held out a map to his father. He'd drawn an orange line through Cobalt.

Paul nodded. There was another knock on the door, and Oma and Papaji entered the bedroom. Papaji walked with only a small limp now. Maija was surprised how fast he'd healed. They both sat on a bench against the wall. Though the bedroom was small, it miraculously held everyone.

"I found an empty mine shaft under the town," Vic said. "The orange line shows how it runs right around PMI, the station, and the school. It covers nearly the whole town. I think it was an old Cobalt mine, or something. Anyway, I found drums inside. They look dangerous. I think they are the key."

"A mine? Please don't tell me you were crawling around down there because if you were—"

Paul cut Maija off. "Does the air down there smell sweet?"

"Yes."

"TCE smells sweet when vaporized. Exposure can cause illnesses from nausea, vomiting, to the worst, cancer." Paul seemed surprised by his own response. "I must have read that somewhere."

"That means toxic chemicals have infiltrated the groundwater," Maija said quietly.

Oma said, "Could this have caused the flu epidemic? Isabella's stomach pain? Oh, God."

"My question is—who owns this land, here?" Paul traced his pointer finger along the area that ran from the station into the forest beyond Main Street.

Maija felt her face go white as her mind turned to the last conversation she'd overheard at the Finch house. She could still hear Eleanora and Herbert's conversation about Tracy.

This is your fault. You couldn't pass up that deal...You're no better than me...Now our daughter has—

"Finch," Maija said. "They did this. They did everything."

"What are you talking about?" Paul sat up higher against the bed.

"I was over there delivering medicine. Tracy is sick. She's dying. It might be cancer." She glanced at Isabella. "I overheard them talking about building here and how they should have known better."

"Michelle," Isabella whispered.

"They put za barrels down there?" Oma asked.

"Well, maybe not, but they bought the land with the knowledge and built the Heights on top of it," Maija said. "That should be illegal."

Paul winced and put his hand to his head.

"Let's let him rest now." Maija shooed everyone out of the room.

On his way out, Papaji placed his hand on Paul's shoulder and said, "This was my fault. I called them. I called PMI and told them I was from the Kwicki Fill."

Paul looked surprised. "It doesn't matter. It could have been anything. I was snooping around. I was so frustrated. At least now we know what is going on." Paul seemed stronger at that moment, as though talking had awakened his spirit.

"You are healing fast," Maija said.

"I am beginning to remember," Paul whispered.

Isabella

There was something about the opening night of a play that seemed to ignite an electrical charge in the air of Cobalt. Though *1,001 Cries* was opening in the afternoon for a matinee, and the incessant rain was still trying desperately to put a damper on the entire village, there was a skin-tingling energy bounding about, and Isabella felt it. The Singh household was bustling in preparation for Isabella's debut.

Isabella slipped her stocking-covered feet into her patent leather shoes as she sat on the edge of her recently made bed. She'd performed this action a thousand times before: left foot into shoe, right foot into shoe, and then slide. Though her dressy shoes weren't as comfortable as her red sneakers, she didn't mind. Today, familiarity and comfort were lesser priorities. The way her mattress bounced when she stood, the storm brewing outside, and even the antique scent of rosewater in the air were all commonplace. Today, however, Isabella felt different, confident, as if all the moments leading up to this particular one finally made sense, and she was ready for all eyes to be on her.

For as long as she could remember, she had preferred the name Isabella to Izzy because Izzy was sharp and, in her mind, would belong to someone who knew how to throw a football and French braid her hair. Since she'd seen her name in its abbreviated form in the play's program, she now thought it sounded elegant, something she never thought she could be. Pretending to be a fictional person allowed her to revaluate her identity. Acting turned her inside out. At first, it had been a game, like charades. But the deeper she went into the character, the more she sorted through her own motivations. To appear sad, she had to recognize what made her heavyhearted in real life. When her character held Erik's hand, she set aside her anxiety and embodied Samantha's confidence. The process of pretending unveiled parts of potential selves beneath her thick hair, glasses, and other invisibility-rendering accoutrements. She felt healthy, too, since she'd stopped drinking water from drinking fountains. The nausea had gone away quickly. And when she slid her feet into her shoes on this day, she filled with a new sensation: courage. Isabella stood tall, puffed up with her new feeling, and went to Oma's wooden box. The necklace was where she'd left it; in its dull gold color, she saw the past.

Maija

The Singh household had changed in subtle ways. Food preparation, for one, was a more involved process because Maija decided they would only eat food grown outside Cobalt and not use the tap water to cook. She wouldn't wait for an official word of warning from the city to tape off her kitchen faucet.

Maija convinced Paul to use his beverage distributor connections to special order two-gallon jugs of Poland Spring water directly from Poland, Maine. The garage, once home to Paul's lair, was now a storage center for gallons of water. Maija was working hard, with a pencil behind her ear and sticky notes stuck to the fridge, computer screen, and car dash. She felt an overwhelming urge to protect her family from poisoned water, nameless attackers, blindness, and, if at all possible, recurrent nausea. Though she was overcompensating for what she considered her personal failures as a mother and wife, her new mantra gave her focus: protect the ones she loved. The water was just the first of many adjustments she made in the household. She added vitamins to everyone's plate at breakfast. To heal her injured stomach and esophageal lining, Isabella received large quantities of raw ginger and holy basil capsules. Maija tested the seatbelts in the car for their durability. She even packed a large emergency box in the trunk filled with a first aid kit, flares, cereal, granola bars, turkey and beef jerky, dog food (she'd heard somewhere that a human could live off kibble for months), and a roll of quarters for potential tolls. Come storm, flat tire, or even car fire, she wanted to be ready. Maija's paranoia grew every second.

"You know, mine dearest, if you put za same energy into feeding za poor, everyone in za world would be fat in a week!" Oma laughed.

Oma was helping Maija draft an emergency checklist mere moments before they were to leave to the theater. It read: "*Fire*: extinguisher under sink. *Blackout*: candles in the garage. *Earthquake*: get under something sturdy and avoid windows. *Hurricane*: tie down porch furniture. *Tornado*: go to the station stock room. *Bioterrorist Attack*: masks, gloves, and hand sanitizer under sink." Maija felt it was overkill, but it was better to be ready than caught ill-equipped. She taped the list to the refrigerator.

Maija's clairvoyance gave her a particular insight into death. She knew now that the lives of those close to her were no different than those of the people who visited her in their spirit form. Evil people weren't the ones who died in burning buildings or tragic accidents. Decent people who thought they'd live at least as long as their spouses died. She'd turned off her psychic ability as best she could, but she could not erase the lessons she'd learned. Maija only wished she could protect her daughter from seeing ghosts. Thankfully her mother had given Maija her pure rosewater cologne; this was one of the only aromas Maija knew of that could keep the spirits at bay.

Vic

Vic was seriously annoyed with his mother. First, she'd demanded that he wear a suit—but he'd managed to finagle his way down to a nice shirt and tie. As he put on his one and only navy-and-white striped tie, he couldn't help but think that he could have pushed for a sweater and slacks; the tie was not a clip-on. He wandered into his parents' bedroom consumed by the difficulty of a Windsor knot.

"Mama? Can you help? I think it's a bad idea I wear this. I mean, it's choking me."

"*Puttar*, you need some help?"

His father was standing before the mirror that was attached to the back of the closet door, straightening his collar on the outside of his sweater. His turban was on his head, hiding his wounds.

"Come here." Paul took Vic's necktie and fumbled with it, at times constricting Vic's esophagus. "I can do this in one second."

"Papa, it's okay. Mama always—"

Paul untied his malformed knot and tried again, with force.

Vic looked at his father's reflection in the mirror. He was here, right here, he thought in disbelief. He felt his father's cold knife in his pocket; he'd meant to give it back to him right when they got home from the hospital, but instead he'd kept it at his side, just as he'd seen his father do for so long. Vic removed it from his pocket and held it in his palm to his father.

"I polished it for you." The knife shone like newly pressed silver in the bedroom light.

Paul let go of the tie and reached slowly for the knife, but then he turned his hand into a fist.

"I have something better for you." Paul went to his drawer and took out a larger, more ornamental dagger.

"Wow, that's a big knife."

"This is the *kirpan* that Papaji gave me," his father said. "And now it's yours. Vic, you're grown up. After I figure out how to tie this tie, I'll teach you how to sharpen it."

"I know how; I've watched you do it."

"See, you already know. Go get your mother for the tie; she's in the bathroom."

When they arrived at the high school, the parking lot was full. The hordes of Cobalt students and their relatives had already taken up most of the asphalt with their Chryslers and minivans. Maija pulled the car into an open handicapped spot near the school. Vic shrugged. Surely they qualified for a placard, with a coma survivor with two healing skull fractures, a blind grandmother, and an elderly man healing from foot surgery.

Vic watched Oma, Isabella, and Papaji scurry toward the theater under the cover of umbrellas. Isabella told her family where to sit so she would know where to look for them in the audience. Maija and Paul shared the last remaining umbrella, while Vic insisted he didn't need the protection from a little water.

With the darkening afternoon light and unending rain, the

structure looked like a watermark, translucently blue against an ever-deepening navy sky. Vic had never been here after the hours required of him. High schools weren't supposed to be populated after classes were out, he thought. The school, usually dominated by rules and watchful eyes, was now just a space being filled by eager audience members.

Vic felt odd in his clothes, like a stevedore stuffed into an older brother's nice clothes. It was the blue-and-white bandana around his hair that gave him a seafaring façade. The gift that his father had given him, so much more than the *kirpan* itself, added to his swagger.

"Hi, Vic."

He turned to see Katie, standing under an umbrella, smiling at him, and he felt his heart leap. "Hey, Katie," he said, trying to sound casual. He stepped toward her.

"I have your coupon. For the photo contest."

Vic had nearly forgotten about the contest. It was strange, he thought, how something like a photo had once seemed so important. "Oh, right. Thanks."

"Your photograph was definitely the best," Katie said. "But then, I have a thing for butterflies."

He remembered the butterfly on her notebook. "Really?"

She nodded, then grinned. "You might even call me Butterfly Girl."

Butterfly Girl—he let the word sift through his brain for a moment. "You're BF Girl? From my blog?"

She nodded again. "It's a great blog, Vic. I hope you plan to keep writing it. Anyway, here's your coupon."

She held out an envelope, and he took it, watching raindrops dampen the envelope. Their fingers touched, briefly.

"E-mail me," she said, then took off toward the theater.

"Pretty girl," he heard his mother murmur, and when he looked at her he caught her smiling her approval.

As they continued along the sidewalk into the school, Vic heard a raspy voice coming from the side of the building. When he turned the corner, he came face to face with Joe Balestrieri and his black eyes. Vic kept walking, leading his family to the high school's entrance. As he was about to collide with Joe, Joe got out of his way.

"You know, bantam weight fighters are even more feared because of their speed." Paul beamed.

Vic understood his father's comment. For a split second, he considered telling him how he'd punched Joe, not once but twice. But he realized he didn't need to. His father was proud of who he was, as he was, completely.

Isabella

The theater was a warm, velvet-lined womb, and Isabella let the room take her in. The scaffolding along the wall and ceiling above the orchestra area was heavy with lights, speakers, and props. Backstage was buzzing with excitement. Stagehands hurried to touch up the set, while actors paced and nervously recited their lines. Isabella peered through a gap in the curtain and watched her father and brother take the aisle seats beside the other family members in the back of the theater. Most seats were full; she was surprised.

The air tingled, and Isabella felt a chill run across her body. She thought of Michelle, and—as the cast gathered among the fake cardboard forest, folding chairs, and holiday props backstage—she silently dedicated her performance to her friend.

Isabella held her wrinkled copy of the script in her sweaty hands and read her lines over and over again. Her brain felt empty. Tewks, who was dressed head to toe in black, with a beret covering his head, took her script away.

"You know it. Just relax." He smiled.

"Break a leg," Tracy snarled. Her skin was pale yellow. Isabella was surprised that Tewks had let Tracy continue in the play, as she'd missed so many rehearsals that he'd shortened her role even more, which meant she was now only in one scene. But it was just like

Tracy not to miss out.

Erik said nothing but squeezed her hand.

"Okay, people. Tonight we do as we've been doing every week in rehearsal. Remember, I'll be onstage just out of sight in case anyone forgets a line. I am so proud of each and every one of you. Everybody knows their job, so let's go out there and show them how it's done." Tewks wiped his damp forehead with the back of his hand, then clapped his hands together. "Places, everyone."

Isabella looked at the set. It was better than she'd imagined it would be. The detailed decorations made the Oval Office come to life, from the busts of former presidents and an enormous American flag to paintings in gold frames and red curtains. The audience's voices quieted to whispers. The lights dimmed, then total darkness blanketed the room. Tewks gave her a little push, and she rushed out to her mark on a stool. The curtain slid slowly open. In a few moments, a spotlight illuminated her and her shiny black shoes. She felt the yellow light in the darkness funnel the audience's vision; it was reminiscent of falling, she onto them, they onto her, like moths drawn to a light.

"There is a certain silence that settles in before a firestorm. Waiting for the inevitable, and knowing the size of the explosives the enemy has, freezes the air molecules into place. Your ears ring, heart throbs, as you wait for the wailing cry of the airplane."

She was poised, serious, and eloquent. A student sitting in the scaffolding pressed a button on the sound system. First came a rumble evocative of an earthquake, a metallic wail, and then an airplane engine seemed to roar from one side of the theater to the other. The light on Isabella dimmed, she stood, and a figure dressed in black removed the stool and ducked off the stage. She ran to her next mark and hoped Erik moved to his. Spotlights lit the entire stage, and the audience gasped. In the background was an enormous window with a digital image of two mushroom clouds projected on the horizon; fire conflagrated in the foreground. In the Oval Office, it looked as if gravity had been turned off and on again: All the furniture was upside down, papers were charred, and books were scattered across the floor. Erik, dressed in a suit that had seen better days, stood off to the side, and Isabella sat on the floor shaking.

"I should have acted faster," Erik said. "After the first bombs dropped, it was my responsibility."

"Mr. Vice President, we need to get underground, please. There is no doubt that the next bomb will come soon."

"They're all gone. They killed our families. I should have pushed your father to nuke them first."

"The President was stubborn. You're still here, and it's your responsibility to stay alive."

The play continued through three acts, and Isabella felt herself becoming absorbed into the role, until she felt as if she inhabited the character of Samantha completely. And then came the final scene, when Samantha and the Vice President emerged from the bomb shelter and saw the sun for the first time. And when the last line was spoken, Isabella felt a weight lift from her shoulders. She turned toward the lights and bowed, and she felt the applause surround her, escalating, until the very floor beneath her began to shake. And then she realized that it *was* shaking. Everything was shaking.

And suddenly, there was an enormous cracking sound, like a tree trunk splitting in half. The sound-effects student shrugged at Tewks, who was frantically looking around the stage. Isabella searched for the source of the noise, and she saw that Erik looked just as startled as she was. The noise grew in volume; then they heard a woman in the audience scream.

Tewks manually switched on the lights in the theater and illuminated the cause of the sound. The red-carpeted aisle that divided the theater into two seating areas had fractured like a fault line and exposed a deep hole. Huge pieces of concrete, red carpet, and wood had already plummeted into the expanding abyss.

The stage shook beneath Isabella's feet, and she and Erik got separated in the chaos. She froze, paralyzed by the magnitude of the scene, and watched for a few seconds as mayhem ensued; people ran frantically toward the exits all at once. Some fell. She saw a few people get trampled by the panicking crowd.

Isabella watched as the fissure expanded and water spewed from the chasm. Soon some were knee deep in water. She saw her parents in the back of the theater, waving for her to follow them. Oma and Papaji must've already made it out.

She headed toward them, but her path was blocked by the swaying scaffolding that was dangling from the ceiling. She saw Vic push past their parents and begin to maneuver his way over the seats toward the stage. The ellipsoidal lights short-circuited and flashed different colored lights until they showered the entire scene in throbbing red. Sirens wailed from the PA system. Isabella made her way to the front of the stage and looked for the best way down. There were still many people in the front, climbing over the seats, trying to get out. She saw Mr. and Mrs. Finch making their way through the crowd from the first row. The ground shook again, and Isabella gasped as the red lights fell from their support onto Mrs. Finch. Isabella watched, stunned, as Mrs. Finch fell to the water-covered linoleum, her floral dress flailing wildly, the water rising around her. The red luminescence made the water look like blood, and Eleanora's body was now motionless.

Vic reached the stage, helped Isabella onto stable ground, and signaled to their parents to get outside. A few minutes later, the entire Singh family was huddled in the Cutlass Supreme. Isabella looked out the window and saw Erik jump into Tewks's van with some of the other actors.

Her mother backed out of the parking spot. As she drove over the slick asphalt, Isabella turned around just in time to see the sinkhole swallow the entire theater and part of Cobalt High. Water splashed up like a great whale's blowhole and drenched the already sopping campus. Her mother continued down Main Street, maneuvering around signs that blocked off parts of the town from street traffic. She turned onto Peregrine Court, and when they approached The Commons, she pulled over. Brown water was rushing up to the front windows of their house.

"Maija, the water's coming," Paul said. "The river is breached. We need to get to higher ground!"

Oma closed her eyes.

Her mother drove up the back roads that zigzagged through a hemlock forest in an old part of Cobalt. When they reached the top of the mud-covered hill that overlooked the entire area, she put the car in park. Though it was raining, Isabella rolled down the window, and they all looked down at Cobalt in awe. If it wasn't for the devastation caused by the flood, the homes now submerged, it would have been beautiful. The trees were the only obstinate survivors of the cataclysm; their saturated, naked limbs interrupted the singular plane of gray sky and water. The PMI campus, most of Main Street, and even the lower portion of the Heights had been softened by the deluge. Manmade edges of concrete and steel were no challenge for the water.

"Everything's lost now." Oma dabbed tears with the back of her hand.

"Not everything." Isabella drew the Star of David necklace from inside her shirt and showed it to Oma. "I borrowed it. Hope you don't mind."

"Darlink." Oma placed her hand on Isabella's.

"Where are we going, Mama?" Vic asked.

"I don't know, dear. I don't know." Her mother's voice shook. "There are supplies in the trunk. We can last for at least a day or so in the car."

Oma sniffed. Papaji held her hand.

Isabella and Vic watched the horizon as Cobalt disappeared behind the last hill.

Paul looked at his family. "I am tired of the rain."

Maija drove on.

ON THE WING

Extinction

Posted on November 14

I found a sad little picture of a dried Xerces Blue corpse online, and beside it was a photo of the fat French entomologist Boisduval. He supposedly "discovered" the Xerces Blue, though I imagine it existed long before the robust man found it. (I think someone sent him the specimen, but I'd rather imagine history with him discovering it in the wild.) Boisduval was dressed in a long coat and shirtsleeves, typical of mid-nineteenth-century attire. He looked proud and confident as he leaned unnaturally against an oversized leather wingback, as though he were Napoleon.

Let me paint the picture for you: a fat French man trampling through the coastal lupine with a net chasing a butterfly no larger than an inch across. The butterfly coasts low above the ground looking for nectar or a salt puddle. He catches it, admires it, impales it with a pin, and declares it a relative Persian king of long ago, naturally. In reality it probably went like this: a fat French man opens a package with said dead butterfly inside, impales it on a pin, and declares it Xerces. Did he see himself in the butterfly and want to draw a connection between his own lineage and the name Xerces? Perhaps he just wanted to lengthen his own name: Jean Baptiste Alphonse Dechauffour de Boisduval. To him, it probably would have been folly to name a discovery after anything less than a crown, and Monarch was already taken.

I learned about the Xerces Blue's last flight recently. It was last seen on San Francisco's Presidio in 1941. I wonder if W. H. Lange, the last recorded person to see the Xerces Blue almost one hundred years after Boisduval's "discovery," knew he was witnessing its last flight. Perhaps he caught the last lonely butterfly, the omega Xerces, as it searched for companions that no longer existed. His habitat was gone, no eggs were laid, and that was that. The more construction in San Francisco encroached upon the Xerces' land, the fewer flowers were available to drink, and the fewer eggs it laid for the next season. The Xerces Blue was unique in that it was a sub-species that only lived in that one small location; studying it would have offered some insights into evolutionary theory.

I see ghosts all around me. From our escape from Cobalt to our drive south to Florida, to my family's new home, I see them. They crowd me. There in Cobalt it was the Singh Blue and the endangered Karner. Here in Florida, it's the Miami Blue that's vulnerable, and the Schaus' Swallowtail is nearing extinction. In the history of the planet Earth, scientists have identified five mass extinctions. These vast annihilations of species have killed around ninety percent of all living creatures on the planet. Some extinction is natural, or caused by a massive cataclysmic event like a meteor. However, hunting a species to death (buffalo, Queen Alexandra's Birdwing, gray wolf, etc.) or destroying habitats through slash-and-burn agriculture is not natural. The rate of our CO_2 emissions has altered the planet's atmosphere. Climate change is natural, yes. Our acceleration of a natural process is not. Some scientists believe that we are upon our sixth extinction. I don't know about this. That no one will ever see another Xerces Blue drinking nectar from the lupine is a loss for us all. All I know is what I see. And what I see are ghosts.

Glossary

achchhá (Punjabi): *good* or *excellent*, used when one is in agreement

ad sach (Punjabi): roughly translated as *truth/God was true in the beginning*

ajuni (Punjabi): roughly translated as *beyond the cycle of birth and death*

akal murat (Punjabi): roughly translated as *the truth is a shapeless form*

anddá (Punjabi): *egg*

ārprāts (Latvian): *mad, insane*, or *crazy*

bachchá (Punjabi): male child

bháí (Punjabi): brother

bháíjis (Punjabi): Sikh preacher or holy person

bahut kharáb (Punjabi): *very bad*

badmásh (Punjabi): *evildoer*

chaliá/chalo (Punjabi): *to go, go on, let's go*

daal (Punjabi): lentils

dacoit (Punjabi): a member of an armed band of robbers in India

dátrí (Punjabi): handheld sickle

dhí (Punjabi): daughter

dūre (Latvian): fist

ēzelis (Latvian): donkey

fiftee (Punjabi): the first layer of cotton wrapped around the head under a turban

frikadelu zupa (Latvian): dill and meatball soup

goonda (Punjabi): a gangster or individual involved in corruption

gurdwárá (Punjabi): a Sikh temple

gur prasad (Punjabi): roughly translated as *his grace extends to all his creations*

hánji (Punjabi): *yes* or *okay*, with respect

haveli (Punjabi): a private mansion in Northern India or Pakistan

hai be sach (Punjabi): roughly translated as *it is true today as well*

ik (Punjabi): one

ik onkar (Punjabi): roughly translated as *there is but one God*

ik mint (Punjabi): one minute

Japji Sahib (Punjabi): Guru Nanak's poem in the *Sri Guru Granth Sahib* that one recites usually in the morning

jap (Punjabi): to recite or chant

jhutá (Punjabi): liar

ji (Punjabi): sign of respect, can be added to words and names

jugad sach (Punjabi): roughly translated as *was true in the primal age*

kaccha (Punjabi): one of the elements of the Khalsa, a loose-fitting undergarment like shorts or boxers

kara (Punjabi): one of the elements of the Khalsa, a simple metal bracelet

khanga (Punjabi): one of the elements of the Khalsa, a small wooden comb used and worn in one's hair

karta purakh (Punjabi): roughly translated as *only the truth can give creation existence*

Khalsa (Punjabi): meaning *pure*, Khalsas are Sikhs who have undergone the sacred Amrit Ceremony initiated by the tenth Sikh Guru, Guru Gobind Singh

kesh (Punjabi): one of the elements of the Khalsa, the practice of not cutting one's hair

khichuri (Punjabi): a combination of lentils and rice

ki halle (Punjabi): *how are you?*

kirpan (Punjabi): one of the elements of the Khalsa, a ceremonial sword or knife

kokle (Latvian): Latvian string instrument related to the zither

kurta, kurta pajama (Punjabi): long and loose shirt that falls around the knees and pants worn by men and women in India

labrīt (Latvian): *good morning*

mané Sikh han (Punjabi): *I am a Sikh*

mans zvirbulis (Latvian): my sparrow

mazmeita (Latvian): granddaughter

mazs dēls (Latvian): little boy

meita (Latvian): daughter

mundá (Punjabi): boy

Nanak hosi be sach (Punjabi): roughly translated as *Guru Nanak says this truth shall be forever*

neyji (Punjabi): *no*, but with respect

nirvair (Punjabi): without hatred

nirbhao (Punjabi): fearless

pakora (Punjabi): battered and fried snacks usually made with vegetables

págal (Punjabi): crazy person

paranthas (Punjabi): stuffed flatbread made with whole wheat flour

patka (Punjabi): the under-turban that Sikh boys begin to use in preschool; they can tie the larger turban, called a *pagri*, at any age

pavan guru pari pita maataa dharat mahatt (Punjabi): roughly translated as *air is the guru, water the father, the great earth the mother of all*

pippal (Punjabi): fig tree of India noted for great size and longevity and regarded as sacred by Buddhists

piyar (Punjabi): love

potrí/potrá (Punjabi): granddaughter, grandson

putns (Latvian): bird

puttar (Punjabi): son

samajhna (Punjabi): *understand?*

saibhang (Punjabi): *the truth is self existent*

sardarni (Punjabi): female Sikh

satnam (Punjabi): *whose name is truth*

sat sri akal (Punjabi): a greeting between Sikhs, *sat* meaning truth, *sri*, an honorific, *akal*, the immortal being, God; the whole phrase may be roughly translated as *God is the ultimate truth*

sohná (Punjabi): *pretty*, also means *gold*

spec piragi (Latvian): small yeast rolls stuffed with bacon

starpība (Latvian): difference

svieki (Latvian): welcome

sivēna galerts: (Latvian): an aspic loaf usually made with pork head, feet, and neck meat

tabla (Punjabi): a pair of drums played by hand

tatha (Punjabi): fabric worn around the jaw to fix the beard in place

tatte (Punjabi): testicles

uz redzēšanos (Latvian): goodbye

vīratēvs (Latvian): father-in-law

wahe guru (Punjabi): is a term most often used in Sikhism to refer to God; also a greeting, it means *wonderful teacher* in Punjabi

wie ist (German): *what is?*

yár (Punjabi): friend, between men

zeķe (Latvian): sock

Acknowledgments

I am forever indebted to:

My parents, Kiki and Kanwar, whose belief in me has made my path so clear even through the gathering of occasional clouds. Ranjit and Kavita Chadha for tough love, generosity, and wisdom.

Dave Miller, for finding me in this lifetime and inspiring me in more ways than there are stars in the night sky. Kristin Salamack, a true friend and travel companion. Gina Lynch, dear friend, for answering my science-ish questions—over a beer, of course. Angie Pelekedis for generously reading early drafts, and for many conversations about the craft. *That* novel workshop at Binghamton University led by John Vernon, and the great bunch of writers I was fortunate to meet.

John Vernon, your critiques and expectations made me a better writer. Susan Strehle, thank you for encouraging my global literary studies. Libby Tucker, thanks for encouraging my interest in folklore and all things haunted. My wonderful teachers at the University of Colorado, Boulder: Jeffrey De Shell, Elisabeth Sheffield, Marcia Douglas, and Sidney Goldfarb. Thanks also to the College of Creative Studies at the University of California, Santa Barbara, for offering an amazing undergraduate program in literature and amazing teachers: John Wilson, Robyn Bell, and Caroline Allen. Thanks to the Francis X. Newman grant that partially funded my research in Latvia and my parents for funding the rest.

In regards to sources, I must acknowledge the *English-Punjabi Dictionary* by Rev. W. P. Hares published by Asian Educational

Services. Punjabi is a difficult language to document in Romanized English, and this was a great help. Also, the *Anglu-Latviešu Vārdnīca* by Zvaigzne ABC was a useful source for the Latvian terms. For firsthand accounts of the Partition, *The Other Side of Silence* by Urvashi Butalia was excellently informative.

Thanks to Dr. Richard J. Sanders for putting my body back together, *twice,* and Dr. Stephen Annest for fixing me. Thank you, Terri Nishimoto, for being my guide through movement.

Thank you, Norbert and Judy Retch, for sharing family histories and priceless documents. Thanks to Baji for telling and showing me your story, and to Darji whose journey inspired elements of this novel. Oma, your tales grew my imagination and my perception of the natural world.

My publishers, Midge Raymond and John Yunker, thanks for your keen eye, kindness, and for believing in books that have something to say.

Hansel, my Griffy, you're my kind of weird.

…and to those of you who are fighting the good fight to put the planet right again.

About the Author

Photo by Brian Mark

Olivia Chadha began her writing career with a stint in Los Angeles writing comic book scripts. *Balance of Fragile Things* is Olivia's first novel, and some of her other works have appeared in *Pinyon, Damselfly Press*, and *Every Day Fiction.*

Olivia holds a Ph.D. from Binghamton University's creative writing program and has taught writing at Binghamton University and the University of Colorado, Boulder.

Like her stories and characters, Olivia brings a boundary-blurring perspective to her writing: She was born in Illinois, raised in New Jersey, and grew up in Southern California. Her family is of mixed Latvian/German and Indian descent.

About the Cover Artist

Photo by Pam Daniel

Pegi Smith is an artist who works in acrylic in warm, rich colors. Her work has been profiled in *Ashland Magazine*, *Revels*, and the *Ashland Daily Tidings*, among others. The original painting "On the Wings of Butterflies," which appears on the cover of *Balance of Fragile Things*, was completed in 2010 and is on exhibit at 38 Central in Medford, Oregon. To learn more about Pegi, visit www.PegiSmith.com.

Ashland Creek Press is an independent publisher of books with a world view. From travel narratives to eco-literature, our mission is to publish a range of books that foster an appreciation for worlds outside our own, for nature and the animal kingdom, and for the ways in which we all connect. To keep up-to-date on new and forthcoming books, subscribe to our free newsletter at www.AshlandCreekPress.com.

CPSIA information can be obtained
at www.ICGtesting.com
Printed in the USA
BVHW070905290620
582501BV00004B/221